What the Parrot Saw

T0204536

DARLENE MARSHALL

Cover Design and Interior Format

WHAT THE PARROT SAW

" A NOTE ARRIVED FOR THE CAPTAIN, ma'am, and it's marked urgent."

St. Armand read the rumpled paper, a frown creasing the lean face.

"There's no time for further debate. I'll dispose of this person for you, Baarbara, and make sure the body's well hidden."

"What? You can't kill me!"

They ignored such a patently ridiculous statement, but Mrs. Simpson shook her head.

"I must insist."

"Oh, very well. Woodruff, you're coming with me. Your only choice is whether it's bound and across your saddle, or riding."

He appeared ready to argue, but after one look at St. Armand's set face said, "I'll ride."

"You'll find a way to turn a profit on him," Mrs. Simpson said, rising to her feet as well, "I know you."

"There is that," St. Armand said cheerfully. "He could have an unfortunate and fatal accident aboard ship, and I know a surgeon in Nassau who pays well for fresh cadavers. Don't look so pasty-faced, boy. If you follow orders, you should survive long enough to keep scribbling. The first order is this... The captain is always right, and when I give an order, I expect it to be obeyed. Say 'Aye, Captain' if you understand."

Woodruff looked at him and swallowed.

"Aye, Captain."

PRAISE FOR THE NOVELS
OF
DARLENE MARSHALL

"I adore Darlene Marshall's books—I can always count on her to make me laugh, make me sigh, and leave me happy."
—Courtney Milan, *New York Times* and *USA Today* Bestselling Author

"I encourage you all to try this author's voice. (She has a great backlist, too.)"
—*USA Today* Books

"I seriously doubt that any summer experience can possibly be more delightful than sitting on the beach while reading *The Pirate's Secret Baby.*"
—Smart Bitches, Trashy Books

"*Sea Change* is original, fun, and a bit eccentric —I definitely recommend it!"
—*New York Times* bestselling author and RITA award winner Eloisa James

"I love a good girl-poses-as-boy story. Add in a pirate captain and a slow simmering attraction, and I'm hooked. (Resign yourself to the marine allusions.) Darlene Marshall does both in her wonderful *Sea Change.*"
—*New York Times* bestselling author and RITA award winner Connie Brockway

"I would totally stow away on any ship Darlene writes about."
—Book Binge

"Great Fun - Pirates, a shipboard romance, a new father upended by his unexpected responsibilities and a woman who manages to keep her head and agency? Sign me up, Captain."
—Dear Author on *The Pirate's Secret Baby*

"5 Stars!... Set in 1820, *The Pirate's Secret Baby* is a well-researched historical romance spiced with humor. The story of Robert, Lydia, and Marauding Mattie weaves an invisible spell that tugs at your heart strings, and I particularly liked Robert's non-violent, but oh-so-typically-piratical solution to thwarting Lydia's nemesis...I've read several of Marshall's previous pirate tales, but this is the best written and most intriguing one."
—Pirates and Privateers

"Recommended Read—I love that you've staked out early 19th century...sea captains, privateers and pirates. David and Charley are...matched perfectly with strength meeting strength."
—Dear Author on *Sea Change*

5/5!—"I can't say enough how wonderful this book is. The ending is just perfect—and will have you laughing and sighing, and not wanting this adventure to come to an end...A wonderful tale full of humor, adventure, and a lovely romance that will sweep you away."
—Smexy Books on *The Bride and the Buccaneer*

ALSO BY DARLENE MARSHALL

Pirate's Price
Smuggler's Bride
The Bride and the Buccaneer
Captain Sinister's Lady
Sea Change (High Seas, #1)
Castaway Dreams (High Seas, #2)
The Pirate's Secret Baby (High Seas, #3)

THANKS
AND
ACKNOWLEDGEMENTS

WRITING IS A SOLITARY BUSINESS, and my dachshund is no help at all when it comes to constructive feedback (although she does get me up and moving away from my keyboard, and that's a good thing.) Without these lovely folks my book wouldn't exist:

Janice and Dr. Amy—The best beta readers around.

My editor, Catherine Snodgrass, who saves me from myself and from stupid syntax errors.

Alachua County (Florida) Library District, especially for all the InterLibraryLoan books.

The Matheson History Museum in Gainesville, Florida.

Agent Barbara Collins Rosenberg, whose sage advice made this novel far better than it could have been.

The LitForum.com for Bookworms and Wordsmiths. Compuserve went away, but we're still hanging around.

RWA Beaumonde and RWA Online, the best chapters in Romance Writers of America.

The Gainesville Area Romance Writers.

My readers—your notes and comments recharge my batteries.

And finally, most of all, that wonderful man I married decades ago, the one who pays the mortgage each month so I'm not a starving writer in a tiny garret. As the Yiddish saying goes, "Love is good. Love and noodles is better." Thanks for all the noodles, hon.

CHAPTER 1

1839

"I DON'T NEED A USELESS WHITE boy. Find someone else to take him off your hands."

"Not a boy, a man. The sort you favor, captain—golden curls, pouty mouth. He's quite pretty, I know you'll agree."

Captain St. Armand stretched out long legs clad in close fitting buckskins, admiring the shine on boots freshly polished. The brothel on St. Martin offered a variety of services to its clients, from excellent meals to boot-blacking, along with the usual amenities one expected from such establishments.

"If I bring a pretty lad aboard ship, everyone will want one. I don't share my toys."

"You'll take him," the madam said. "I'm calling in my marker for the incident last year."

"That wasn't my fault!"

"Your ship, your crew, your fault, St. Armand."

"Really, that man needed some excitement in his life."

"That's not the excitement Mr. Carlson sought at this house. He never expected a goat."

St. Armand snickered at the memory. "I still say what you're asking is excessive."

"I thought you'd turn me down." Barbara Simpson took a sip of the sherry she'd served herself. Her guest was drinking Jamaican rum, as usual. "You should know though, the young man in question is Bunny Rathbone's relation."

"Bunny Rathbone! How is the dear old boy?"

"He's well, moving up in the world. He wrote me to say his cousin was touring the islands and if he came here I should treat him as an honored guest. Bunny implied Mr. Woodruff needed to experience more of life. To put it bluntly, he called the young man a 'stuffy, boring stick.' I invited him to the house, but first he ran into a spot of trouble and I brought him here for safekeeping."

The doors to the parlor were open to catch the afternoon breezes rustling through the bougainvillea—a restful pause before business commenced for the evening. Comfortably rounded and middle-aged, Mrs. Simpson was a shrewd businesswoman whose motto was to give the clients what they desired—within reason—and to treat her girls as she'd wanted to be treated when she'd worked there. She'd miss Captain St. Armand, a favored customer setting sail for Nassau after a stop to provision and catch up on mail and messages from home. A packed valise waited near the door.

"The two of us have fond memories of Bunny's visits to this house, but I'm sailing on the tide, so bring your package out here and let me see for myself."

The madam's bully boys were summoned and returned a short while later with their "package" struggling between them in a futile attempt at freedom. It was a young man in his mid-twenties, and, as promised, he had bright gold hair and sky-blue eyes. One of those eyes was blackened, and a bruise discolored the left side of his face. He was also gagged with his hands tied in front of him.

"As you see, I need your help taking him away, and you could use a cabin boy. You told me so yourself. Mr. Woodruff has an unfortunate habit of speaking intemperately, and there were people who took exception to what he said."

"People?"

"Americans. Ah, I thought that would interest you."

"I am *slightly* tempted," the captain said, looking the young man over. "I may have a use for him, other than the obvious one. As always, you have an excellent eye for the goods."

The captive made a noise muffled by his gag.

"Don't look so horrified, Sunshine. The work's not onerous and it comes with special benefits. If he's annoying the Americans I'm thinking of, it makes him far more trouble than he's worth, Barbara. I'll pay you for the goat incident and leave him to his own devices."

"The goat incident set me back twenty-five pounds, not to mention the free services Mr. Carlson received for his embarrassment. You owe me, but if you take Woodruff with you to Nassau we'll call it done."

She directed one of her men to get the captive's gear. The captain pulled a fine cigar from the mahogany box on the table, taking time to light it and inhale before answering.

"Twenty-five pounds? I don't care how pouty his mouth is, there's not a man alive worth that amount."

The bound man squawked again, jerking against

the hold on his arms.

"Untie the gag, James. Maybe Woodruff can convince me of his worth."

The gag removed, the captive worked his square jaw back and forth, glaring at them.

"I demand you release me at once! I am a British citizen and I will notify the authorities!"

St. Armand looked at Mrs. Simpson, then both laughed aloud. Even the guard chuckled.

"How do you intend to back up that demand?" St. Armand asked. "Did you happen to bring a knife with you? Or guns? Or friends with guns?"

"Friends with guns are good, Captain."

"Indeed they are, James, but I don't believe Woodruff has friends here, with or without guns."

"You cannot hold me here! I did not come to the islands to end up in a bawdy house!" he protested.

"Well, that's your problem right there, Sunshine."

Woodruff took a deep breath, then looked at the mistress of the house.

"You are not responsible for me, Mrs. Simpson. I am not unappreciative of your protecting me by keeping me here, but I can take care of myself."

"You don't seem to be doing a good job of it so far."

He glared at the sea captain.

"I do not know what your interest in my affairs is, sir, but I do not need your assistance." He started to step forward, but James's heavy hand on his shoulder kept him in place.

St. Armand set down the cigar.

"It's not up to you. Hold out your hands."

Almost reflexively the man thrust his arms out. St. Armand's knife sliced through the knots, but when Woodruff tried to pull his arm back, the captain gripped his hand and turned it over.

"Soft and smooth as a nun's arse. You've never hauled lines or done work harder than holding a pen. Don't look so astounded. I can tell you're a scribbler from this callus on your finger." Cold eyes scanned him from his face down to his feet. "Soft all over. I only take crew and cargo aboard my vessel. You are worthless to me."

The brothel owner delicately cleared her throat.

"Goats, St. Armand. Remember the goats. You don't have to keep him forever, like a pet. Take him to Nassau or Jamaica and leave him there. You owe me, and I owe"—she paused and looked at her guest—"our mutual friend, so let's be reasonable about this."

Woodruff stared at the sea captain. "You are Captain St. Armand? *The* Captain St. Armand, of the *Prodigal Son*?"

Before he could answer, the brothel's majordomo knocked at the door.

"A note arrived for the captain, ma'am, and it's marked urgent."

St. Armand read the rumpled paper, a frown creasing the lean face.

"There's no time for further debate. I'll dispose of this person for you, Barbara, and make sure the body's well hidden."

"What? You can't kill me!"

They ignored such a patently ridiculous statement, but Mrs. Simpson shook her head.

"I must insist."

"Oh, very well. Woodruff, you're coming with me. Your only choice is whether it's bound and across your saddle, or riding."

He appeared ready to argue, but after one look at St.

Armand's set face said, "I'll ride."

"You'll find a way to turn a profit on him," Mrs. Simpson said, rising to her feet as well, "I know you."

"There is that," St. Armand said cheerfully. "He could have an unfortunate and fatal accident aboard ship, and I know a surgeon in Nassau who pays well for fresh cadavers. Don't look so pasty-faced, boy. If you follow orders, you should survive long enough to keep scribbling. The first order is this... The captain is always right, and when I give an order, I expect it to be obeyed. Say 'Aye, Captain' if you understand."

Woodruff looked at him and swallowed.

"Aye, Captain."

"Good lad. Wait for me outside."

Oliver stood on the veranda, rubbing his sore wrists. To be fair, he'd not been mistreated by the brothel keeper or her staff. They'd kept him locked in a hut on the back of the estate, but they'd cleaned up his cuts and bruises and fed him.

His head buzzed as he tugged on his jacket, thankfully still in one piece. Out of the corner of his eye he could see the guard, lounging against the wall but watching him. He wasn't going to run off. He'd thought Captain St. Armand a story made up by old salts cadging drinks from gullible travelers. Some stories put the notorious sea rover in the middle of the wars against Napoleon, some said he'd fought the Americans, others said he'd outrun the Royal Navy in his schooner. All the tales said men who crossed him didn't live long enough to regret it.

That seemed impossible. Yes, St. Armand had the look of a pirate about him, but his lithe form and light

voice showed him to be far too young to have fought
for or against Napoleon. He was tall and clean-shaven,
with startling blue eyes. The French name combined
with ebon hair and tan skin made Oliver think he was
from Mediterranean lands or a mulatto. In the islands
it was best not to pry.

St. Armand clearly had secrets though, and the open
windows to the house's parlor made it easy for Oliver
to eavesdrop on the couple inside.

"I might have a use for him, beyond the obvious.
I've been looking for a man like that."

"I worry about you. You cannot keep this up, my
dear."

The woman's taffeta skirts rustled, and he imagined
her moving in closer to her lover as she added, "Stay
with me, St. Armand. You know how much I want
you."

"It was a delightful interlude, but this could not be
a permanent diet for me, Barbara. I am what I am.
Some things are beyond my control."

"What a waste. No man can do for you what I can,"
she grumbled.

Oliver's skin flamed as he listened. He wasn't naïve.
He'd been sent to school, heard tales of sailors and
their ways. Was Mrs. Simpson worried St. Armand's
perversions would be exposed? Even worse, given the
"cabin boy" remarks, did he fancy Oliver for himself?

There was no further conversation from the room
behind him, but his hearing was excellent and he
suspected the couple was sharing an intimate moment,
kissing as they prepared to part. It was confirmed
when he heard St. Armand speak tenderly in a low
voice.

"Goodbye, Barbara. I don't know when I'll return,

my dear, but I will always treasure these days with you."

"You know you have a place in my heart as well, love. Goodbye, Mattie."

CHAPTER 2

HORSES WERE BROUGHT TO THE front and St. Armand emerged from the house, strapping the valise behind him before smoothly mounting the chestnut.

"Mount up, Woodruff."

Oliver secured his own case, glad again he'd chosen to travel light. Without another word, the captain set off, and he hurried to catch up. St. Armand was quiet and alert, his eyes scanning the shrubbery and rocks as they rode.

It was dusk. The tropical light gave a soft haze to the road, and they didn't need torches. St. Martin was like most of the other locales Oliver had visited in the Caribbean—run-down and neglected, but bright with flowers and lush vegetation.

A perfumed note from Mrs. Simpson had arrived within a day of his ship docking, inviting Oliver to the house, saying an unnamed mutual acquaintance had recommended him to her. The offer had piqued his curiosity, but he was pummeled in the tavern before he could act on it on his own.

Now his adventures were taking a very different turn. St. Armand seemed exactly the sort of picaresque character who'd do well in a novel or travel journal, though Oliver would sooner die than give in to the pirate's advances. Perhaps St. Armand was simply an opportunistic hedonist, enjoying the company of women as well as men.

"Captain, I appreciate your helping me to leave that establishment, but I don't want you to have a"—he struggled for words that wouldn't insult this well-armed man—"a false impression about me. I am not interested in, in…"

The words trailed off in the dusk.

"Yes, Woodruff, what is it you're not interested in? I'd be fascinated to find out," St. Armand said, glancing over his shoulder at the road behind them.

"I don't want you to have a false impression about me, about why I'm accompanying you. I couldn't help but overhear your farewells with Mrs. Simpson."

There was silence while he seemed to mull over Oliver's words.

"Let me be certain we're clear on what it is that does not interest you. You eavesdropped on a private moment, and now you're warning me not to have designs on your fair young body. Is that correct?"

"I'm trying to have a serious conversation, sir! I've heard about you and your ship. You have a reputation as a notorious libertine, a voluptuary…"

"And you're not that kind of boy? I can fix that."

Oliver's teeth clenched and he could see the man next to him enjoying his discomfort.

"See here—"

"Stifle it. I need to pay attention to the road, and I don't have time for your maidenly airs."

St. Armand was listening for something, occasionally looking over one shoulder. They rode along in silence until he said, "Woodruff, do you recall your first lesson for life at sea?"

"Always obey the captain's orders?"

The captain looked behind them, then grinned at Oliver.

"Ride like your arse is on fire, Woodruff. That's an order!"

Two shots rang out, followed by a shout from behind them.

"Halt, you blackguard! You're under arrest!"

"Someone's shooting at us!" Oliver yelled unnecessarily, but St. Armand was already ahead of him, the horse's hooves beating a cloud of dust on the road. The gold braid decorating the captain's coat kept him in Oliver's sights, and he caught up after an eternity of hard riding.

"Who is shooting at us?"

"Do you want to wait here and find out? Decide fast, because if they catch you, you'll be hanged as a pirate."

"I'm not a pirate!"

"Good luck explaining that on your way to the gallows."

St. Armand pulled forward again, and Oliver concentrated on riding and keeping his head down. Another shot whizzed by his ear and he cursed the pirate, but their pursuers were falling back. More importantly, he could see the lights of the bay ahead of him.

St. Armand leaped off the chestnut onto the dock, then unstrapped his valise as a ragged boy ran forward to take the reins.

"The horses go back to Mrs. Simpson," the captain said, flipping a coin the boy neatly snagged out of the air.

Oliver dismounted and ran over to St. Armand, already headed to a boat bobbing in the water. Three sailors waited there and one caught the captain's bag as it was thrown in.

"Come aboard and take your chances, Woodruff, or stay here and chat with the gentlemen behind us."

"Trouble, Captain?" asked a sailor.

"Nothing out of the ordinary."

Oliver climbed into the boat and hunkered down, looking over his shoulder. The rest of them did not seem overly concerned, even when the pursuers reached the docks and started yelling for a boat of their own.

The sailors rowed them out to a schooner with raked masts. *Prodigal Son* was painted on its bow. They ignored the hollering from the docks and chatted with their captain as Oliver climbed aboard to the stifled snickers from one of the sailors following him, then St. Armand shimmied smoothly up the ladder, taking Oliver by the arm and standing him at the rail.

"Stay here until I figure out what to do with you. You can wait. The tide will not. Mr. Turnbull, get us underway."

Oliver did as instructed, his bag at his feet, taking in all the activity. The mate, Turnbull, was a grizzled salt with half an ear missing and the remainder of his face looking as if it was put together on a bad day for faces. The crew responded smartly to the barked orders. Oliver pulled his notebook and his pencil from his jacket, trying to appear unobtrusive and unthreatening as he jotted down notes. He'd expected the crew of a pirate ship to be oozing evil out of their pores, but these men sang as they raised the anchor, hauling away at an arcane arrangement of ropes and pulleys. If he could capture the moment on paper he'd be better able to reconstruct the scene later.

The sails stretched out, reaching for the wind, and the schooner soared through the water like an osprey after a fish. He stood at the gunwale, taking it in. He'd been beaten, shot at, held prisoner in a brothel (without enjoying any of its usual services), and hauled aboard an alleged pirate ship. He'd longed for adventure when he was confined to the dreary offices in Manchester, and now he was getting it in abundance. The creak of canvas and rope, the sailors' chanteys, the mystery of the ship's captain... He looked over his shoulder at St. Armand, talking with the helmsman.

The captain wore a finely tailored frock coat of navy blue wool with a high, black velvet collar. It was crusted with gold braid, gleaming buttons moving down at an angle from the wide padded shoulders to a tapered waist. He sported a black silk dotted neckcloth against his white linen, a red satin sash girdled his waist, and the smooth buckskins were tucked into high boots. His curls fell across his forehead, though he eschewed the side whiskers so many other young gallants favored.

Oliver tugged nervously at his torn shirt cuff, even as he knew he'd never be able to compete with such sartorial splendor. The captain studied him in turn as if pondering what to do, then motioned him over.

The mate joined them.

"Shipping a new man, Captain?"

"We're transporting Woodruff here to Nassau, Mr. Turnbull. I've explained I don't carry passengers, so you'll find him a hammock and show him the ropes."

There was a rush of air overhead and Oliver ducked reflexively, avoiding a collision with a flashy green parrot swooping down to perch on St. Armand's shoulder.

"Good evening, Roscoe. Who's a good boy?"

The parrot ruffled his wings as Turnbull passed over a handful of nuts he'd pulled from a pouch at his waist.

"That's a lovely par—"

"Don't say it!" Turnbull and St. Armand said at the same time.

St. Armand reached up to scratch the bird under his beak. "This is Roscoe, the ship's cat. Who's a good kitty? Who's a good boy?"

Oliver could deal with being shot at, beaten, evicted from a brothel, kidnapped by pirates, but there were some situations he was not willing to accept. "I realize I may not survive this voyage in one piece, but I must speak my mind, Captain. That is not a cat."

"When I want your opinion, I will tell you so. Roscoe's a prime mouser and a valuable member of the crew. Last I checked, your greatest value to me may be in selling you to the anatomists. Do not confuse our ship's cat about his duties aboard this vessel."

The bird cocked his head and eyed Oliver.

"Lubber! Lubber!"

"Ain't that the truth." Turnbull sighed. "You don't want to be more useless than the cat. It could end badly for you. Can you peel potatoes?"

"Peel potatoes? Certainly not. We had servants for that."

"Wrong answer. Try again."

Oliver looked around at all the hard-working sailors, then swallowed and turned back to the mate. "Aye, Mr. Turnbull."

"That is the correct answer. You'll assist Cook in the galley for now. Daly!"

St. Armand watched this byplay with a sardonic smile, or perhaps it was only the crescent-shaped scar at the corner of his mouth pulling his lips into a quirk. A red-headed sailor hurried over, and Turnbull told him to take Oliver below and show him where to hang his hammock. Daly was close in age to Oliver, and his brogue made his origins clear.

"Welcome aboard the *Prodigal Son*," the sailor said cheerfully. "I'll put you with the starboard mess. That's where I am, and we've the best mates there. Watch your head. I've seen green men knock themselves out cold below decks."

It was dim below, filled with the scent of brine, men in close quarters, and oil lamps. Oliver's eyes adjusted as Daly introduced him to the other crewmen—a polyglot mix of Africans, a Dutchman, Spaniards, Englishmen, an additional Irishman, an American or two, and a Chinaman. A sailor with a tight cap of white curls on his head and a weathered face wrinkled and dark as a walnut only grunted at the introductions, then went back to carving scrimshaw.

"Don't take it personal, Woodruff. Daniel Green here ain't the friendly type, but he's the best when we're reefing the topsails. He's a hero of the Royal Navy, he is, saw a lot of action during the wars."

"Is this a British ship then?" He'd seen the flag, but St. Armand's speech was a mélange of American and English rhythms with a hint of island patois. Turnbull sounded like he'd been born in sight of Dover's cliffs.

"Well now, that's kind of a tricky question and best not explored too deeply, if you know what I mean. Ah, Mr. Nash, let me introduce you to…"

"Oliver Woodruff," he said, extending his hand. The other man shook it. He clutched a sheaf of papers in his left hand. It was missing two fingers. The ones remaining had knuckles swollen with rheumatism, a common complaint in the damp and cold environment of a sea going vessel. But his eyes were keen over the spectacles pulled low on his squashed nose.

"And your place on this vessel?"

Oliver tugged at his ear. "I believe I rank somewhere below the ship's...cat, and for now I'm to assist the cook."

"Mr. Nash here is the quartermaster, among other tasks," Daly explained. "If it has anything to do with the ship's business of buying, selling, doling out the shillings or what have you, he's the man to see."

Nash pulled out a pencil from over his ear and made a note in the numbers on his papers.

"I'll sort it out with Mr. Turnbull. Get some slops, keep your gentlemen's gear for when you're ashore. Welcome aboard."

The ship was settling into its evening routine and Daly found Oliver a mess kit in ship's stores to go with his slops—loose duck trousers, worn but clean, a knit shirt like the other sailors had, and a blue jacket torn at the shoulder but a reasonable fit.

Daly looked at Oliver with approval after he'd changed into his new gear.

"That's more like it. No place for a gentleman down here, only us sailors."

The crew had eaten earlier in the day so the Irishman took Oliver to the galley, where he said with a wink that he'd cajole the cook into giving the new man a bite to eat.

The cook was short and so black his skin gleamed

blue in the lantern light. He appeared singularly unimpressed by Daly's blarney, but after the sailor left he cut off a hunk of cheese and a wedge of a meat-stuffed pastry to go with it. He put it in front of Oliver along with a cup of coffee, motioning him to pull up a cask to sit on. The cook had one foot and a wooden stump, and while he had a crutch under his arm, he had no trouble navigating the rolling decks.

"They call me Cook, but ashore I'm Mr. Cicero Holt," the cook said. "Mr. Turnbull tells me you're my new helper. Show me your hands."

"What is it about my hands that fascinates people?" Oliver muttered, but he popped the last bite of pastry into his mouth and followed orders.

Holt, whose own hands were tough and wiry as the rest of him, shook his head, then reached for a small knife off a rack.

"Start peeling, Woodruff. I've work to do to prepare for tomorrow." He pulled out a bag of vegetables and showed Oliver where he'd save the scraps for the ship's animals. Some of the odors belowdecks weren't only from the two-legged crew members.

Oliver was hacking away at a potato when Holt barked at him, "We'll be roasting the ship's cat before landfall if you keep wasting food like that!"

He showed him how to remove skin and leave potato behind, and eventually there was a pile of tubers cleaned and set aside for the next day. Oliver stood and put his hands at the small of his back, stretching muscles complaining from the unexpected manual labor.

"Glad that's over," he said, turning toward the door. "Ow!"

The cook whacked his arm with the end of his

crutch.

"You ain't done until I say you're done. Now, start on those pots."

Oliver towered over the cook, his blistered hands clenched at his side.

"See here, I am not a scullion—"

This time the tip of the crutch landed on Oliver's throat when he tried to move.

"If those pots ain't cleaned to my satisfaction, you're leaving here feet first. You got that?"

He jerked his head for yes, the pressure of the crutch keeping him from speaking.

When the cook finally released him from the galley the pots shone and the food was organized for the next day's meals. Oliver fumbled his way into the hammock as the starboard watch snored around him. He rubbed his aching arm, and as his heavy eyes closed, he offered a brief prayer for fair winds to speed him to Nassau.

CHAPTER 3

"**S**HAKE A LEG, WOODRUFF. THE men want their victuals."

Oliver blearily pried one eye open, hoping it was a bad dream. Holt was standing next to his hammock. The luxury of being a passenger and sleeping the morning away seemed a distant memory as Oliver pulled on his shoes and yawned his way to the galley.

The parrot was there, perched on a chair back, eating fruit from a cup, still eyeing him suspiciously.

"Are you concerned Roscoe's going to fly around and do something in the porridge, Mr. Holt?"

"Don't be foolish, lubber. He uses his sandbox like a proper ship's cat. 'Sides, this lot probably wouldn't notice anyway."

Oliver pretended he didn't hear that as, under Holt's direction, he carried pots of porridge to the mess, and a second trip with steaming coffee. Conversation was limited as the men hurried through their meal to get to their tasks, and Oliver returned to the galley and gulped down his own breakfast while the cook readied a tray.

"Take this to the captain's cabin, smartly now."

The captain had mostly the same as the men save

for the addition of fine china and silver rather than tin plates and cups. There was a pot of coffee, porridge with a small dish of honey, and cheese from the ship's goat.

He hesitated outside the cabin, trying to figure out how to knock and balance the tray while the deck rolled beneath his feet. Fortunately, the door opened and Mr. Turnbull looked down at him, then raised an eyebrow.

"Your new cabin boy is here."

"I am not the cabin boy," Oliver said, setting the tray on the captain's table, wincing as the handles chafed his blistered hands. "I'm the cook's assistant."

St. Armand was dressed but didn't look fully awake, and nearly snatched the cup of coffee from his hand.

"You're the cabin boy if I say you're the cabin boy."

"Meow."

Oliver paused from putting out the porridge. "Did your animal just *meow* outside your door?"

"Isn't that what cats do? Let him in."

Roscoe flew in once the door was opened, settling on an oak perch fastened to the deck. He gave Oliver a glance, then turned aside to groom himself. Turnbull dropped nuts in Roscoe's dish, and the bird mumbled and began cracking them.

St. Armand, looking more awake now, watched him through the steam rising from the coffee cup. The captain wore a less flamboyant jacket than the previous day, dark green with only a satin edging at the collar and cuffs.

"Are you enjoying your voyage, Woodruff? Everything comfortable and cozy for you?"

Oliver mulled over the best response that wouldn't get him flogged or keelhauled. They were away from land. The captain had fulfilled his obligation to get him off St. Martin. After all, he had bragged about his ability to dispose of bodies. What could be easier than feeding one complaining Englishman to the sharks?

"I am finding the voyage interesting, and I'm learning things."

"How to peel potatoes?"

"That, and also about life belowdecks. It's quite the adventure." He scratched his ear ruefully, startled to see the parrot imitate the gesture with his claw. The bird watched him, its head cocked to the side. Oliver didn't know if that meant it was about to attack, or whether it was viewing him in a new light.

"Will there be anything else, Captain?"

"Yes. Tell me about the men who beat you on St. Martin."

He almost pulled out the chair to seat himself but stopped at a growl from Turnbull. Passengers might sit in the captain's presence, cabin boys and galley scullions did not. Turnbull went back to examining charts and Oliver took a deep breath, collecting his thoughts. It had been hot and dank that painful evening in Marigot, with insects flying into eyes and ears and contributing to the short tempers.

"We were in the tavern. It started out easily enough, but then the talk turned to slavery and Britain's emancipation of its Negroes. The men who confronted me were drinking through most of the day. They did not like my point of view."

St. Armand nodded. "Politics and brandy aren't a good combination, particularly when Americans are involved. They were American, were they not? From the Southern states?"

"How did you know that?"

"You'd be surprised what I know."

Oliver didn't know why those simple words sent a shiver down his spine, but the captain was still talking.

"Are you anti-slavery then?"

"I am, though it is not a popular position in Manchester. I am not afraid to stand up for what I believe in. I even wrote a strongly worded letter to the *Times* condemning the practice."

"Good to know you're a man of action, Woodruff. Here in the islands fledgling nations are fighting to get out from under European control and political discussions are dangerous. The United States in particular stomps around like a belligerent drunkard, looking to take on anyone they think is standing in their way. Most annoying."

"Speaking of belligerents, Captain… Why were men were shooting at us on St. Martin?"

"People shoot at me all the time. One gets used to it."

"They do not shoot at me!"

"You dwell on the past far too much. You're here, you're not a cadaver—*carpe diem*, Woodruff. Seize the opportunity to expand your horizons."

"As a pirate?"

"Good heavens, lad, none of us are pirates. That is against the law. We are enterprising merchants. You'd do well to remember the distinction," he finished gently, holding out his coffee cup for a refill.

Despite the mild tone and the warm air in the captain's cabin, Oliver willed his hand not to shake as he poured.

"Do you expect more people to shoot at you—us on this voyage, Captain?"

As if responding to a stage cue, there was a knock

on the door.

"Mr. Turnbull, it's as you thought," said Jonas, one of the sailors Oliver had met over the morning porridge. "That was the *Salacia* you spotted."

"Very good, Jonas. Find Mr. Nash, then stand by."

"Aye, sir."

"Let us see what Nash has to say, then we'll proceed," Turnbull said to the captain. "Are you done with him?" he added, jerking his head toward Oliver.

"He does brighten up the cabin, but I would not want to get on the bad side of Cook by keeping his assistant. You are dismissed, Woodruff."

Oliver busied himself gathering up the dishes and disposing of the scummy water St. Armand used to wash before breakfast. It smelled of sandalwood, probably from shaving soap.

In the galley he asked the cook about the ship they'd spotted.

"The *Salacia*? Are you certain?"

"It's not a common name, so yes, I'm certain that's what they said."

Holt mulled this over while he worked on the meal for midday.

"There's history with our ship and the *Salacia*. Captain Jensen and Captain St. Armand... Well, sometimes they're friendly toward each other, other times you want to check to make sure your powder's dry and your blade's sharp. If they called for Mr. Nash, then there's going to be some trading going on. In the meantime, we need to get everyone fed. Back to work."

Once he was finally released from the confines of the galley with its heat and interminable turnips, he went up on deck to get some fresh air. A blur of green rushed past his ear and Oliver reflexively ducked. The parrot perched on a coil of rope in front of him and dropped something at his feet.

It was a dead rat.

"Roscoe only brings gifts to people he likes, and he doesn't like many people," the captain said from behind him.

The bird preened its feathers, confident the offering would be accepted with good grace. Oliver eyed the rodent for a moment, then turned and looked at St. Armand.

"May I ask what I'm supposed to do with this bounty?"

St. Armand nudged it with a booted toe.

"You could put it in your pocket in case you get peckish later, but if not, you can toss it over the side. Just be sure Roscoe doesn't see you doing it. It will hurt his feelings, make him feel rejected."

"We wouldn't want that, not when he's already suffering a crisis of identity." He bent and picked up the rodent by its tail, shuddering slightly, then strolled away, keeping the rat hidden from sight so the bird couldn't see it.

It slipped over the rail and hit the water without making much of a splash, and the bird didn't squawk, so Oliver rejoined the ship's master.

"Walk with me."

Oliver gratefully obeyed, cramped muscles loosening as they paced the ship. St. Armand watched everything, but it was Turnbull who gave the men their working orders. They looked different from the sailors aboard the vessel that brought him to the islands. The men of the *Prodigal Son* went about their work cheerfully, their clothing wasn't in rags, and they didn't have the pinched faces of sailors subjected to verbal abuse or even a clout with a knotted rope like those on his last journey. He realized he hadn't paid much attention to those men. He played cards with other passengers in the saloon, dined at the captain's table, exchanged pleasantries with the officers. The sailors were there, part of the ship's machinery, but not part of his life.

"Why are you in the islands, Woodruff? I'll ferry you to Nassau, but after that if you want to get yourself killed, it's none of my concern."

Oliver stopped and rubbed his hand along the polished rail.

"I came here wanting a change from England. My father was sickly for many years and I could not leave the family. Now my father's gone and I must take up my responsibilities, but I promised myself that before that happens I would do something—something just for myself. So here I am."

St. Armand moved next to him, looking out over the waves. "Nothing wrong with wanting adventure and change. The world is a vast place, and England is only a small part of it. Some of the men are aboard because they wanted change, and some are here because they want to be paid to see a bit of the world."

"To be honest, Captain, I'd hoped for more adventure and fewer turnips."

"Keep your eyes open. The day's not yet over."

Oliver returned to his duties below, and when he carried in a fish stew, the mess cheered to see it. Leaving port with fresh ingredients and a lucky catch earlier that morning meant they'd dine well.

"See, that's one of the reasons the *Prodigal's* a good ship. Mr. Turnbull and the captain, they take care of the crew, don't pinch coins until they holler just to get a touch more profit for the owners," Daly said.

Oliver filled his own kit as he took a seat.

"Who owns the *Prodigal Son*?"

"Captain St. Armand is part owner, as are Mr. Nash and Mr. Turnbull. Some nob in England also has a share. I've crewed on ships where the owners short the crew's mess to cram in more cargo. Don't see that here."

"What about the other ship out there—the *Salacia*?"

"You could see some action, youngster." Green didn't say anything more as he reached for the coffee. There was an air of heightened anticipation among the men, and Oliver wondered if the charges of "Pirate!" along with the tales of the legendary Captain St. Armand had validity.

Released from his galley duties, Oliver joined his shipmates on deck as they drew closer. The *Salacia* was larger than the schooner, carrying more canvas, and Green said it was a merchantman out of New York.

Nash stood next to the captain and Turnbull at the larboard rail, going through the papers in his hands.

"And molasses and coffee from Cuba."

"I like coffee."

"So do people in London, Captain." He scribbled some notes with his pencil, doing quick calculations. "With the *Salacia's* coffee added to what you already have, you could make a tidy profit on this voyage, even without the other cargo."

"Good thing about coffee, Mr. Nash, is everyone wants it. Perhaps I'll sell it in New York. First though, let's chat with Captain Jensen. Woodruff!"

"Sir?"

"You'll row over with us. You said you wanted a change from turnips. Go see Green."

Green, issuing weapons from a locker, frowned when he saw Oliver in line, but passed him an axe and said, "Try not to poke anyone in the arse with that, lubber."

Oliver watched how the others secured their various blades at their waist and followed their example.

"Are we going to have to fight?"

"You never know," Daly said cheerfully, "but being prepared and alive is better than being surprised and dead, ain't it?"

The *Salacia* backed its sails and no threats were shouted at them, but they were carrying fewer guns than the *Prodigal Son*. Swivel guns amidships seemed to be the extent of their armament, though there were probably small arms available to them as well, along with pikes to repel boarders.

Oliver took an oar, the captain sat in the bow, and a ladder was lowered for them when they came alongside. Oliver followed St. Armand and saw the crew of the *Salacia* watching, but not pointing weapons at them. They looked to the bearded barrel of a man emerging from below, broad through the torso but shorter than St. Armand.

"So it is you, you scoundrel! Have you come to rob me then?"

"I seem to recall you owe *me* from our last encounter, Jensen."

"I owe you? You have a lot of gall, you sharkbait!"

The tension rose as Oliver stood near his captain, sweat prickling down his back.

St. Armand looked up at the American flag flapping above Jensen and rubbed his chin. Then he shrugged and pulled a pistol out of his pocket.

"Clearly we disagree on this. I'll make it simple. Pay me what you owe me, or I'll shoot Woodruff."

It took Oliver's brain a moment to process the captain's words. Everyone was staring at him, and the sailors nearest him were inching away from the gun pointed at his head.

"What? What? Wait! Damn it..."

He sputtered to an incoherent finish as the two ship's captains politely watched him, then a guffaw burst out from Jensen and he bent over with laughter, slapping his knee.

"I swear, the look on your man's face. That was priceless!"

St. Armand grinned at Oliver and lowered the pistol.

"That enough excitement for you, Woodruff?"

Oliver put his hands behind his back to keep from stomping over and punching that louche fool in the snoot. He kept his temper in check and inclined his head to the two commanders.

"Well played, Captain. If I'm not about to be shot for your amusement, do you have orders for me?" Oliver asked.

Jensen looked at him with interest. "A new pet?"

"My cabin boy," St. Armand purred. "What else he is remains to be seen. But that will have to wait. Do you have information for me?"

Jensen sobered. "I do, but I don't know if you want to take this one on, Matt. There's risk."

"Merciful heavens, a day without risk is like a day without coffee. And speaking of that, if you have some to trade I could make room in my hold."

As they turned to go below St. Armand looked over

his shoulder.

"Your orders, Woodruff, are to assist Green with anything he needs."

Simple enough, and the crews of the two ships appeared to be on good terms. It looked unlikely that he would use his axe today. He could see the benefit of it on a vessel where it could hack through rope, wood, or men, though he shuddered at the last thought. Killing sailors because they stood between the crew of the *Prodigal Son* and coffee was not the excitement he wanted.

Sacks were brought up from the *Salacia's* hold, and with an *oof* he hoisted one over his shoulder to load in the boat. Based on what he'd seen aboard ship, coffee more than grog was the pirate drink of choice. They followed the navy custom of a ration of the rum drink each evening as well, carefully doled out under Mr. Nash's watchful eyes.

The two captains returned and Oliver watched them talk, their heads close together. Jensen put his hand on St. Armand's arm and said something, but St. Armand shook his head.

He glanced up and met Oliver's gaze, looking straight into his eyes, and heat rushed through him. He was being evaluated, he knew, but for what?

"Get that to the boat."

"Aye, Mr. Green." Oliver turned away, feeling... He didn't want to think about how he was feeling. St. Armand was taking a personal interest in him, which, on one hand alarmed him, and on the other...

He hadn't felt a fascination like this since his school days, that period of confusion and turmoil. He'd later dismissed those feelings as the sort of things many boys go through, based on his observations of his peers, and hadn't considered those moments since. Not really. Not until now. Too much was happening to him, and each day he was in danger of drowning, or being consumed by a blue-eyed shark.

CHAPTER 4

"TRY THE FIGURE EIGHT."

"That one's easy," Oliver said, neatly weaving the strands of rope.

"You think you know the ropes now? Give me a running bowline," Daly said.

Oliver scrunched his brow as he willed his hands to remember the twists and turns.

"There. A running bowline knot."

"That's a running fockin' disaster, mate." Daly snickered, leaning back against the bulkhead and picking up the mending. He had a tidy side-business sewing clothes in exchange for favors such as extra pudding or small coins, though the exchange of money was strongly discouraged by Nash. Now he was the proud owner of a silver penknife, a trade Oliver mourned every time he sharpened his pencil to make notes in the journal, but he'd needed a shirt without holes more than he needed the knife.

His writing was coming along, though most days he looked at what he'd written and despaired over ever getting it published. He'd never realized how difficult it was to capture a mood, a moment, an air.

Take the captain. It was clear he would be the

central figure in any story. The pirate drew all eyes like a lodestone drew iron. It wasn't just his stylish wardrobe, or his countenance—so handsome and finely constructed it bordered on pretty. It was the man's air of command, his presence. He looked at home aboard his vessel—his quick smile at one of Turnbull's dry remarks, his comments to the crew that made them stand a bit straighter, pull a bit harder.

When Oliver brought the supper tray, he sensed the captain watching him as he moved about the cabin.

"Tell me, Woodruff, do you have someone waiting for you at home, a sweetheart, perhaps?"

Oliver fumbled the plate as he set it down. He turned to find St. Armand leaning against the wall, close enough that he could see the long-lashes framing eyes dark as the sea outside. The scent of his sandalwood soap twined with the smell of coffee, and Oliver knew he'd never smell the drink again without thinking of this man.

"No. There's no one I'm attached to in England."

"You are such a fine-looking young man, I would have expected you to have a sweetheart…or someone special. But then, you're here for adventure, aren't you, Sunshine?" The pirate reached for the coffee cup, his arm brushing against Oliver's. "One can experience many new things when one's away from the confines of people who know you. People who judge you."

A ripple ran up Oliver's back and he was aware of how very alone they were in the small cabin, how quiet the evening was, how the nearness of the captain made his pulse speed. "I'm afraid I don't understand what you mean."

He knew exactly what the captain meant. Those long fingers cradled the coffee cup as he looked up from beneath his lashes, the ghost of a smile flitting on his mouth. Oliver swallowed, his mouth dry, and could feel his body responding to St. Armand in a way that would put lie to his statement.

But if he'd thought himself in danger before, madness lurked here, and before St. Armand could say—or do—anything else Oliver gathered up the tray and hurried out the door. He stood there, his hands clenched on the metal, the sound of the captain's low laughter echoing in his wake.

After a restless night of disturbing dreams and a near spill from his hammock, Oliver was bleary-eyed when Holt shook him awake, but he knew better than to complain. He took up his duties in the galley and while there was much about his current situation that disturbed him he knew one thing... If he never saw another turnip or potato, at least in its raw state, he wouldn't regret it. He must have said the last aloud for Roscoe chimed in, "Neptune's balls!"

"You, sir, are unfit for polite company. Have a turnip."

The bird watched him from his perch atop a chair back. He was seeking him out now, following Oliver around more. He suspected it was cupboard love since the cook's assistant had so many tasty treats at hand.

Holt stumped back into the galley, then prepared the tray for the captain's meal. By now their relationship was comfortable enough that Oliver could ask something he'd wondered for days.

"Mr. Holt, did you lose your foot here aboard ship?"

Holt stopped what he was doing and looked at Oliver for a long time, considering the question.

"I didn't lose my foot. I ran off and got caught by patrollers. Master James said I needed both hands to cook, but I didn't need both feet. Now take this to the captain."

"Aye, Mr. Holt," Oliver said with new respect for the dour freeman.

Turnbull let him into the captain's cabin and he arranged the meal on the table. The sunlight streaming in through the stern windows brightened the space, making the colorful pillows and rugs glow. The captain kept his own cabin neat, everything stowed away, and there was little for his cabin boy to do other than serve meals. Oliver paused as he poured the coffee, recalling the last meal he'd served and its tense aftermath. But the first mate was here now, and he smiled to himself as he imagined the pirate playing chaperone.

Today the captain was dressed in a coat of deep navy, with fawn trousers and a scarlet cravat flattering his tan skin and black curls. The jacket was waist length and something about his overall appearance jarred, but Oliver couldn't put his finger on what it was until St. Armand set the coffee cup down and reached for a chart in a cabinet near the table.

He almost dropped the coffeepot. "You're a woman!"

The cabin became far too quiet and Oliver wanted to bite his tongue off. If he was wrong, St. Armand wouldn't take kindly to having his masculinity questioned. But if he was right, he had the makings of a bestselling book in his grasp. Piratical sea captains were picaresque. A woman in that role—

A heavy hand came down on his shoulder, and he looked up into the unsmiling face of the first mate.

"Do you have a problem being aboard Captain St. Armand's vessel?" Turnbull asked politely.

"Yes! I mean, no! I don't have a problem with the vessel or Miss—Captain St. Armand or anyone—I don't care what the captain wears or who he—she— kisses or...or..." The words ran down as he saw his life washing away like rainwater down a drain. "I'm going to be sold as a cadaver, aren't I?"

"Are you certain you want Woodruff here to make it to Nassau, Captain?"

St. Armand leaned back against the table, arms crossed over a bosom Oliver would not stare at, not if his life depended on it. Which at the moment, it did.

"I promise, I won't tell anyone!"

"It's not a secret." Captain St. Armand—he was going to have to think of her as Captain St. Armand, no matter what—said in that contralto voice. "All you need to know is I'm the commander of this vessel. Everyone aboard knows it. You will continue to say 'aye, sir' or 'aye, Captain,' and we'll muddle along."

There was something in the underlying tone that still brought images of scalpels to mind, so Oliver gulped and said, "Aye, Captain," and gratefully followed Turnbull's order to come back later for the tray. This was too much to think about, especially after all the jumbled emotions of the past days.

"If that lubber was any thicker you could use him as a plank."

Mattie snickered at the mate's comment, but her mind was still tossing around the idea of putting Woodruff to use at something more productive than peeling potatoes, pleasing her in bed, or feeding sharks.

"All I'm saying is, he may be the best opportunity

we have. Well-spoken Englishmen don't drop into our lives every day. You know what happened to him in St. Martin. He's the most likely candidate and time's working against us."

John Turnbull scratched his ear.

"What if he doesn't go for it? Have you thought about how you'll keep him from peaching to the authorities in Florida?"

Mattie walked to the window, looking out over the turquoise waters of the Caribbean, waters the same shade as the eyes of her cabin boy. She pushed that thought aside before glancing over her shoulder.

"It's regretful, but accidents happen all the time, aboard ship and on land as well. I would weigh Woodruff's life against our needs and make the decision I need to."

"You're the captain, lass."

"Indeed. I took this on. I'll live with what I have to do. In the meantime, let me think about how best to approach the problem."

Turnbull returned to his duties, leaving Mattie with her thoughts and her meal. She was honest with Woodruff—her gender wasn't a secret aboard the vessel—but it had been a long time since she'd thought of herself as Miss St. Armand. She may not have been comfortable in society, but she knew the sea, and she knew ships, and she knew how to fight. Captaining the *Prodigal Son* was the life she'd been born to, and most days she focused solely on being the ship's commander.

However, she could be distracted by a pretty face, and Oliver Woodruff *was* pretty. His thick gold hair set off a slender visage with a straight nose, a square chin sporting a pleasant gilded scruff, and eyes a paler blue than hers.

The rest of him was equally well put together, not overly muscled, well-balanced to her in his height. She could look him in the eye, and if she had him bent over a table…

But she was getting ahead of herself. Pretty boys could be purchased in any port for fun and games, but right now she needed him for work. Fun with Woodruff could come later.

If he survived.

CHAPTER 5

"THAT MESS OF PEAS IS burning, boy!"

"Sorry, Mr. Holt." Oliver stirred the pot in question while questions bounced through his mind. Who was Captain St. Armand? Mrs. Simpson called her "Mattie," but that could be a boy's name or a girl's name. Captain Jensen had called her "Matt," so maybe he didn't know about her. They'd seemed well acquainted though, and when their heads were close together aboard the *Salacia* there'd been an air of intimacy. He recalled the madam's remarks on Captain St. Armand preferring the company of men, but it was clear from that interlude she also enjoyed the intimate company of her own sex.

He did his best to keep his eyes to himself when he was in the captain's presence, but it was difficult. At night he scribbled notes so he'd be able to reconstruct it all later. He knew she was aware he watched her, and sometimes he saw her watching him in return, her deceptively sleepy-eyed gaze making him uncomfortably hot, not only because of the possibilities it raised in his mind, but because she reminded him of a cat watching a mouse hole, patiently waiting for the right moment to pounce.

Then the thought of Captain St. Armand pouncing on him made his situation even worse. Some men relieved their tensions in their hammocks in the dark. Everyone pretended it wasn't happening, but it was quite common. Any more thoughts of pouncing and he'd be joining his shipmates in "boxing the bishop," as they quaintly termed it at school.

Matt? Mattie? St. Armand was well spoken, though the mixture of accents and phrasing in her speech made her hard to pigeonhole. Usually one could identify someone in England by speech. Where they lived, what stratum of society was theirs, but she could be self-taught or she could be a gentleman's daughter, it was hard to say.

He still suspected Captain St. Armand was a pirate, and that the *Prodigal Son* was well armed for reasons other than the safety of the ship and its cargo and crew. That theory was put to the test later that day when the lookout spied another vessel off the starboard bow. Oliver was in the galley with Holt when the call came, "All hands on deck!"

"That includes you, Woodruff. I need to take care of the fires here, but you want to move smartly now."

Oliver took off as other men raced up with him onto a deck crammed with well-armed sailors.

"Woodruff, can you shoot? Never mind. If you've never handled a pistol on a rolling deck you're liable to blow someone's head off. With my luck, it'd be me," Nash grumbled. "Here, take this and try to look threatening."

He shoved a pistol at Oliver and sent him over to starboard where he did his best to stay out of the way of the others. That seemed like an even better plan after he checked the pistol and discovered it wasn't loaded.

The ship they pursued was a merchant brig flying United States colors. A shot from the bow gun caused the brig to back its sails, and it was clear they were no match for the pirates—because it was ridiculous for Oliver to think of his shipmates and their captain as anything else when they were all standing around armed to the teeth, threatening another vessel.

A bewhiskered officer aboard the American vessel took a speaking horn and yelled across the water. "Why have you opened fire on us?"

Turnbull took up his own horn, his deep voice resonating through the tube. "We've come to trade with you. That was just to get your attention."

Oliver could see the Americans frowning and arguing amongst themselves. Before they could respond, Turnbull picked up the horn again.

"If necessary, we can repeat our knock on your door. Can't guarantee the gunner's accuracy though. I've seen him put a nasty hole in a hull by accident. We're sending over men now and suggest you meet them properly."

While this discussion occurred, Nash moved among the men, distributing heavy weather gear, even though the temperature was well into tropical levels.

"But—"

"Stow your questions and do as you're told, Woodruff!" Nash snapped.

Oliver put on the oiled jacket, heavy trousers pulled over his duck ones, a woolen cap and a scarf around his neck. He feared he'd pass out from the extra layers, but the men around him acted like this was a normal way to dress in the Caribbean.

They entered the boats, and when Daly was

distracted Oliver lifted his pouch and loaded the pistol. He'd be damned if he was going to enter into a fray with an unloaded gun, orders or no.

They climbed aboard the *Betsy Anne* to find the first boat, the one carrying Captain St. Armand, had secured the ship's crew on deck. Daniel Green motioned for the others to follow him below, and when the American officers objected, St. Armand said, "We're here to buy some of your molasses. Don't make a fuss or negotiations could end badly."

This was said in a reasonable voice, but the threat was explicit and it shut up the Americans.

Below it was dank and dark, and Oliver took a breath, nearly fainting from the miasmic atmosphere.

"What is that stench?"

"Quiet," Green whispered harshly.

They moved aft until they came to a barred door. Green nodded at Fong, the big Chinaman, who took a breath, then kicked the door in at the latch. Green followed immediately, and there was a flash and an explosion as he shot an armed guard lifting his own pistol to bear on them.

Nash rushed in behind, and Oliver's eyes adjusted to the dim light and the smoke. The room held a dozen people—men in chains and three women huddled together. The stench was their unwashed bodies and the refuse of days at sea without proper sanitation, seasickness, and bad food. They stared at the sailors, hollow-eyed, but Nash was already working on the chains, picklocks in hand.

Green addressed the slaves in Spanish. Whatever he said made the men sit up and look more alert while Nash freed their shackles.

"Strip," Green said.

At first Oliver thought he meant the slaves. Then he saw his shipmates yanking off their gear down to their trousers and he followed suit, shivering now after being swaddled in heavy wool. The clothes were passed to the slaves, who pulled them on, the women covering their heads with the caps.

"Daly, Woodruff, you take the lead. Green and the others will bring up the rear. C'mon, men," Nash ordered.

Green said more to the slaves, who gathered in a knot in the middle, the men on the outside, and they headed up the companionway.

When they reached the deck Nash said, "Stand here with me, Woodruff. This is where it gets dicey."

Oliver took his position and as the crew emerged from below, the *Betsy Anne's* captain moved forward.

"You pirates can't take our cargo!"

St. Armand stared at him, backed by the guns of the men of the boarding party as well as the guns of the *Prodigal Son*.

"Says on your papers you're carrying molasses from Cuba to Savannah. It's legal to import molasses into the United States, but last I checked, you couldn't import contraband. Contraband like Africans, for example. Those sailors behind me? Those are my crew. We'll head back now and let you get on your way. A shame we couldn't come to agreement on purchasing your molasses, but some days are like that, aren't they?"

St. Armand was speaking in accents straight off the Liverpool docks, making it harder than ever for Oliver to pin down where the captain originated. None of that mattered to the American captain, who looked ready to fight as a fortune in human chattel was spirited away, but he knew he could do nothing except fume.

A younger officer was more impetuous.

Oliver saw the movement from the corner of his eye as the man pulled a knife and rushed St. Armand from behind. Oliver fired his pistol into the deck at the man's feet and the officer skidded to a halt.

The air rang with the sound of the gunshot, but St. Armand calmly said, "That's the only warning you'll get, Captain Mallory. It would give me pleasure to sink this scow to the bottom of the ocean so you cannot import *molasses* into the United States again. Do yourself a favor. Act prudently and you'll live to sail another day."

"Woodruff, stay with the captain," Nash said as Green helped the Africans into the waiting boats.

"Aye, Mr. Nash."

One of the men passed Oliver a pouch. He reloaded before joining St. Armand, who silently watched the activity around her. She was more masculine looking today, her hair sleeked back under her hat, her breasts bound beneath her brown jacket. Her sex might not be a secret aboard ship, but he could see where it was to her advantage to keep people guessing about the legendary Captain St. Armand.

She rested her gloved hand on the blade strapped to her thigh. The knife was over a foot long, an unusual design, double edged and curved at the point with a substantial guard at the hilt, and a heavy brass pommel.

"Like it? It's a Spanish hunting blade I won in a card game in Cuba," the captain said as if they were standing in the park conversing, instead of aboard a slaver they'd just hijacked. On the other hand, he doubted he'd be discussing wicked-looking knives while strolling through Hyde Park in London.

"It looks like more than I need for slicing turnips, Captain."

"Spend time with my crew and you'll be surprised at what you can learn to do with a good knife. Back to the boats," she called out, and they left the *Betsy Anne* as rifle-wielding crew members in the rigging of the *Prodigal Son* kept watch.

The schooner clapped on sail, leaving the brig lumbering in its wake. The slaves were on deck, scrubbing down from their days forced to lie in filth. The men went first, laughing among themselves as they cleaned off, and they were issued clean trousers and shirts from ship's stores. A canvas partition was rigged for the women to wash behind, and they were given loose calico dresses. Ship's biscuit and drink was distributed and they fell on it with ravenous speed.

At first he'd suspected they were pirating away the slaves for their own profit, but now he wasn't sure. Having seen the care for the enslaved people, knowing how Mr. Holt felt, it made him wonder more than ever who the captain was and what role she played in events in the Caribbean.

The Abolition of Slavery Act had become law only a few years back. For the mill owners in England, the issue of slavery in the United States was still tied to cotton production and hotly debated even as Britons congratulated themselves on being morally superior to their upstart cousins across the Atlantic.

Was St. Armand's involvement more personal, her sun-dark skin bespeaking an African background rather than a Mediterranean one?

Turnbull called him over.

"You'll be responsible for this lot until we're in Nassau. Make sure they're fed and that they're not wandering about, getting underfoot. There's a place in the hold for the men, quarters for the women. Show them how to hang their hammocks."

"I don't speak Spanish, Mr. Turnbull."

"That's your problem. You're still working in the galley with Cicero, unless one of those women is kitchen trained."

Oliver approached the group of slaves, sitting on the deck nearby and talking amongst themselves in low voices. They fell silent at his approach. He eyed them and sighed, scratching his head.

"I'm Oliver Woodruff. I know you can't understand me, but I mean you no harm." He put his hands on his hips and stared at the silent group. "Does anyone speak English?"

One of the men looked at the others, then jerked his head in a nod.

"That'll make it easier. You are…?"

"Joe."

He waited, then realized many slaves don't have surnames. Holt had named himself, he'd told Oliver so.

"Very well, Joe. As I said, I'm Oliver Woodruff, and I could use your assistance. You heard Mr. Turnbull say I'm to see to your needs, so let's start with the most important—is anyone in need of medical attention?"

At their blank looks he said, "Is anyone sick? Injured?"

Joe spoke in Spanish to the group, then said sardonically, "We're valuable property, Mr. Woodruff. No one beat us the past few days because we might fetch less money."

"Follow me then—do any of the women have experience in kitchen work?"

Turned out they didn't. One of the women had been a child's nurse until her services weren't needed, the other two were field workers on a coffee plantation. Turnips still loomed in Oliver's future.

He showed them how to hang the hammocks, hilarity ensuing as he demonstrated how to enter a hammock to sleep. One of the men made a remark to his companion after glancing at the women, but Joe said something sharp to him and he shut up. The women huddled together, away from the men, and when Oliver took them to their quarters he asked Joe to come with him to translate. He spoke softly to the women, not at all like he spoke to the men, and they relaxed.

"You're good with people, good at calming the women."

Joe nodded at the one he'd identified as a child's nurse.

"That gal, Teresa—she was a wet-nurse because she birthed her own babe and could take care of both. When little master started schooling, her boy was sold away. She has nothing now."

Oliver had no response for that, so he let Joe explain the hammocks, which the women eyed warily.

He finally had them settled, but there was still the evening meal to serve. When he entered the galley, everything was ready, all the vegetables washed and prepared.

"You did enough today, boy. I managed before you came. I can manage for an afternoon."

"Thank you, Mr. Holt. I was beginning to feel like a galley slave."

As soon as the words were out of his mouth, Oliver wanted to punch himself. The room went deathly silent and he slowly turned to see Holt's black eyes boring holes into him. He was reminded that the cook was standing next to all the knives.

Then the older man whooped and slapped his knee.

"Galley slave? That look on your face! I swear, I thought you were going to piss your pants. Never seen a white man turn that shade of gray. Heh. Galley slave. I'll remember that. Now, get to work serving this, the larboard mess won't want to wait for you."

"Aye, Mr. Holt."

Oliver grabbed the food and hurried out before he said something else life threatening.

He saw to the slaves after the crew, bringing food for them and eating with them up on deck. At first they were put off by him sitting with them—the women in particular eyeing him before cautiously eating their own food—but at that point he was so tired he didn't care.

A hand gently shaking his shoulder brought him out of a doze.

"You fell asleep over your food," Joe said, and for the first time Oliver saw the glimmer of a smile on his face. "Teresa was ready to grab your leftovers."

Oliver pushed the tin plate over to Teresa with a gesture for her to eat, and she fell on it, eyeing him all the while.

When all were finished, the women began to sing a song softly, clapping their hands in rhythm to the music. One would sing a line and the others would respond in a dialect that sounded like a patois of Spanish and other languages. The men joined in, one of them bringing a bass voice so deep Oliver thought the deck beneath his feet vibrated.

The singing lifted him up. He was awake now, able

to appreciate what he'd been a part of that day. He didn't know where the slaves were bound, or what their futures held, but he knew he was wrong to think of them as slaves any longer. They were free, as free as anyone aboard the vessel, and he'd been a part of the events that freed them.

CHAPTER 6

"FETCH THE CAPTAIN'S TRAY, BOY."
    At Holt's command he set down the pot he'd been scrubbing, the last of his galley duties for the night. The tray was not outside her cabin, and when she said "Enter" at his knock, he took a moment to run his hands through his hair, trying to bring his curls into order before presenting himself to Captain St. Armand. At least his clothes were clean, a fresh shirt and his own jacket since the clothes he'd stripped off aboard the *Betsy Anne* waited laundering. His face bristled with his new and itchy beard, and he'd have to ask Green or Daly how they managed shaving aboard a rolling ship without cutting their own throats.

St. Armand wore a white shirt and a waistcoat of blue leather tooled in gold, along with her usual buckskins. She was covered more than ladies wore in their bodices at fashionable evenings, but her shirt was open slightly at the neck, and that glimpse of white linen against her tanned skin drew his eye. She leaned back against her table, watching him.

He busied himself loading her supper tray, but she said, "Leave it outside the door. I wish to speak to you."

He did as instructed, then hesitated at the open door.

"Close it."

The cabin was quiet, the parrot was somewhere else on the ship, but he could hear the normal night noises of the *Prodigal Son*, the never-ending creak of the rigging, the wind and the waves, along with the voices of the men. He gave a brief thought to the closed door and being alone with the captain in her cabin, then dismissed this vestigial concern for propriety.

He was, as he'd been so often reminded, of very low status aboard the ship. He almost smiled at the thought of his own virtue being at risk. St. Armand retrieved a bottle of rum and two glasses, motioning him to sit as she took her own chair across the table from him. Her hands were ungloved, clean, but scarred from old wounds. No sailor had smooth hands and he glanced down at his own, cracked and reddened from kitchen work, tougher now than when she'd hauled him out of the brothel.

She poured him some rum and some for herself, peering at him over the top of her glass as she drank, then set hers aside.

He drank and tried not to choke on the fiery liquid, looking at her with new respect. Anyone who could drink that and walk afterward had bottom. He wanted to ask her about herself, about the varied speech that made her hard to identify, about how she became captain of a band of rogues and pirates who knew she was a woman but accepted it in stride. But it wasn't the right time for his questions. He was here at her command.

"You acquitted yourself well aboard the American

ship," she said, leaning back in her chair. "I was impressed, both by your handling of the pistol under stress and by your quick thinking."

He shrugged, though her praise gave him a warm feeling. She'd also seen him stripped down to his trousers, and he would be less than male if he didn't hope she liked what she saw.

"Did you intend to fire at his feet or was it luck that you didn't hit him, or me?"

"There was more skill than luck in my shot," he said confidently. "Shooting is something I do well, although I'm still becoming accustomed to the ship moving."

He did enjoy taking his pistols out when he could get away from his responsibilities. The combination of having to clear his mind, steady his hand, and rely on his eyesight and muscles relaxed him. Of course, he'd only shot at targets, not at foes trying to kill him, and he knew she thought the same thing by the small smile turning up the corner of her mouth.

That smile brought the delicate crescent scar at the corner into focus and he wondered how she acquired that, what it would be like to put his lips there... He reined in his wayward imagination.

"What will happen to the people we brought aboard?"

"They're black gold. Strong men, women who are proven breeders. Smuggling slaves into the United States through Florida territory is highly profitable, and given the poor standards of the navy and the Revenue Marine, not too great a risk. I could go to Fernandina, Apalachicola, even New Orleans—any of those ports would give me easy access to slave dealers."

"You did not stop the *Betsy Anne* to steal the slaves for yourself and resell them."

"No?"

"No," he said firmly. "I've only spent a short time aboard this ship, but seeing the crew, and seeing how they acted, how you acted... I think you took those slaves to do something else with them. I don't know what, but I suspect you're working with anti-slavery forces."

"Interesting," she said, taking a sip of her own drink.

She watched him again and he realized he wasn't used to sitting with a woman who didn't chatter. The young women of his acquaintance, the ones he saw at church and social events and assemblies, they twittered like a flock of birds, preening before the young men or their peers.

Captain St. Armand—Mattie—just *was*. She was in command of the ship, of herself, of the situation. That's what struck him—he'd known men who had what a naval acquaintance referred to as "command presence," projecting authority and confidence, the ability to lead others, but he'd never met a woman who had that quality. Until now.

It intrigued him, and it excited him, and he'd be lying to himself if he didn't acknowledge the attraction she held for him. He could only hope it was reciprocated because a misstep with this woman would end with him suffering something more fatal than an admonishing tap on the wrist with a folded fan.

She rose from behind the table and came around to where he sat, perching herself on the edge, one booted foot swinging as she examined him. Her hair was neatly slicked back against her head and he was tempted to reach up and tousle it, to see it spring out and curl around his fingers.

She leaned forward and his glance flickered down to that open collar and lower, to her breasts. He suspected they were bound, flattening them against her chest, and he itched to unbutton her shirt and see for himself.

"Ahem."

His lifted his gaze to a knowing smile crinkling her eyes at the corners.

"I invited you into my cabin for a reason."

"Oh?" he said, striving for an insouciant tone.

"I need a man. But not just any man. I need a special man...one willing to do things others cannot."

Her throaty voice sent shivers down Oliver's spine, and into other places. He glanced at the glass of rum, but resisted reaching for it, instead relaxing back into his seat with a smile.

"Am I the man you're looking for?"

"You have the most important qualification. You're white."

"I'm quite flatt—what?"

"You are white. White like bird droppings. White like pastry flour. White like rice—"

"Yes, I understand all of that. What does my skin color have to do with anything?"

"So speaks a man who's never had to think about the color of his skin. Being white can open doors and shut mouths."

She stood and refilled her glass, and his, and he didn't hesitate this time as he took a drink.

"In a day or two we will be in Nassau. You will be free to leave the ship at that time, but I want to offer you an opportunity to stay on for a job I have in mind."

Poor Woodruff. His confusion was writ all over his handsome face, but Mattie kept her smile to herself. She was certain nothing in his comfortable life in England had prepared him for the ship, or for dealing with her.

That was good. Life taught her to seize every advantage she could and putting those men she encountered on uncertain footing helped. She knew what they saw when they looked at her, and most of them could not move beyond trying to slot her into a comfortable category. She wasn't a wife or a relative or a lady or a maidservant or a shopkeeper, and for most of the men she encountered that left only "whore" as a classification.

Aboard the *Prodigal Son* she was Captain St. Armand. Anyone who wasn't happy with that didn't last long aboard the schooner, and some had found it a long swim back to shore. The ones who stayed gave her the respect she was due, respect she knew with no false modesty she'd earned. Her hands weren't soft like Woodruff's. They were calloused from gripping her cutlass, from climbing the rigging, and there was tar ground in that would never come out. She bore the scars of encounters where she'd been a shade slower than her opponent, but she was here in her cabin, alive to tell the tale. Most of those whose knives had left scars were not.

She took a moment to savor the sight in front of her. Woodruff's face and form were easy to admire, and the golden bristles on his chin made her itch to run her fingertips down his face, to see if the skin was as soft beneath.

That could wait. Right now there was business to discuss. She returned to the massive chair behind her table, an indulgence in the tight quarters, but one she knew increased her consequence in the eyes of any crew who stood before her. She was *always* aware of how much appearances mattered, which was one reason she'd asked this reluctant crew member into her cabin this night.

Of course he glanced at her tits. He was a man, after all, and he hadn't had the time to grow used to her as had her regular crew. She'd allow him that liberty, this time, so long as he didn't make a habit of it. Right now her conscience was warring with her brain, telling her bringing this lubber into harm's way was selfish. The right thing to do would be to leave him in Nassau, pat him on the head, and send him on his way with a few tales he could tell over the evening port when he returned to his comfortable, safe life in England. But doing the other work she did, and being captain, meant weighing the needs of one against the greater good.

"Enter," she said to the knock at the cabin door.

Turnbull came in, and Woodruff jumped at the interruption. Poor lamb. When she'd said she needed a man, he had clearly hoped for a different outcome this evening.

"I was about to explain to Mr. Woodruff here why I need a white man."

Turnbull made a disgusted noise, but she wasn't about to back down. He agreed with her on the need for their work. It was her methods he disapproved of.

"There are other ways, Captain, ways that don't put us at risk from him tripping us up or running to the authorities."

"I'm sitting right here."

Turnbull ignored him and fetched his own glass, his ochre skin gleaming in the lamplight. Mattie turned back to Woodruff.

"I am taking a chance telling you of our plans, as Mr. Turnbull points out. Of course, if you betray my confidence, it goes without saying you will suffer a—"

"'Tragic and fatal accident,' yes, I know. Tell me what it is you want."

"Captain."

"What?" he turned to Turnbull.

"Do not interrupt again, and finish that statement with either 'Captain' or 'sir' or I might think you're being disrespectful to the ship's commander."

Woodruff took a breath, getting himself under control.

"What is it you want from me, Captain St. Armand?"

Oooh, someone was beginning to show some spine. It didn't bother her. Taking command of a man with no backbone wasn't a challenge. Bending a strong man to her will...that was exciting, and potentially quite rewarding.

"As you figured out, I did not take those slaves off the *Betsy Anne* to resell them. I will, however, profit from today's events. There are people in England, and in parts of the United States, who help enslaved people obtain their freedom. Some slaves run away on their own, using deception to make their way to freedom, but as long as they're in the United States they're still at risk."

"And you steal them off ships?"

"If you're smart, you won't use the word 'stealing' when speaking of Captain St. Armand's business."

"Mr. Turnbull is correct. 'Stealing' is such a strong word, with severe legal consequences. Let us say instead I impress them into my crew and take them to where they have a better chance at living free. Your responses aboard the ship today, your assistance with our passengers, and the reports I have from Mr. Holt and the others lead me to believe I can have confidence in you."

Turnbull leaned back against a cabinet, his arms crossed over his chest, and Mattie took a swallow of her rum.

"When we reach Nassau you must make a choice. I will have done what I promised Barbara Simpson and you'll be free to go your own way. However, if you choose to sign aboard the *Prodigal Son*, you will assist me in my next job. I don't know how much news from this area reaches you in England, but Florida Territory is embroiled with a conflict with its Seminole Indians, many of whom are maroons or escaped slaves. Their conflict is my opportunity."

"Maroons?"

"Black Seminoles or their relatives. Because of the conflict, and because the owners are worried about uprisings in general, it's becoming harder for slaves to run south and hide in the wild. They have a better chance of getting to freedom if they can get across the water to the Bahamas or other British land. Indeed, there are some in England who believe building up the black troops on Jamaica makes a good check on American expansion in the Caribbean. The Americans are terrified the black regiments will turn up on their shores and start a full slave revolt."

Woodruff absorbed all this and Mattie watched the landsman as her ship hummed around her. So much of her life had been spent aboard this vessel, or ones like it, that it was hard for her to now imagine a life on the land year in, year out.

"Why me?"

Mattie looked at Turnbull, then back at Woodruff. The mate didn't need to be here. He wasn't her duenna—a thought that made her smile inside. But he was an excellent, if harsh, judge of character. How Woodruff responded to tonight's conversation, how much Turnbull believed him, could determine whether he'd be appropriate for the task ahead.

What he didn't realize is a wrong answer or attitude could still result in him never making it to Nassau.

"What do you know about me, Woodruff?"

"Nothing. The crew does not gossip about you." He looked at her intently. "I suspect your involvement in helping these slaves could have a... personal connection?"

"Personal. Yes, you could say that." She steepled her fingers again, debating how much to tell him. Giving him the truth, if not the whole truth, was the best.

"I have, as you might have guessed, black blood. In New Orleans I'd be called a 'yellow gal,' an octoroon. It is thanks to my father that I'm free and not a slave. He bought my mother's contract when she worked in a brothel in St. Martin—the very brothel where we first met."

"So your father was Captain St. Armand. Is he French? Or British?"

She debated telling him, then shrugged.

"He's British, but he has nothing to do with this, or you. Unlike that earlier Captain St. Armand, I cannot go everywhere, do what I need to do in the United States or Florida Territory because I'm a woman, and because I'm not white."

"I can see why you'd need a white man, but why me? There are other white men aboard this ship."

"Yes, but they're not gentlemen. Daly, Nash, they're excellent crew members, but I need someone who's well-spoken and comfortable in society. We'll invent a false identity for you, something to explain who you are, why you're traveling, and why you'd be in Florida."

"We could set him up as a member of the peerage. The Americans are impressed by titles and such."

"Not a bad idea, Mr. Turnbull. Hmmm...how would you like to be a viscount, Woodruff?"

"I have a radical idea. Let's tell the truth."

He looked rather smug saying this, as if the idea of telling the truth meant he had one up on them. Turnbull growled, but she put up a hand.

"What truth would that be?"

Woodruff stood, pacing the small confines of her cabin as Mattie leaned back and enjoyed the view. Barbara was right, he was a pretty boy—no, he was an attractive man and that was a very different thing than a pretty boy. Pretty boys were had for a song in any port, but a man who carried himself well, who exuded confidence, that was more to her taste. Bringing him aboard and involving him in her schemes might have unexpected benefits, and she quashed the pang of conscience that said a good girl would not put someone like him in harm's way.

It had been a long time since anyone, herself included, considered her a good girl. A good girl wouldn't be watching his arse as he moved, the graceful play of muscles beneath the cotton trousers. She'd seen him today stripped down to nothing but those trousers, hanging low on lean hips with sculpted bones, and she liked what she saw.

"You haven't asked me about myself, Captain—who I am, why I'm here,"

Turnbull looked at him keenly.

"In our world, you don't pry into a shipmate's background or ask too many questions. Not safe."

"Yes, I've come to appreciate the wisdom of that," he said wryly. "But I may be of more help to you than you suspect. I'm from Manchester, where my family owns a mill. Perhaps you've heard of Moffett Mills?"

Mattie sat up, her senses alert. "I have. Your family is connected?"

"My mother's family. My uncle has no children so I'm being groomed to take over for him. My own father is dead, but he was connected to the peerage. I'm not in line to inherit a title, but my grandmother was an earl's daughter. So no, I'm not Viscount Somebody, but I have connections. Legitimate, truthful connections that buy cotton from the United States."

"That could be a problem."

"How so?"

"What we're doing is dangerous," she admitted, wanting him to know what was at stake. It was one thing to use some poor dupe, but there would be repercussions if someone connected in society turned up missing or dead, repercussions that could not only affect her work here, but the lives of other people in England.

"If you're well-known in business circles, or in society, there may be people in America who will know too much about you. There's a great deal of cross-fertilization, if you will, among Southern planters and their cousins in Great Britain."

He thought about this, then shrugged.

"That will not be a problem. The mill owners work through brokers in Liverpool, and the planters deal with factors in New York to sell their crops. While my family is known, I haven't been working publicly for my uncle. He's not keen on my assuming control of the mill," he admitted. "Uncle Braswell termed me a radical and an ungrateful wretch biting the hand that fed me."

He looked at them and didn't appear boyish at all.

"Our family is locked in embrace with the slave states of America, as they produce the cotton we need at a cost we can afford. What you're doing is noble, helping a handful of people escape bondage, but it will not change the system. America will use slaves to grow cheap cotton, and Englishmen will buy cheap cotton. The public only cares about saving a shilling or two on fabric, not about the blood staining their calicoes and muslins. You cannot free all the slaves."

"You're right." Mattie twisted her glass of rum. "I cannot free them all. But I can change things for some. In addition," she added briskly, "I'm being well compensated for the work I do. This gives me a lucrative option in place of other profitable forays that bring too much attention from the navy. There's still risk, of course."

She hesitated, then plowed on. She couldn't throw Woodruff into harm's way without him having a sense of what was at stake.

"Those men shooting at us in St. Martin were after me because they'd connected Captain St. Armand to a slave-stealing incident. While today was a success, the risk all around is increasing and it's becoming more difficult to conduct these operations as myself. I need a confederate who can give me suitable cover."

"A white gentleman."

"Exactly." She stood and crossed her arms over her chest, looking at him, *seeing* him. He offered her opportunities she hadn't considered, and she needed to think this through, find the best way to work with him, not just use him.

"Do not give me any answers now. When we're in Nassau, if you want to learn more, if you want to do more, we'll talk then."

"How would you manage if I said no?"

She shrugged. "Maintaining a ship like the *Prodigal Son* takes a great deal of coin, and the work I do is profitable, so I would find a way."

Woodruff watched her silently, then looked at the mate. "Mr. Turnbull, you oppose my involvement. Why?"

"You've managed to fit in well enough," Turnbull acknowledged. "But this is dangerous work." He looked at his commander and something on his face softened.

"I've known the captain here for a turtle's age, and taking risks is nothing new to Marauding Mattie, but you need to know what's at stake. We do," he finished on a serious note. "Men die in our world. You need to know that before you agree to anything."

"Men die every day, everywhere, Mr. Turnbull. They die in mill accidents and carriage accidents and from war and from disease. What matters is how you live your life until that moment. We will talk later then, Captain. You've given me a great deal to think about."

She nodded her dismissal and Woodruff left, the

parrot flying in through the open door. Roscoe went to his perch and ruffled his feathers, settling in for the night. Mattie walked over to the bird and scratched him in the spot he favored, and he made the little clucking sounds that reminded her of a cat purring.

"He's not what we expected," Turnbull said.

"No, but he may be what I need. I will know more after New Providence."

"He considers himself part of the crew now."

"It's different," she said. "The men who sign aboard are after gold or a steady meal and grog. Woodruff did not sign aboard. I took him like a parcel to be delivered. He's staying with us because we intrigue him, and perhaps now because it's something he believes in."

"He knows there is danger involved."

"Like a young man who takes the king's shilling knows there's danger involved? Do you think the recruiting sergeant says, 'Here you go, lad, a good opportunity to get your legs blown off or your brains shattered'? No, he says, 'Sign up, boyo, see the world, get glory, meet pretty girls.'"

"You've developed a conscience, sprat," Turnbull said, pushing off the wall. "Me, I've never had much use for one. See, it's like owning a carriage. Nice to have when you need it, but too much upkeep for day-to-day use. Speaking of people who keep carriages…"

The big man paused and she looked over her shoulder at him. The silver bristles on his face caught the lantern light and she was reminded again that while she'd grown up under his watchful gaze, he'd grown older.

"They want you to come home."

"Have things changed that much, my friend?" she

asked. "Is my place there more comfortable than it was ten years ago?"

"Life will always be difficult for you, just as it's never been easy for me. But you will make your own safe harbor. You're not a little sprat anymore. You're a woman grown. More importantly, you're Captain St. Armand. No one can ever take that away from you," he said. "Just be careful of yourself with Woodruff. He's different from most you deal with."

"Because he's a gentleman?"

"That, and for other reasons. He could be a risk to you in many ways, lass. I don't want to see you get hurt."

"You realize there's no one else I let talk to me this way?"

"Aye, and that's why you keep me around."

"That and your handy ways with a blade, Mr. Turnbull." She turned back to the bird, who eyed her with a hopeful gleam, and she reached over to her table to get some fruit for the cup on his perch. The bird had a simple philosophy where she was concerned. Guard her, bring her vermin, let her feed him.

So much less complicated than dealing with men.

"For now, let's get our latest consignment unloaded in Nassau and then we'll see where Woodruff stands."

"Oh, he'll sign on. That boy is aching for adventure. It's written all over him."

"That is one of the things we do best—add excitement to people's lives. What would they do without us?" she added lightly.

"Grow old and die in their own beds?"

"Instead we offer 'A short life, but a merry one.' Remember Bartholomew Robert's motto?"

"Aye, but that age of pirates is past, Captain."

"So everyone keeps reminding me. Good night, old friend."

CHAPTER 7

OLIVER CONSIDERED WHAT CAPTAIN ST.
Armand—Mattie—said to him as he peeled turnips the next morning. A soft knock at the galley door brought him and Holt looking up from their work. Teresa, the woman who'd been a wet-nurse, stood there, eyes cast down as she twisted her hands in her dress. Joe was behind her, and he said something to her, then gave her a gentle push forward.

"Teresa says she wants to help here. She's grateful to the ship's people for taking her off the slaver and doesn't like to sit around all day."

Holt gave her a long, considering look, then nodded. "Work is good, keeps your mind off your troubles. Boy, find someone else to annoy."

"Aye, Mr. Holt," Oliver said, happy to pass his apron and knife over to Teresa.

When he and Joe went above, they found Daly showing the other rescued blacks how to pick oakum. One of the men looked rebellious at the idea of working under orders again, but Joe spoke sharply to him and he stopped grumbling.

"What did you say?"

"If you want to eat, you have to work. Not the same

as field work, but we all have to work at something. I work as a carpenter mostly. Only time a man stops working is when he dies and goes to heaven."

Joe and Oliver joined them at the never-ending task, as the tarry fiber was used in seams throughout the vessel to keep the water out. Daly started humming a chantey and the others picked it up. The Irishman had a lovely tenor voice, and soon the former slaves were singing "Round the Corner, Sally."

Out of the corner of his eye Oliver saw Captain St. Armand talking to Daniel Green. The sailor went below and returned with two cutlasses, one of which he tossed to his captain, who caught it neatly. The men stopped what they were doing to watch the weapons practice.

St. Armand took a stance and saluted Green, who snickered—the first time Oliver had ever seen anything approaching a smile on that dark face— then rushed the captain with a yell. Green's reach was shorter than St. Armand's, but he was fierce in his attack and the blades flashed in the sunlight.

St. Armand grinned as she ducked beneath a back-handed blow which could have taken off an ear at the least, but then Green stepped into her guard, clouting her on the jaw with the cutlass hilt, sending St. Armand to the deck.

Silence froze the new arrivals as they watched a black sailor knock down his captain.

St. Armand climbed to her feet and shook her head, then wiped blood off her chin with the back of her hand and picked up her weapon.

"You old seadog, you've learned a new trick. Show me how you did that."

"Watch and learn, youngster," Green huffed.

He took a moment to catch his breath, then slowly repeated the attack, repositioning St. Armand's arm at one point, then feinting up to her chin.

They repeated the maneuver twice, then St. Armand shook out her arm, narrowed her eyes and said, "Now, try that again."

This time it was St. Armand who knocked Green down, helping him to his feet with a laugh.

"Good enough, Daniel. I like it. I want you to demonstrate that move to the crew later, starting with Daly and Fong. One's quick, the other's big, and I want to see how they handle it."

"Aye, aye, Captain."

There was a sharp pain in his palms. Oliver looked down at his hands, only now realizing he'd fisted them so tight during the fight his nails nearly broke the skin.

"Woodruff!"

He looked up at St. Armand, wiping sweat off her brow with her sleeve, her chin still smeared red. Where most of the sailors were stripped down to shirts and trousers, or shirtless in the case of Fong, she was dressed in a fully fastened white shirt, a blue neckcloth tucked inside, a waistcoat of burnished gold satin over it. It dawned on him that even though her crew might know she was a woman, if she dressed and carried herself as a man, they could more easily ignore her sex.

He was certain he'd never reach that point.

She shrugged into her coat, a rich tobacco brown shade of superfine. The padded shoulders enhanced the masculine look of her gear, drawing the eye upward rather than to her trim waist and bound breasts.

"Fetch me hot water from the galley."

"Aye, Captain," he said, and as he walked away he realized two things. Like it or not, he was serving as her cabin boy, or at least her steward. He also realized he was used to women who coaxed and cajoled men into doing what they wanted, though he'd certainly heard the cook at home give the servants the sharp edge of her tongue when they didn't move fast enough to suit her.

The scene in the galley made him pause. Holt and Teresa were sitting side-by-side, peeling vegetables together. Holt said something to her, then showed her a different angle for her knife. There was no scolding as there had been for him, he pointed out.

"If you brightened the galley as much as this pretty gal does, I wouldn't have scolded you either."

Teresa didn't smile, but she appeared less apprehensive when she looked at the cook. She wouldn't look at Oliver.

"Captain's sent me to get hot water, Mr. Holt."

Hold fetched a can and filled it from the boiler, then put together a plate of cheese and sliced ham along with the still chewable ship's biscuit. Oliver appreciated the benefits of sailing closer to the islands, though he was longing for fresh water when they made land. He'd never realized how much one took things like fresh water for granted until his sea voyage. He vowed the first thing he'd do is soak the salt out of his skin and drink his fill of water when he was safely ashore.

Holt covered the plate with a cloth. "I want you back here for luncheon. I'm not sending this little gal out to serve that lot."

Oliver left for the captain's quarters, setting the steaming can on the deck and knocking before entering. She was alone, peering into a mirror set into the wall near her oversized bed. There was no hammock for the captain, but a large, comfortable looking structure with pillows and a silk coverlet, somewhat faded from its time at sea, but still holding jeweled tones in its fabric. An Oriental rug softened the planks on the deck. It looked lush, but unlike the other sailors, he wasn't barefoot, so he couldn't check for himself. Being barefoot aided in climbing the rigging, Daly said, but Oliver wasn't comfortable with that yet. His feet were as soft as his hands, seeming to attract every splinter aboard ship.

He set the plate on the table and at her gesture, poured the hot water into her washbasin. She dipped a cloth into it and dabbed at the blood at the corner of her mouth, flexing her jaw back and forth, testing it after Green's punch.

"You missed a spot." Oliver reached over to take her chin in his hand, freezing as the implications of his act struck him. He'd put his hands on her without thinking, as he would for a friend or a shipmate below deck.

But she wasn't either of those things. Mattie St. Armand was the captain, and she was a woman. A most attractive woman who watched him now, her sapphire eyes darkening as they stood so close. He took the cloth from her hand, dipped it in the water and wiped the fleck of blood from her cheek, the area reddened from where she'd been struck. It wasn't the first time she'd taken a blow.

"How did you get this scar?" he asked as he gently ran the cloth over her chin, the crescent alongside her mouth giving her smile an interesting twist.

She wasn't smiling now as her lashes fluttered

down, fanning out over her expressive eyes. "I trusted someone I should not have trusted. A business associate. He made an attempt to slash my throat and keep our profits for himself."

Oliver's fingers tightened on the cloth he held, water trickling down his arm. "Where is he now?"

"He's no longer a threat to me, or anyone else. I have strong feelings about betrayal."

"Are you warning me because of our plans?"

"No. I have a good sense for who I can trust, and who I shouldn't trust, but it's not infallible. I trust you enough to share my plans with you, Woodruff. If I thought you'd betray me you wouldn't be standing here now. You certainly wouldn't be standing in my cabin, close enough for me to do this."

She touched his face, only the tips of her fingers, but it bloomed all the way to the base of his spine as she smoothed them down his skin to his jawline. The cabin was so quiet he heard his beard rasp against her fingertips.

It was the simplest of caresses, but it changed everything between them, everything that had happened until this point. He'd not been bold enough to touch her, and even now, he was still, awaiting her command, awaiting her pleasure. He tipped his head to the side, a smile rising from his chest.

"And what do you risk if you trust me with more?"

"'Trust you with more?' You're cheeky for a cabin boy."

"I'm not your cabin boy."

"So you say, yet here you are."

He let the smile out, but stepped away from her, gathering the water can and dirtied cloth.

"Will there be anything else, Captain?"

She leaned back against her table. "What if I said I wanted you to stay?"

"Is that an invitation? Or an order?"

A smile quirked up the corner of her mouth. "It was a question."

He looked at her a long moment, then set the can down, walking across the few planks of deck separating them. It was quiet in the captain's quarters, and he could hear her soft breathing as he carefully ran the back of his knuckles along her jaw, lifting it as he angled her head for a kiss.

She went still as his lips touched hers, learning the taste of her, the sweetness and tartness in one package. He barely grazed her mouth, not pushing, not rushing, living in the moment as he'd learned from her, and her hands rose and held onto his shoulders, her lips soft beneath his. She was the right height for him, the right shape beneath his own hands as he held her face, careful of her injury, careful of her, aware of the strength in her slim hands as she slipped them around his neck, holding him against her.

He took his time, but at the end, he put his hands on her shoulders and stepped out of her embrace, his breath coming fast, her chest rising and falling beneath her bindings. Her eyes were heavy-lidded as she watched him move away from her.

He braced himself for an attack—verbal or physical—but she cocked her head to the side, running her finger over her swollen lips, drawing his eyes down to that movement.

"Interesting..."

Her gaze shot down to his trousers.

"I can see what your answer would be. You may leave, cabin boy."

He cleared his throat, and picked up the can, holding it in front of him. He didn't want to have anyone questioning what he'd been up to here.

"Woodruff?"

He turned at the door.

"I have a house in Nassau. You will stay there if you make the commitment to come with me. Mr. Turnbull and Mr. Nash will be there as well."

"Aye, Captain."

She waved him out, and as he walked back to the galley he tried to parse her words. Was she warning him about Turnbull and Nash being nearby? Was she letting him know there would be other opportunities?

He suspected Captain St. Armand was used to getting her own way, aboard her ship or in port. She knew men, but she didn't know him. He was willing to wait and bide his time. He didn't know if there had been cabin boys with "special benefits" in the past, but he was not about to become another addition to a long string of lovers. If anything was to happen between them, she would remember Oliver.

Chapter 8

THE TAVERN IN NASSAU HAD no name or sign outside the door, but everyone knew it. Almost everyone. *It's a shame the place isn't known to any decent brewers*, Oliver thought, trying to drink some lackluster ale.

"I told you to get the rum."

"I don't have your tolerance for that beverage yet, Captain."

He shifted uncomfortably while she sipped from her own mug.

"You keep doing that and he may relieve himself on you out of spite."

"I'm not used to wearing a live animal," he protested, as the parrot preened on his shoulder.

St. Armand looked at Turnbull.

"'Bring him along,' you said. 'It'll be good for him to get out and about.'"

"I meant Woodruff, not the pa—not Roscoe."

She snickered. "Well, Woodruff, are you enjoying being out and about?"

He took another sip of the ale, worried that if he tried to respond he'd break out into a huge grin. He was sitting in a disreputable tavern in the Caribbean, with two dangerous pirates, *and a parrot on his shoulder.* Being here today brought home to him how gray, structured, and boring his life was in Manchester.

"Stop staring, Sunshine. You don't want to make me nervous."

Oliver pulled his gaze away, but it was hard not to stare. The most exciting aspect of this most exciting voyage was getting to know Captain St. Armand, and the more time he spent with her, the more he wanted to know her in all her guises.

Today she'd changed her appearance again, penciling in darker, thicker brows, and her distinctive blue eyes were hidden behind spectacles with smoked lenses. More than ever, she looked like a young man of color.

"The people we're meeting haven't met me. They don't know I'm a woman," she'd explained as they'd disembarked from the ship. "This gives me an advantage, and I learned early to use whatever weapons were at hand to put the odds in my favor during a fight, or a negotiation."

"What is it we're negotiating? Or are we fighting?" he'd asked.

"I have no intention of fighting today, but you have to be prepared."

Turnbull had rumbled agreement from behind them. They'd started out with the bird riding on Mattie's shoulder, but the parrot switched allegiances when he saw Oliver in the group. He still hadn't figured out why the parrot was attracted to him, but he had to admit it gave him a feeling that he was fitting in better with the crew of the piratical vessel, now that he was properly accessorized.

The knife at the captain's hip was a sober reminder. They weren't playing pirate. They were serious.

Deadly serious, and they expected him to be as well. He was a mill owner, not a pirate, and when the mate told him yesterday that he'd be coming with them, Oliver had spent restless hours in his hammock wondering what he would do if trouble broke out. Could he have shot that sailor aboard the *Betsy Anne*, if that was what it took to stop him attacking the captain?

"You can still leave," she said quietly as they sat together now. At his startled look she added, "I can read your apprehension on your face. You did not ask to be brought into this. You don't have to stay."

"Captain—"

She held up her hand to silence Turnbull while she watched Oliver. He looked at her, really looked at her, seeing beneath the paint and false identity. She needed him, and while he wasn't entirely comfortable with her methods, he could not help but admire her commitment to a cause greater than herself, greater than either of them.

"I'll stay."

Her expression didn't change, but he saw her relief in the relaxing of the lines around her mouth. Odd, he would have thought a woman whose face bore the marks of years in sun and salt spray at sea would be unattractive. All the women he knew were careful of their complexions, careful to look as well-preserved and girlish as possible.

Mattie St. Armand wasn't careful. Today she wore a straw planter's hat, but it was part of her costume, shading her face and making it harder to see her features. She lit a cheroot, the smoke wreathing around her and adding to her "masculinity."

The tavern was dim and far from clean, but the

clientele appeared at ease with the sailors from the *Prodigal Son*. In addition to Turnbull and St. Armand, and Roscoe, Oliver spotted two of the crew dicing in the corner near the door. He doubted they were there because the food and service brought them back.

They sat with the parrot in the shadows against the wall where they had a clear view of the door. Roscoe squawked and mumbled "lubbers" when a pair of men entered dressed in clothing perfectly respectable and appropriate for a London bank, but which stood out in the tropics like a signboard saying, "Take advantage of me."

One was a white man with heavy salt-and-pepper whiskers along his jaw, red-faced and sweating in the heat. The other was a black man, soberly dressed and sporting a clerical collar.

They looked around nervously, then spotted Oliver and the others in the back. After making their way among the patrons the men stopped before the table, and the whiskered stranger stuck out his hand at Oliver.

"Captain St. Armand. It's a pleasure to meet you."

The real St. Armand said nothing but raised an eyebrow at Oliver. She flicked an ash off the cheroot, rising to greet the newcomers.

"I'm St. Armand. You must be Mr. Foster and Reverend Michaels."

Roscoe mumbled "buggering beets," a seeming non sequitur, then left Oliver's shoulder for the rail on the wall behind him. Oliver slipped him some mango, and the bird settled in with his treat, ignoring the humans.

Foster looked flustered at his error, but after a moment shook St. Armand's gloved hand.

"I see. I expected someone different."

"Of course you did. You gents pull up a seat and we'll talk."

St. Armand's usual precise speech was gone again, the tone and inflection now a mix of island and Liverpool.

"Want anything?"

Reverend Michaels looked around the tavern and frowned.

"No, thank you, Captain. You have the...packages?"

"All neat and tidy and aboard my ship. You have my money?"

Foster reached into his valise, but Michaels put a hand on his arm.

"Captain St. Armand—allow me to appeal to your conscience," he said, and Turnbull snorted at the plea. "You could do a great deal more to help your people if you'd forego payment and allow us to use these funds to further our cause."

St. Armand took a drink of rum and gazed at the preacher, then set her mug down.

"Let me make something clear to you, Reverend," she said in a soft, chilling voice. "*My people* are the sailors on my ship and we have an arrangement. If you're thinking of going back on our agreement, it will not end well for you, savvy?"

"You'd threaten a man of the cloth?"

She shrugged. "I don't threaten. I do know your abolition society doesn't have a boatload of sea captains you can hire. I suggest you pay the one you do have, and we'll all be smiling at the end of the day."

Foster pulled a handkerchief out of his coat and mopped his red brow. He was clearly unused to the tropical heat and looked anxious to conclude as quickly as possible and adjourn to a more comfortable venue. He took out a leather envelope and passed it to St. Armand, who lifted it, judging its weight, then passed it to the mate.

An uncomfortable silence settled before Foster cleared his throat. "Can we talk in front of these men, Captain?"

"Mr. Turnbull is my second-in-command and this fellow here is my cabin boy. They're trustworthy."

The disgusted look Reverend Michaels gave him nearly made Oliver speak up and deny he was the cabin boy aboard the notorious *Prodigal Son*, or anyone of particular utility to the captain, but he stopped himself. St. Armand was testing him, testing his loyalty and his willingness to follow through on his commitment. He sat there, gazing steadily at the men.

"Very well. We have another job for you. The one I mentioned in my letter," Foster said. "You're to pick up two packages in Fernandina at our usual rates."

"When?"

He looked around the room, then lowered his voice.

"Christmas time. I anticipate it will take them four days to reach the site, if all goes well."

"You want the usual services?"

Michaels muttered something.

"You have something to say, preacher? Speak up, so we can all hear it."

"I said, 'And now abideith faith, hope, charity, these three, but the greatest of these is charity, Captain.'"

She gave him a steely glance. "God loves a cheerful giver. I heard that's from the Bible too. You keep giving cheerfully to me and we'll all be good."

Reverend Michaels looked ready to rain down

hellfire and brimstone on the pirate and the crew, but Foster put a restraining hand on his coat sleeve.

"The Society is prepared to meet your fees, Captain. We will do whatever it takes to scourge this evil from the world. You will be paid."

The sour expression on Reverend Michaels's face made it clear he had no taste for this devil's bargain, but they finished the arrangements and took their leave, scooting out of the tavern as quickly as they could. Turnbull left to join the men at the other table.

Some of the tension flowed out of Oliver, and Roscoe hopped back on his shoulder.

"Meow?"

"Yes, I have more." He passed the bird a slice of mango, ending up with sticky juice dribbling down his jacket. "I can't imagine why they thought I was the captain."

Mattie drank some of her rum as she watched him gently scratch the parrot.

"Roscoe does make you look more commanding, but it's simple. They thought you were the captain because you're the only white man at the table."

Her words were crisp once again, and he wondered if he'd ever know the real Mattie St. Armand. If that was even her name.

"What was the purpose of the playacting? I know you're doing good works. You're not just in it for the money."

"Really?" She leaned back now, hooking one arm over the chair back. "You know me so well then? Or are you trying to convince yourself of something you want to believe because it makes you feel better?" she said.

He started to reply, then shut his mouth because he

didn't have a good answer.

"The *playacting* as you call it, is part of what's kept me alive and in business so long. What will Reverend Michaels and his friend remember about Captain St. Armand today? If they ever bring up my name, they'll say I'm a conscienceless and arrogant mulatto who cares only for money and rum. I want them to have a certain image of who Captain St. Armand is, and that image suits me just fine. Sometimes staying alive is all about image, and reputation."

"What happens to the people we took off the *Betsy Anne*?" Oliver asked.

"They'll go to quarters set aside for them until they can be settled. Some of the men join the army, and that can be a good choice for them. Others will be put to work, sometimes the same as what they did as slaves."

She leaned forward and looked down at her rum, a troubled expression on her face. "It's not much better than what they had. The Society does what it can, but times are hard."

"At least they're free."

"Free to starve. However, I've never had a one say they'd trade freedom and difficulties for slavery. All these people have seen loved ones sold like cattle. Some of them are fresh from Africa, taken away from their homes and all they know. Freedom's a dream, but it's a dream that requires hard work for all involved."

The bird hopped back on the rail and Oliver mirrored the captain, leaning forward so they wouldn't be overheard. "Tell me more, Captain, about what to expect when we reach Florida. Will the slaves need assistance? The men tell me you do the physicking aboard your ship."

"It's not uncommon for captains to be the apothecary, surgeon, and physician at sea. There are medicine chests for ships with instructions on what purge to dispense and when. I'm fortunate, and my men would say they are also, because I had better training."

She was speaking more freely than usual, and he noticed the level of rum in the mug was considerably lower. He suspected she'd never have opened up to him otherwise, but like a good pirate-in-training, he wasn't about to let an opportunity pass.

"How did you receive medical training? Was your father a surgeon?"

"My father?" She snickered. "He's skilled with a blade. I'll give him that, but no, he's not a surgeon. Do you ever wonder how I came to be a sailor, Woodruff?"

"All the time."

A smile quirked her lips, emphasized by the scar at the corner.

"The *Prodigal Son* was my father's ship before it was mine. He didn't give it to me, I had to earn my place, and then I had to purchase it from him. When I was an adolescent I became..." she paused and scratched her chin. "*Unruly* would not be a bad word to describe me. Obnoxious also would be appropriate. I ran away from home. Twice. To stave off further drama, my family followed the example of countless British families before them. They sent me to sea."

He paused from lifting his own glass. The ale was bad, but at least it was wet.

"Generally it's sons who are sent to sea, not daughters of the house, Captain. Daughters are usually sent to school, or a governess hired for them."

She shrugged. "My parents were not entirely

without sense regarding the appropriateness of sending a girl to sea. They shipped me aboard an American merchantman, a hen ship they knew of through a mutual acquaintance."

"Isn't that what they call a ship where the captain's wife and family lives aboard?"

"Correct. Captain Fletcher is a one-eyed old sea dog, as tough as a side of salt beef and about as attractive, but he was a fair captain. More to the point, his wife is a skilled doctoress. I learned about being a cooperative member of the crew from him, and about shipboard medicine from her."

Mattie twisted her mug in her hands, remembering those days. Aboard Captain Fletcher's *Harpy* she was not special or different. She was simply a member of the crew. She bunked with the Fletchers' daughter Frances, and she learned doctoring from Mrs. Fletcher. Those lessons changed when Mattie grew in height, grew breasts, and developed an eye for the handsome boys in the ports. Then the blunt doctoress lectured her on how to avoid unwanted consequences from dallying with young men. After hearing the descriptions of the "diseases of Venus," Mattie had been tempted to cross her legs and not open them for anyone, but her own nature and the opportunities presented in the various ports led her to choices that weren't always prudent, but, so far, had not complicated her life. It was the Fletchers who placed her in contact with the abolitionists, creating a lucrative smuggling opportunity for the *Prodigal Son*.

"Where are they now?"

She was wrenched out of her memories by

Woodruff's question.

"Captain and Mrs. Fletcher? Last I heard they were in China, or maybe in the Sandwich Islands. They also talked about sailing to New South Wales. I preferred to stay in this hemisphere."

She finished her drink and slammed the mug down. "Let us take advantage of our stay on dry land, Woodruff. I'll show you some of the local sights."

Going ashore with Turnbull and Nash was like seeing the sights with one's kindly uncles. Deadly, well-armed uncles, but not her idea of a good time. The pretty boys in port she hired for a few hours were entertaining enough, but most had run together into a faceless blur, and lately she'd found none of them even tempted her.

She realized that she longed for conversation, conversation with a person who was smart, and educated, and her age. Not a crewman, or a merchant trying to take advantage of her, or someone who thought she was a whore or a pirate and nothing more.

Woodruff looked at her in a way she found intriguing. He saw her as a person, and his regard made her want to look at him. That was easy enough to do. His glowing hair and fair skin turned pale gold by his time aboard ship made him look like a statue she'd seen of a young athlete from ancient Greece—polished marble carved to display a slim, lithe physique.

When she'd taken the soft Englishman aboard she'd braced herself for whining and complaints, but to her surprise and pleasure he'd worked hard to become part of the crew. His patience and concern for the freed slaves also intrigued her. More and more, she was beginning to think of him not as a dupe to be used and discarded on her next slave-stealing run, but as a partner. Mr. Turnbull would always put protecting her first—that was his job. Woodruff—Oliver—listened to her and offered comments or arguments, but didn't try to dissuade her from her actions.

She knew why she hadn't approached him after that one momentary lapse—it would never do while he was aboard ship. The upcoming trip, with all of its excitement and danger, could prove most interesting.

For now there was money in her pocket, a handsome man at her side, and the satisfaction of a job well done. She would enjoy the moment, because all of those things could be gone tomorrow.

The captain didn't appear impaired by the rum as she rose from the table. Oliver admired her stamina. Perhaps it came from long practice. He wanted to know more about her. Who was her family that they'd placed her aboard a ship when she was a young girl? What kind of people did that? Her normal speech, well-spoken and educated, made him more curious than ever. She was an enticing mystery, and he was in no hurry to leave the *Prodigal Son* and return to Manchester, not when each day aboard ship or ashore was an adventure, even when there were turnips to peel or oakum to pick.

He blinked in the sunlight, bright in his eyes after the dim tavern. Mattie removed her spectacles and adjusted the brim of her hat, and it prompted him to say, "I need one of those."

"You covet my hat?"

She grinned at him and the flash of white teeth nearly stopped him in his tracks. When she smiled it changed everything about her. He saw the woman beneath the penciled facial hair and padded shoulders, and he realized it was one reason why she smiled so seldom. She looked younger, more carefree, more feminine, and he felt privileged she shared one of these rare moments with him.

"Let's get your headgear taken care of so you don't get sunstroke," she said. "The market up ahead has what you need."

Roscoe hopped off his shoulder onto his mistress's, looking about him with interest.

"Do you always take the parr—Roscoe out with you?"

"Not everywhere, but he's a good lookout."

He looked at her quizzically.

"Atop my shoulder he can see over the crowd, and if he recognizes a threat, he'll let me know. Roscoe's not only a good mouser, he's an excellent watch-kitty."

"You're having me on, Captain."

"It's true. Animals of Roscoe's breed are quite intelligent."

"Where did you acquire him?" he asked.

"He was a gift from an admirer," she said, leaving it at that.

He found the oddest feeling growing in his chest. It was jealousy. He was jealous that some lover in her past had gifted her with a bird, and he feared he'd never be able to compete for her affection, with either Roscoe or her past admirers.

He looked at her sideways as she strode along, her long legs eating up the dusty road, one hand on the massive knife she wore conspicuously displayed at her hip, her eyes scanning the crowd for danger. Her skin was browned and weathered, but it gave her beauty an edge, a sharpness akin to her knife, something shiny and lovely and deadly all at once.

He could not envision her bundled and corseted and constrained by village life. But what did he know? She had the airs of a lady, the speech of a lady. Perhaps in her background was a girl who longed to return to England, to have a place of her own.

They'd reached the market and examined the straw hats cunningly woven by the ladies seated on the ground, each calling out in the charming island lilt for the gentlemen's business. St. Armand took him to a beldame wrinkled enough to have greeted the first Englishmen to set foot in the islands. They knew each other, and soon fierce bargaining ensued. Oliver wanted to chime in that he could afford a straw hat, but he realized the two of them were enjoying themselves, and the other vendors contributed their comments as well. Soon coins were exchanged and he now possessed a straw hat similar to that worn by the planters he'd met. He fancied it gave him a rakish air.

A quieter conversation led to a packet of something else being passed over for more coinage, and St. Armand tucked it inside her coat.

"Herbs," she said at his questioning glance, but then they went to another stall where she bought additional supplies for the medicine chest aboard ship.

The market was filled with sights and sounds— flowers blooming in scraggly shrubs, gulls fighting over scraps of fish, frying food that tempted them into purchasing conch fritters served so hot he had to juggle them from hand to hand before eating them. The smell of the dust and the lush greenery, the whiff of sea breeze, all were an assault on his senses, along with the bright foliage and the vivid colors of the market ladies' dresses and headgear.

Some of them were former slaves, only recently granted freedom by Great Britain. Many had continued to labor in near-slavery conditions as "apprentices," but others had established themselves as farmers and fishermen, barely getting by but selling their own products for themselves in the market.

All the vendors seemed to know the captain, and some of them even called out greetings to Roscoe. They handled their business and Oliver found himself loaded down with bags and parcels. He grinned as he thought of how it would be exactly the same if he was home with his mother and sisters, but then he realized they wouldn't be keeping their hands free to be close to a blade.

St. Armand directed him down a side street where sea grapes shaded the dusty avenue, the residences fewer as they headed away from town. She seemed to shed cares and years as they walked along together, away from the ship and its obligations, and he hoped he'd played a part in adding that jaunty stride to her step.

"You seem to be at home here, Captain."

"The islands have long been a pirate's playground," she said as she turned her head. The parrot squawked and resettled itself on her shoulder. "I'm only the latest in a long line of seafarers who've put into port."

"Is it difficult for you, being the only woman aboard a ship full of men?"

She was a few steps ahead and looked at him over her shoulder, an amused expression in her eyes.

"Why do you think I'm the only woman sailing aboard the *Prodigal Son*?"

That took the wind out of his sails and he stopped

in his tracks. "I'm making assumptions again, aren't I?"

"Keep walking, Sunshine. We've things to do. Yes, you're making assumptions, and if I were you, I wouldn't stare at my shipmates as you puzzle it out. Makes them nervous. Privacy's important aboard ship, and people go to sea for all sorts of reasons."

He couldn't help it. As they walked together he began running through the crew in his mind. First he eliminated the ones with full beards, then he scratched off the ones he'd seen bare chested as they worked. It still left a handful of "men," and he knew he'd be thinking about it when they returned.

The captain was correct though. One of the first things he'd learned aboard ship was to keep his eyes to himself. Many of the men did not share stories of their background, and he'd come to understand that no matter what you'd done before, once you were a sailor you proved yourself every day by your actions.

"You have to admit, Captain, any person would be fascinated by your tale. You cannot deny that you are unusual, a woman in command of a vessel of rough sailors, some of whom are also women in disguise."

"I would rather my life not be turned into entertainment for the masses. I really would rather not. I hate to think of harm coming to some scribbler who might write about me." She looked at his hands—the hands where she'd already remarked on his penman's callus.

"Are you warning me? Or threatening me?"

"More the former than the latter. As I said, we value our privacy aboard ship. No need to go telling tales."

"You could do a great deal of good telling your stories, Captain."

"As cautionary tales for rambunctious young girls?"

"I was thinking more of the work you're doing to help the enslaved. People need inspiration, and you could bring home to them how important your work is."

"I'm not a writer," she replied.

"I am. We would collaborate. A partnership. In fact, it could be written so no one need know you're a woman, if you prefer."

"Do not push your luck, Woodruff. You're in a better place than you were when I first fetched you aboard ship. You no longer have to worry about being sold as a cadaver."

"I don't?"

"No. With your family money you are much more valuable to me if I hold you for ransom."

"You jest, of course."

She just smiled at him.

"Beets! Beets!"

The parrot leaped off her shoulder, straight up into the air, flapping its wings and squawking before perching on Oliver.

"Bloody hell," St. Armand muttered, coming to a stop. Two men were approaching, sailors from their gait, focused on the captain. They ignored Oliver.

One man was short and rotund, sweat pouring off a face reddened and chapped from the elements. He spread his stocky legs apart as they blocked the road.

The other man was older and was dressed finer, but was no cleaner than his companion, and Spanish or part-African from his looks.

The shorter man grinned, displaying a disturbing lack of teeth, and his speech whistled as he said, "We was watching you in the tavern, laddie. Looks like you might have something weighing down your pockets. We've come to help you with that burden."

His companion said nothing but watched the captain. It was clear neither of them considered Oliver a threat, which annoyed him as he set down his bags. Earlier he'd worried whether he could kill a man, now he was tempted to put it to the test.

"Do you know who I am?" St. Armand asked in bored tones.

"Looks like you're some shirtlifter out for a stroll with his bumboy. If you give us your gold we won't try to steal a kiss, sweetie."

"Idiots," she said under her breath. "I'll give you one piece of information, and what you do with it is on you. I'm Matt St. Armand, captain of the *Prodigal Son*."

At Mattie's words the taller of the two straightened and put his hand on the other's shoulder.

"Boney, you need to stand down."

The dumber one shook off his companion's hand.

"What're you scared of, a skinny boy with a knife? We can take the likes of them!"

"You should listen to your mate there, Boney. If anything happens to me, my crew will cut you up for chum."

"They have to catch me first, molly boy. I'd say two against one is even odds," he added, pulling a wicked looking knife from his belt.

That was enough. Oliver removed the pistol from where it was hidden by his coat and cocked it.

The taller thief put up his hands and backed away, keeping his eyes on them.

"I'm not having any of this. You're on your own, Boney."

"Oliver! You clever, clever lad. You brought a pistol to a knife fight!" she said, and he nearly blushed under her approving gaze. The remaining thief sweated profusely as he stood there with his knife in his hand, his eyes darting back and forth.

"You're thinking about throwing that knife at me, which would be your last and stupidest mistake," St. Armand said. "I've been dodging knives since I was a nipper, and you're not fast enough to outrun me or my friend's gun. Leave now, and we'll call it square."

Frustration plain on his face, Boney gave her an ugly smile and shoved his knife back in his belt.

"No harm. We're done here then," he said, backing up to join his mate.

Oliver put the pistol back in his coat. Out of the corner of his eye saw a blur hurtling past him.

"Aaargh! Get it off'a me!"

Boney wrapped his hands over his head, Roscoe clawing at him until he dropped the knife he'd pulled out when Oliver had turned away.

"Pardon me, Woodruff," St. Armand said, pulling the pistol out of his coat pocket, cocking it and taking aim at the thief.

"No! Don't shoot him!" Oliver shouted.

She ignored him, her eyes narrowed on the man whose hands were back up in the air. A trickle of blood ran down his clawed scalp.

"You have a disturbing number of scruples," she said, but lowered the gun. "You're in luck, Boney. His soft heart will keep me from shooting you. For now. But if you ever cross my path again, I guarantee your luck will have run out."

St. Armand looked at his companion, still standing with his hands in the air. "You're clearly the one with the brains, so take your friend and go."

"Yes, sir," the thief said, hustling his bloody companion back towards town.

The captain watched them until they were out of sight, then turned to Oliver.

"Well done, Sunsh—Mmmf!"

It took his brain a moment to connect to the rest of him as he grabbed her by the lapels and pulled her in for a kiss, nearly yanking her off her feet. His pistol was still in her hand, digging into the back of his neck and she might shoot him for his presumption.

It was worth it.

Her lips were soft beneath his, so soft, but her body was firm and he came alive like a millwheel on a rushing river. The sensations flowed over him and crashed through him, inflaming him. She moved her hand behind her back, tucking the pistol away, then she brought it back to his face, cupping it gently. He angled his head to deepen their kiss, to wring every iota of feeling from holding Mattie St. Armand in his arms.

She was unlike anyone he'd ever known in his quiet, circumscribed life, and that made her kisses all the sweeter, the feel of her hands against his bearded face all the more exciting. Even standing as they were on a public road, where any passerby might see two "men" kissing, it added to the excitement. This wasn't a kiss stolen at an evening musicale. This was a kiss with all the intensity of an island summer day, with heat, and moisture, and the sunshine beating down on them. He let his hands roam down her back, over her coat, turning and pushing her up against a tamarind tree, taking the risk of putting his hands on her hips and pulling her in tighter so she could feel his desire for her, how much he wanted her.

"Kissy kissy! Kissy kissy! C'mon, sweetie, give us a buss!"

They froze, and Oliver lifted his head.

"I am going to strangle that animal," he said.

St. Armand cleared her throat, and he was gratified to see the color high in her cheeks, her eyes soft and dewy as she unwrapped her leg from where it draped over his hips.

"Don't. He did well today."

She pulled her coat down and picked up her fallen hat from the ground, then raised her arm and the bird flew to her.

"We have people and tasks awaiting us, Woodruff. And did you learn anything from today's encounter with those idiots?"

"Not to turn my back?"

"Correct. You already know the most important detail—always bring a gun to a knife fight. I confess, I am quite impressed by your foresight."

Her words shouldn't make him proud, since she was referring to a man almost being shot, but he nonetheless stood a little taller. A thief threatened him with a knife and all but called him a sodomite, but she'd called him Oliver and kissed him. He was cheerfully strolling down the path to piracy, but for that look on Mattie St. Armand's face, the feel of her mouth caressing his, he'd load himself down with a flotilla of weaponry.

Roscoe fluttered his wings, and Oliver suspected the bird was looking at him rather smugly out of its beady little eyes.

"Roscoe's a good boy. Roscoe loves you. Kissy, kissy."

"Yes, you're a good boy, Roscoe. I love you too."

"Not I," Oliver muttered.

She grinned cheekily at him and gave him back his pistol. "You and Roscoe are both my heroes today. You don't mind being grouped with the ship's cat, do you?"

He fell into step next to her. "Considering at one time you judged me less useful than the animal, it's a step up."

"I like your attitude."

"When we were threatened, why did your parrot cry, 'Beets! Beets!'?"

"It was the first obscenity I taught him.

"Beets are not obscene."

"They are to me."

He let this odd conversation go to deal with more important issues. "Will those men come after you?"

"It's unlikely. They were under the impression we were a pair of molly boys who would break down and cry if they threatened us. They won't try it again," she said grimly. "If I worried about fools trying to rob or assault me, I'd never leave my ship."

They continued down the sandy path until the salt breeze brushed his face as they stepped through to the beach. There was a sprawling house, built up off the ground, a deep veranda wrapping around it and windows open to catch all the air and sunshine. The upper story had balconies fronting long shutters. It looked comfortable and homey until he spotted a sailor with a rifle, keeping watch on a little railed platform on the roof.

The house was painted a warm salmon shade and was surrounded by shrubbery displaying riotous blooms in all shades from fuchsia to raspberry to melon. He slanted a glance at the fearsome pirate walking alongside him.

"I like pink," she said diffidently.

"Nothing wrong with that."

The guard on the roof waved to them, and the door opened as a tall, extremely dark man dressed in livery awaited them.

"Welcome home, Captain," he said with a crisp London accent.

"It's good to be back, Wellington." The captain passed her hat to the butler. "This is Oliver Woodruff. He'll be our guest for a while."

Wellington inclined his shaved head and said, "Welcome to the islands, Mr. Woodruff."

Oliver could imagine few things less comfortable on a Bahamian afternoon than a full wool suit, but the butler looked impeccable, and he was all too aware of his own scruffy and piratical appearance, complete down to the parrot back on his shoulder. St. Armand spoke up, almost as if she'd read his mind.

"Have word sent to the tailor's shop. Woodruff here lost his wardrobe in transit and we'll need to outfit him, and fairly quickly. We'll head there first thing in the morning."

"Of course, Captain," the butler said, looking at Oliver with new respect. The captain's words clarified his status as an honored guest. Roscoe abandoned him to fly up the broad staircase where he no doubt had his own lodgings.

"Will you be dining with us tonight, Captain? There's souse," he said apologetically.

"Mrs. Oldman's pig feet souse suits me fine, Wellington. I know our arrival was unexpected. Ask Mr. Nash and Turnbull to join us. In the meantime,

I'd like to bathe, and I imagine our guest would like that as well."

Wellington motioned over one of the housemaids, who dropped a quick curtsey and said, "Welcome home, Cap'n. We'll heat the water for you."

Oliver ran his hand over his bearded face. "Was my gear brought over from the ship? I can handle my razor now that there's no deck shifting beneath my feet."

"It's in my room," St. Armand said, starting up the staircase.

Oliver followed, and he would have been dead and buried not to enjoy the view of her pert backside and long, long legs in trousers clinging and moving with her up the stairs. Wellington may have been cool and collected, but Oliver was feeling every bit of the tropical heat and then some. He considered asking for cold water to douse himself, but the thought of a hot bath soaking the dirt and salt out of his pores was too enticing.

"Your room, Woodruff." She pointed to an open door.

It was airy and large, opening onto a balcony. White linens covered the bed, and the wide planked floor was the same bleached color as the sand at the water's edge. The windows had no glass, just shutters that could be adjusted for shade, and there was a chair and a lamp in front of a small writing desk.

"Will this do?" she asked.

"After sleeping in a hammock surrounded by farting sailors?" He stopped himself. This wasn't how one spoke to a lady, but it was exactly how he would speak to a companion and fellow traveler. She was looking at the room, smiling to herself at his rude quip.

He knew how to talk to men. He knew how to talk to women. He was still learning how to talk to Mattie St. Armand. He'd been at this woman's side today, helping her to secure safety for the slaves she'd taken, fending off robbers, reveling in her kisses, and he knew every day with her on this adventure would be a challenge, and a new experience.

"Yes, this room is perfect. How long will we be here?"

She shrugged. "Depends. We need to be in Florida by Christmas, but that gives us some time to make preparations. If you're in on this venture, you're still under my command. You are not to go into town on your own, savvy? There's too much at risk. Are you going to have problems with that?"

"Worried I'll get into another fight with Americans?"

"It's more likely than you think. Traffic is heavy between here and the southern United States, particularly East Florida. If we're going to pull this off... —We'll talk more at supper."

She left him and entered the room next to his. He glanced back through the open shutters to the balcony and stepped out into the sunshine. As he'd noticed when they'd approached the house, the two rooms shared the balcony. Her shutters were also open, and he could hear her in there, clothes rustling, dresser drawers opening.

A knock on the door disturbed his fantasy of crossing over to her room, and three brawny men came in carrying cans of hot water and a tub. They put down mats on the floor, filled the tub, left a can for him to shave with, and the maid came in with towels and a bar of soap. One of the servants returned with Oliver's bags, dropping them on the floor.

The maid was the last to go, and she looked at him saucily over her shoulder.

"Welcome to the island, sah. You can leave your clothes outside the door for washing. If you need anything, just send for me. I'm Trudy," she said, closing the door behind her.

Oliver stripped off his sailor's gear, gratefully depositing it to be laundered. He'd never fully appreciated what hot water and being clean meant to him until he sank into the tub and scrubbed himself from head to toe. So many things he'd taken for granted in his swaddled life in England. Servants who carried in hot water, clean clothes, food. Safety.

What kind of life had the captain left behind in England, a life so unpleasant that she'd put up with the dangers and rigors of life at sea as a better option? The pert housemaid, Trudy, might have tempted him once, but a girl like that was nothing next to a woman like Mattie St. Armand.

He was about to doze off as the water cooled when the door to his room was flung open. He sat straight up, expecting the housemaid, but what he found was the frowning captain.

"I just had a thought. Don't shave after your bath. I need you to stay bearded for now." She paused, sweeping her gaze over him. He was as bare as the day he'd been born, hunched down in a tub that felt suddenly far too small.

"You are supposed to stand in the captain's presence, Woodruff."

After giving him a long look while he tried unsuccessfully not to redden, she snickered, turned on her heel and left.

He sank back into the water, scratching his beard.

It had only started to itch once she'd said he shouldn't shave, but no doubt she'd explain herself. Five minutes later he was toweling off, his mind suddenly full of witty ripostes he'd wished he'd thought to say when she was admiring his form.

Supper was served in the dining room with the shutters open wide to take advantage of the evening breezes. In addition to the pig's foot souse, there were pigeon peas, yams, and fresh mangoes served with cake and cream. Oliver had heard Englishmen complain about their travels, bringing their own food and not wanting to eat "foreign nonsense." He wondered what the point of travel was if you only mingled with people like yourself and ate foods you ate at home?

St. Armand also had a selection of quality wines, which he especially appreciated after the bad ale earlier in the day. He sampled claret while Nash and Turnbull finished their meals and quaffed better ale than the tavern swill.

A pair of footmen served under the butler's quiet direction. They too were dressed impeccably, their white-gloved hands quietly whisking plates away.

"The lads are coming along, Wellington," the captain said as the young men left the room. "Will they be ready to move to another household soon?"

"Yes, Captain. Adam is ready now, and the governor has requested him for his house," Wellington said proudly.

"We train young men and women who wish to go into service," she explained to Oliver as the butler poured coffee. "Our people are in high demand, and some leave for other islands and households there. A few have even gone to England with their employers when they return home."

The table was set with gold-rimmed china, sparkling crystal and spotless table linens. Oliver breathed a happy sigh as the muscles in his back relaxed. Travel was all well and good, but one missed the comforts of home.

"My compliments to your cook and the staff on an outstanding meal, Captain. Has Wellington been with you for long?"

"You could say he came with the house. I received the residence as payment for a debt, and the butler was working here. He wasn't a slave," she added quickly, "but had left service in England to return to the islands. Said he'd never get used to the damp and cold there. The man who lost the house to me was returning to England, and Wellington wanted to stay on."

"Always has his nose in the air like he's smellin' something bad," Nash grumbled.

"That's because when you're aboard, he *is* smellin' something bad," Turnbull said.

"Gentlemen," St. Armand said as the two old mates fell to bickering. "We have business to discuss regarding the next Florida run. Mr. Nash, you're aware that Oliver will be joining us. Do you have any comments?"

The quartermaster gave Oliver a keen glance over his eyeglasses.

"Woodruff here is a good choice, Captain. I've been observing him and I have no complaints about his service aboard the *Prodigal*. He's fit in well with the crew and pulls his weight."

"Really?" Oliver said, sitting up straighter in his chair. Nash had never spoken to him except to give him orders. The approbation of a seasoned pirate was not to be taken lightly. "Thank you, Mr. Nash."

"Don't get cocky, youngster. The real battle's ahead of you."

"Aye, Mr. Turnbull."

"So." St. Armand pushed herself to her feet and waved the men back to their seats. She started pacing in front of the table, hands clasped behind her back. It was such a typically masculine stance that Oliver wondered if she ever acted the woman, and what it would be like to see her in that guise.

"We will proceed then as planned. Tomorrow I'll take Oliver to get outfitted for his role. We need to be in Fernandina by late December. Mr. Nash, contact our people there and see to it that all is in order."

"Aye, Captain," Nash said.

"While your suggestion that we tell the truth would be an interesting change of pace, it won't serve, at least not completely," she said, studying Oliver's face.

"You were bearded for the meeting at the tavern, introduced as my cabin boy, and we've established that identity here. You'll shave in Florida. With the new clothes and your changed appearance and status we'll manage the deception."

She reached into her pocket and pulled out a creased and water-stained paper that she held aloft.

"This was given to me by Captain Jensen."

It was a handbill from Florida Territory, offering a reward of $200 for information on an unknown slave stealer.

"'Wanted for stealing three slaves in Pensacola: About 25 years old, five feet ten or eleven inches, dark haired, spectacles, a downcast, sly look, may be a mulatto,'" she read from the paper. "Signed by Governor Call. I'm getting quite the reputation."

"That description—that's similar to the look you had in town today," Oliver said.

"I like that they have the 'sly' part in there. It would be demeaning to be labeled 'looks three turnips shy of a bushel.' But this is why we need to exercise caution in Florida."

"I know I'll be a British citizen with connections to mills. What about you?"

"All will be revealed soon enough," she said, reseating herself.

Wellington came over with box at that point, three of them selecting cheroots while Nash waved them away. After the butler left, St. Armand leaned over and lit hers off the lamp on the table, inhaling the fragrant smoke before responding.

"I don't like this," Turnbull said. "You're risking yourself, over and over. Have you already forgotten what happened to Dr. Cotton?"

Mattie said nothing and sipped her wine, so it was up to Oliver to ask, "Who is Dr. Cotton?"

Turnbull looked at him, his battered face grim.

"Cotton was suspected of being the ringleader of a slave revolt and was lynched along with a slave in the Territory. Ever since the Murrellite scare a few years back—"

"John Murrell was a Mississippian suspected of plotting a revolt so he could steal slaves," Nash chimed in.

"Ever since, Florida's been scared and watchful, not hesitant to use men who take justice into their own hands. They don't care if you're stealing slaves to resell them or to free them, it's all the same."

Turnbull's voice gentled as he looked at Mattie.

"You cannot stop slavery, not in the United States. It's too powerful a force, earns too much money for all involved. Even Woodruff here, his mills couldn't run without cheap cotton, and that's all coming from America. They keep expanding their cotton land, Florida, Alabama, Texas, everywhere they can plant seeds and pick bolls. It won't go away because we wish it."

"I know that, Mr. Turnbull. Most days I feel like King Canute trying to hold back the tide," the captain said.

Oliver paused from where he was lighting his own smoke, looking at her sharply. One didn't expect to hear references to English history from pirates in the Caribbean. He thought of what Mattie St. Armand might have become had her life been one of slavery. Given her stunning looks and light skin, it was all too easy to imagine her being sold in New Orleans. She would sit in a little house like a gardenia waiting to unfold, spending her day pampering herself in anticipation of pleasing some loutish merchant or planter who owned her body.

It turned his stomach—this woman, born to command, to lead, having to pretend to be a fragile flower, to hide her true nature, to daily live with the fear of punishment or being sold if she didn't please a man.

Turnbull's question took him out of those thoughts.

"Do you agree with what we're proposing, Woodruff? Do you fully understand you could be captured and sentenced to the pillory or a whipping if caught? And that's the mild punishment. You're more likely to be hanged out of hand by a lynch mob than ever see a courtroom."

"That is barbaric! It's the nineteenth century, not the Dark Ages!"

"That is justice on the frontier. It's unsettled and unpopulated and whites are frightened of Indians, slave insurrections, and Britain invading, especially in Florida."

The fine dinner he'd enjoyed now tasted like the cigar ashes in the dish in front of him. He'd wanted some excitement on this journey, a colorful story or two to tell back home. He'd never planned on getting himself in a life-or-death situation where he could find himself at the wrong end of a gun or a noose.

"You can change your mind until we leave for Florida, Woodruff," Mattie said.

She didn't call him Oliver as she had before. He set his cigar aside and ran his hand through his hair. If he backed out now he'd be alive, but not the man he wanted to be, especially not the man he wanted Mattie St. Armand to see. He wanted to see the admiration in her eyes, the special light that he now hoped might be for him alone.

"I am aware, Mr. Turnbull, that arguing about slavery in the comfort of my home in England is not the same as risking my life for strangers. However, I said I would help, and I will follow through."

And there, it was back. The light in her deep blue eyes as she looked at him.

"Thank you, Oliver."

She turned to the first mate. "The time is also right for another Florida run. There's still upheaval with the Indians."

"Which means people are more suspicious and

watching their slaves more closely," Nash said. "But as you pointed out, the Floridians are worried about slave stealers and abolitionists. They're watching Apalachicola the hardest, so coming in through Fernandina gives us a slight advantage."

"It also means you'll need more training, Oliver." She stubbed out her cheroot. "We'll be up with the morning watch. Meet me on the beach and you might learn something new."

She bade the gentlemen good night and Roscoe flew from the back of the house to perch on her shoulder as Oliver watched her walk up the staircase.

"If anything happens to her, you're going to find it hard to eat with your throat cut from ear to ear, Woodruff," Nash said genially.

"You may be the right man for the job because you know which spoon to use and can talk like a toff, but you're the least trained, least experienced man aboard the *Prodigal Son*. Your missteps could cost Mattie... everything," Turnbull added.

He didn't know what the history was among Nash, Turnbull, and Captain St. Armand, but it was obvious they cared deeply for the young woman. It was more than friendship, more than the respect of sailors for their commander, and he knew if they could take his place they would in a heartbeat.

"I am appreciative of your concerns, but you must have some trust in me also. I can see Captain St. Armand is a special person. I've never met anyone like her," he added, almost to himself. "I give you my word that I will do my utmost to protect her when we're in Florida."

CHAPTER 9

OLIVER WAS ROUSED FROM A delightful dream about lady pirates by a hand roughly shaking his shoulder.

"Up you go, Sunshine. Time to stab things."

He blearily opened his eyes. Mattie stood next to his bed, holding a steaming mug. He reached for it, then remembered he was sleeping in the nude, the Bahamian evenings too warm for the extra layer of a nightshirt.

"Just set it on the table, please."

She raised her shapely black brows. "You didn't think I was bringing *you* coffee, did you? Which one of us is the cabin boy?"

"I thought I'd been promoted to travel companion and co-conspirator."

"Not quite yet, Mr. Woodruff. First we'll get you out on the sand and see how likely you are to kill someone through clumsiness. Out of bed now, chop chop. If you hurry, you can grab coffee and a roll from the galley and meet me outside. Don't make me come looking for you."

On that ominous note, she turned on her heel and left, taking the coffee with her.

He took her threat seriously and threw on his clothes, padding downstairs through the largely silent house. Noises and enticing aromas from the kitchen behind the main building drew him like a lodestone. He paused on his way to the beach, earning a scowl from cook, but purloining his own mug of coffee and a bread roll smeared with guava paste.

"I don't like people coming in here snatching food, instead of sitting at a table like civilized folks," she said, waving a wooden spoon at him.

"As I value my life, Mrs. Oldman, I cannot keep Captain St. Armand waiting for me."

She sniffed in dismissal and turned back to whatever savory stew she was preparing for the midday meal. He hoped he'd survive to enjoy it.

Oliver squinted in the sunshine cresting over the ocean, inhaling the sea air. Mattie leaned on the jamb at the doors leading out of the back of the house. She wore a white linen shirt, a black leather vest buttoned tight over it, and buckskins. Her feet were bare even though there was still a slight chill from the lingering night.

"Carry that case and follow me," she ordered.

"Aye, Captain," he said, regretfully setting aside the coffee and picking up the case.

They were alone on the beach, save for the gulls and terns. A flash of color at the corner of his eye stopped him, and he paused to admire a flock of flamingoes at the edge of the shallow cove.

"They are a sight, aren't they?"

"It's certain there's nothing like them in Manchester," he said, turning to her with a smile. "I can understand why you live here."

"It's a slice of paradise, particularly in the winter.

No snow, balmy breezes, and the smells and sights that always bring back memories for me."

"Of course. You were born in the islands."

"My first winter in England I was convinced the priests had it wrong, and that hell was a place where it was cold and frozen for eternity." She shook herself. "But that was long ago and in a different land. We have things to do, Woodruff."

She led him down to where the sand was firmly packed at the edge of the water, just out of reach of the wavelets. Inside the case were wooden knives.

"I'm going to stab someone with a piece of wood?"

"You are going to practice with the wooden knives. If all goes well, we'll progress to blades. You'd be surprised how many men grab for a blade and end up slicing their own hand. There's skill involved, like anything else. You already know the first lesson of knife fighting—bring a pistol, or even better, shoot your foe from a distance."

"That's not very sporting."

She laughed, startling a sandpiper pecking at its meal. "You did not really say that to me just now, 'It's not sporting'? I wish Mr. Turnbull had been here to hear it."

She snickered again and shook her head. The sun glowed off her black curls, picking out highlights, and he longed to wrap one of those curls around his finger, feel for himself if they were as soft and springy as they appeared. She normally slicked her hair back with pomade, keeping it close to her head to enhance her masculine looks. At her home she was more relaxed, more Mattie St. Armand than Captain St. Armand, at least to his eyes.

She brought him back to reality.

"Pay attention, Woodruff, or you're no use to me and I'll ship you out on the next packet to Liverpool."

"Aye, Captain."

"'Not sporting.' Do you know what we call men who don't fight fairly?"

"Cheats?"

"We call them *alive*. Forget whatever nonsense they taught you in school about being fair." She stopped laughing, her face serious. "This is your new life. You have to be prepared to defend yourself at all times. The only good fight is one you walk away from, and that will mean someone may end up bleeding. You want to make sure that someone isn't you, and for my sake, I don't want it to be me. Now, watch how I hold the blade. The first thing we'll do is practice how to fend off a slice."

They drilled on the sand until the sun was high and sweat plastered his shirt to his back. Oliver's knuckles ached from being whacked with the wooden blade his opponent used, and there was even a cut along the edge of his finger where the practice knife broke the skin. He was short of breath and his wrist ached, but Captain St. Armand looked cool and collected.

"Don't give up, Sunshine. You know what we call men who give up the fight?"

"Rested?"

"Dead," she said, punctuating this with a blow that could have been fatal had she not turned her knife at the last minute to hit him with the edge rather than push the hard wood between his ribs.

"Much better." She jumped back when he came after her. "Use that anger, and the pai—oof—"

As she fell he stuck his free hand forward to help her, only to end up cursing and sputtering from sand tossed in his eyes. The next thing he knew his ankle was twisted out from beneath him and he was flat on his back, with a grinning Mattie St. Armand kneeling on his chest, her wooden knife stuck under his chin.

"Go ahead, tell me it's not sporting to trick you."

He wiped what he could from his tearing eyes and said something to her he'd never said to a woman in his life.

"That's more like it! Get angry, think like a pirate and less like a gentleman. No, don't apologize," she said, getting her knee out of his belly and helping him to his feet. "I've been hard on you today. I can handle a little rough language."

He was still holding her hand, and when she made to tug it back, he did not release her.

"Nonetheless, I am mortified, Captain St. Armand. I should never have said that to you, no matter the provocation."

"Ah well, I've been told sometimes I'm capable of provoking a saint."

"I am not a saint," he said, tugging her closer. The feel of her body on top of his, even with her knife at his throat, was imprinted on his senses and he was aware of her as a woman, no matter how much she tried to hide it. She put her ungloved hand on his chest, and it was as if there was no cloth barrier hindering them, nothing to stop him from leaning in to close the gap separating their lips.

Nothing except the wooden knife under his chin.

"Keep your eyes on the hands," she said quietly. "Do not let your guard down."

He didn't move but looked deeply into her eyes. They were the deep blue of the sea behind them, rich as sapphires.

"There are things worth risking oneself for. Do you ever let someone past your guard?" He leaned in, ignoring the blade he knew could still cause serious harm to him. "I would risk a great deal, even my life, to hear my name on your lips again."

"You are already risking a great deal, Oliver. I have not forgotten that, nor should you."

She stepped away from him, and he let her go, and he fancied he felt some reluctance from her as she released his hand.

"Go get yourself something to eat, and get dressed. We're going into town."

She turned on her heel, tossing her wooden knife into the case. He watched her stride up to the house, her slim hips outlined by her trousers, her movement fluid with a warrior's grace.

She was as sharp and deadly as her knife, and he could not forget that, nor did he wish to. If she hadn't had an edge to her, she wouldn't be Mattie St. Armand.

The tailor's shop was a pleasant combination of masculine style and island sensibilities, the fabrics tending toward linens and cottons rather than woolens. The owner, Edward Digby, greeted Captain St. Armand as an old and valued customer.

"My friend Ned here was brought to the islands on one of my early voyages," she said. "He worked his passage sewing clothing for me and the crew."

Digby was a middle-aged man, small and slender as a reed and balding, but he had a kind face.

"I have a reputation to maintain, Captain, and you showcase my wares as none other can."

If the tailor had the dressing of the captain, then he must be fully aware of her sex, but the camaraderie among the two was that of friends, nothing more.

"I'll take your measurements, Mr. Woodruff. What are you needing?"

"He'll need clothes suitable to an English merchant visiting the islands," she answered for him. "Nothing too fancy, and one or two substantial wool pieces for a trip up north."

"As far north as New York or Boston?"

"I doubt we'll venture farther north than South Carolina, but it will be during winter."

She wasn't revealing all, even to a man she'd labeled her friend. Oliver made note of this, and it reminded him there was another errand in town to see to as the tailor reached for his pencil and paper. He already had his measuring tape around his neck and motioned Oliver to the dressing room in the back.

"Is there a barber you can recommend, Digby? I need a trim, someone who's skilled with beards."

"Just up the street is a good man. I'll give you his direction when we're done here."

Oliver stripped down to his smallclothes and when he returned Captain St. Armand was sitting in an armchair next to the mirror in the back of the shop. She slouched in an armchair, one leg dangling from the side over the arm, leafing through a weeks-old London paper.

"Do not mind me. Carry on."

He looked around, but Digby was still in the front, gathering materials.

"I am not comfortable having an audience when I am standing here in my unmentionables."

She glanced up from the paper and scanned him

from head to toe. "Two arms, two legs, a head—the usual parts. More than some aboard ship. You have nothing I haven't seen before, Woodruff. Do not have the vapors."

He would have argued, but the tailor returned and bustled about, getting Oliver's measurements and discussing various fabrics with him, as well as with the Captain.

"May I enquire as to whether Mr. Woodruff will be dressing for a particular…occasion, Captain?"

"We can speak freely, Ned. He knows of my work. To answer your question, he will be himself—a successful young merchant, not flashy, not too wealthy. Sober clothes, but not those of an old man. We don't want his wardrobe to look entirely suited to the islands. It should be evident he's newly arrived from England."

Digby nodded, then sat back on his heels. "What about you? Do you need clothes for this venture? Any other crew members I need to outfit?"

She shook her head and set down the newspaper.

"I have what I need and it will just be the two of us for the most part."

When Oliver disagreed with St. Armand over a silk waistcoat, Digby chimed in, "I must agree with the captain on this. You have a role to play, and this saffron brocade will be an excellent choice for evening wear."

"Digby's more than a tailor. He used to dress actors and actresses in Drury Lane and knows a thing or two about costumes, paint, and disguises. He understands how to make the man's look fit his circumstances."

"Clothes send a powerful message, Mr. Woodruff," the tailor added. "The people you encounter in your travels will be able to sum you up at a glance based on your attire. My task is to prepare you for that role, just as I prepared actors in London before they ever stepped on stage."

"This goes on my account," St. Armand said, raising her hand when Oliver would have protested. "You are part of my crew, under my command, and getting these things at my orders. Do not argue with me. This is just another ship's business expense. How quickly can you have the clothes ready, Ned?"

"You're in luck, Captain. One of my customers ordered two pair of trousers and a jacket, but his ship sailed and he never came for it. They're close enough to Mr. Woodruff's measurements that with a few alterations I can have it for you this afternoon. Shirts and waistcoats will take longer."

Mattie stood and walked over to Oliver. "You know my measurements. Could he wear one of my waistcoats?"

Digby scratched his head with his pencil and thought. "Yes, I do believe he could. You two are similar enough in size, though you're an inch or two taller."

"What? I cannot wear h—Captain St. Armand's clothing!"

They looked at him and Mattie put her hands on her hips, tilting her head to the side. "I don't see why not. I admit, you're slightly broader through the shoulders and have longer arms, am I correct?" she said looking at the tailor, who leafed back through his notebook and nodded.

"We're of a size, Woodruff. Nothing wrong with using what we have."

Oliver opened his mouth and shut it again. The idea of wearing a woman's clothing was wrong, viscerally wrong. But it wasn't really women's clothing. It was men's clothing worn by a woman. And that wasn't the only thing…

"Are you certain the captain is taller than I am?"

"Yes, I have the measurements right here. Captain St. Armand is two inches taller than you are."

"It's not how long a pikestaff is, Woodruff. It's how skilled you are with it."

"I am not worried about measuring up."

"Now, no need to be snappish," she soothed. "We're done here for now?"

"Yes, Captain. You can come back in"—he checked his notes—"one week for final fittings."

St. Armand shook her head. "Too much time. Hire extra seamstresses. Send the clothes to the house."

"As you wish," Digby said, looking pleased, likely over the extra fees he would charge for rushing the job. Stepping to the doorway of the shop, he called over one of the boys always hanging about looking to earn a few coins. He dispatched the child to fetch additional women to sew.

Oliver dressed himself while the two talked in the shop, then rejoined the captain.

"No frowning, Woodruff. I will loan you my brown waistcoat with the gold stripes. You'll look splendid in it. Now, let's find you that barber."

When they stopped a few streets over he took a deep breath of the barber's shop, the sunlit space and the familiar scent of bay rum and shaving soap washing over him. Whether it was in Manchester or New Providence, there were some places that smelled familiar and welcoming, and a good barber shop was such an establishment.

The barber took one look at Oliver's straggly facial

hair and tsked. "I can have that off for you sir, and warm oil on your skin to soothe and soften it too."

"No," Oliver said, though the thought of being clean-shaven and oiled sounded delightful. "I just need it brought into shape so it's not so wild."

"I can do that. Would you like your hair trimmed as well?"

"Might as well," he said, relaxing into the barber's chair as St. Armand seated herself on a rattan lounge, crossing her ankle over her knee. As the barber worked, he gossiped with the captain about the politics of the islands and what was on people's minds.

"The young queen is being courted by one of her cousins from Saxony, did you hear? Word is she favors his suit."

"She has so many cousins, which one is this, Pompey?"

"Alexander or Albert, something like that."

"It's Albert, the young prince of Saxe-Coburg duchy," Oliver chimed in. "The press in England was buzzing with speculation."

"It must be difficult, having one's every move watched and judged. I would hate to be the man attempting to court her."

"Yes, Captain," the barber said, gesturing with his shears too close to Oliver's ear for him to be comfortable. "Imagine being married to a woman who can order your head chopped off if she doesn't like you slurping your soup at supper."

"I don't think that's quite in the monarch's abilities, but it would take a special person to spend his life tied to such a powerful woman," she said.

Oliver slanted her a glance, careful not to turn his head, but she was leafing through another London paper, not looking at him. The papers were oftentimes months out of date, but still avidly consumed by the islanders and expatriates.

"Did you read about the revolt on the *Amistad*?" she said.

"Poor buggers. If they landed here they would have found shelter and welcome."

"That is what has the Americans in an uproar, Pompey. They don't want word to spread that slaves taking ship to our islands walk away free. After the *Enterprise* incident, that Senator Calhoun nearly had apoplexy, calling it 'a great outrage committed on individuals by a civilized nation.' He was referring, of course, to the slave owners, not the slaves, as the victimized individuals."

"Tweaking their white noses is a joy, Captain," Pompey laughed. "It makes me proud to be an island man. Oh, begging your pardon, Mr. Woodruff. I hope you didn't take offense."

"I would never take offense when a man's holding sharp blades near my face," he said dryly. "Carry on."

The barber trimmed away at the growth on Oliver's chin, and he nodded when he saw his face in the mirror held up for his inspection.

"Much better. Now I look less like Robinson Crusoe," he said. "Well done."

He paid the barber and put his hat on, relishing the feel of being more himself again. He'd realized something in the shop. Here he was a stranger in a strange land, his pale skin and blonde hair marking him as "other." At home, his uncle and the other mill owners of his acquaintance acted as if being an Englishman was the only appropriate status for a gentleman. Naturally, they made fun of the Americans with whom they traded, dismissing them as tobacco spitting bumpkins and louts. Oftentimes, they were correct.

They never thought at all about the people living in America who picked the cotton they depended on for the cloth they turned out. Or if they did, they did not talk about it. In the islands there was no escaping slavery's legacy, especially with emancipation so newly won. You saw it in the dark faces surrounding him, people still speaking in dialects Captain St. Armand identified as African—Ibo, Yoruba—and the rhythms of Africa echoed too in the singing of the freed slaves aboard ship.

He knew now he was seeing a part of the world few of his peers would ever see, nor would they wish to. They did not want their world view shaken, and he had new respect for the abolitionists and reformers whose work he'd admired without ever truly understanding what it was they did. The people they helped were sailors and farmers and cooks like Mrs. Oldman and barbers like Pompey.

"You're quiet, Sunshine. Don't you like your haircut?"

"I like it very much. I was lost in thought," he said, flashing her a smile.

"Good way to get yourself killed," she said, looking around her. She'd left off the parrot today and was dressed more soberly but was still armed with her long knife.

As they walked back to the captain's pink house he kept his eyes open for more robbers waiting to leap out of the bushes and attack them, but either word had gone out or it was their half-day off.

"How would you feel about going out this evening,

but as a simple sailor, not as Mr. Woodruff?"

"Do I have to be introduced as your cabin boy?"

"Consider it protective coloration, Sunshine. People will dismiss you as inconsequential."

"Or a pervert," he muttered.

"An inconsequential pervert, but that's not important."

"If you were the one in this position you'd feel differently."

She grinned, but there was no humor in it. "You have not yet seen me in my varied guises. Do not be so quick to think you are being treated poorly. But the offer is genuine."

"Is it wise? I had the impression you wanted to keep me under wraps until we get to Florida?"

She shrugged. "What's life without a little risk? Sometimes you pick up the best information over a hand of cards, or when a man's had more liquor than he can hold. In addition, you came to the islands to see the sights. A night on the town shouldn't be damaging, provided we're well armed and prepared for action."

"Normally my nights on the town involve nothing more than picking the best cravat and checking my wallet."

"I can see your idea of what constitutes an exciting evening is quite different than mine," she said, looking up at the sun to gauge the time. It was a skill he admired. Mattie St. Armand was comfortable in her surroundings, whether aboard ship or in the islands, attuned to the rhythms of the sea and the shore.

What would it be like to see her in London, or Manchester? Would she be more at ease as Mattie, or as the captain? He suspected the latter, but the idea of squiring around Miss St. Armand, escorting her to the opera or to supper, intrigued him.

It was the idea of introducing her to his mother or the bishop that made his thoughts come to a skittering halt. His association with Mattie St. Armand could be an island interlude, nothing more. It was impossible, given who they were, the lives they led, to imagine anything else.

"You should not worry overmuch about what people will think about us tonight," she said, her eyes always scanning their surroundings for danger. "Island society is different from what you know back home. The white men here are largely exiles sent to the Indies to make their fortune, escape debt, cease being an embarrassment to their families for one peccadillo or another. Take Ned Digby. He was one step ahead of the authorities when he came here—the target of a powerful family. Poor Ned loved, but not wisely, and his affections threatened a betrothal which would have involved a sizeable dowry."

"He was wooing the bride?"

"No, not the bride," St. Armand said dryly. "It was the groom's family that saw Ned as a threat to the marriage going forward. Few men settle in the islands on their own. Disease, drink, and distance from England are what keep them here. But you intend to return to England, don't you?"

"I have to. I have a role there that's been prepared for me. If it's not a role like the one Digby outfitted actors to play, it's still a role I must take on. My family is expecting me to run the mills. The people in our village need the mill to stay in operation and keep them employed. I'm not being immodest when I say they need me, someone who understands the operation of the business but also has an eye toward the future. The world is changing, Captain. England is changing. Steam and coal and water are driving the nation forward, and we cannot hold back the tide, as you pointed out."

The sun dappling through the trees cast her face in shadow.

"I know that. My ship is already beginning to look like an antique compared to the steam-powered vessels. A captain who sails on schedule, not dependent on the wind and the tide, that captain can get more business. Even if I have to give up valuable space in the hold for engines and the coal and wood to fuel them, I can make more profit because of schedules."

"Will you do that? Switch to steam?"

She was pensive, and he thought she'd answer, but she just shrugged.

"Today I will focus on the pleasures I can grab while I'm able to. Tonight I'll show you a side of the island you only see with an experienced guide."

"Will we dine at your home?"

"You can be certain of it. I may be willing to drink in these taverns, but you'd be taking your life in your own hands if you eat the food they prepare. When ships are in and business is brisk, the island's cat population takes a sudden dip."

They were at the house and the lookout gave them a wave, which Mattie returned. Wellington was at the door to greet them.

"Welcome back, Captain. I took the liberty of having the maid mend your clothing, Mr. Woodruff. You'll find it's now clean and pressed as well."

"Wellington, you are a jewel," Mattie said. "Please tell Mrs. Oldman we'll dine at home tonight, but I expect to go out later this evening."

"Very good, Captain," the butler said, taking their hats and St. Armand's gloves. "Will you need particular weaponry for your excursion?"

Oliver stumbled, but they ignored him.

"Put out the brass knuckles, and outfit Mr. Woodruff with"—she looked at him— "one of the Italian daggers, I think."

"I did that well on my lessons?"

"No, but you did well enough that I prefer to have you armed. Do try to look more like a brigand and less like a choirboy though."

"Now I'm sorry I had my hair trimmed."

"Well, what's done is done. The beard helps."

Every time she mentioned his beard it made it itch. So he scratched now, looking forward to the day when he'd be clean shaven again. They climbed the stairs, Oliver a few steps behind and doing his best not to watch the sway of her hips as she climbed, but it was a lost cause.

"And I'll get you appropriate clothing. Stop staring at my arse."

"I'm sorry!"

"No, you're not, so don't pretend. What I said was, your clothing is too fine to wear tonight, and the sailors wouldn't wear their slops for a night out. After supper I'll get you something from my wardrobe."

"I must say, I am not comfortable wearing your clothing, Captain."

"Be reasonable, Sunshine. It's men's clothing and

we're of a size, so it's the logical way to proceed. If you're worried I'll look more dashing than you, put your mind at ease. I *will* look more dashing than you. Always. However, the two of us should make a handsome pair of fellows."

CHAPTER 10

IT WAS A DIFFERENT TAVERN, but much was the same. Woodruff knew better than to order ale, and Mattie watched him as he took his time with his rum, seeming more interested in watching the patrons than in drinking.

He was a most observant fellow, her Oliver. That thought stopped her cold as she raised her mug to her lips. When did she start thinking of him as *hers*?

She smiled to herself, remembering the look on his face earlier when she'd come down to supper in her London-tailored coat, the high collar crusted with braid, the golden buttons gleaming against the dark wine broadcloth. Her waistcoat was sky blue silk embroidered with roses whose threads picked up the color of the coat and the gold of the buttons. Her trousers were gray and narrow through the leg, but his eye was drawn to the flap in front.

"*What* do you have between your legs?"

"That's a rather personal question, don't you think?" she'd said. She had hibiscus in her garden that didn't blush as pink as poor Woodruff.

"It gives my appearance the verisimilitude needed to help people see exactly what I want them to see—a fully equipped young man on the town."

At the words "fully equipped" he'd turned such a bright shade she feared he'd burst into flames, which only spurred her on. She put her hand on his shoulder and leaned in to whisper in his ear, "If you are a very, very, good boy, Sunshine, someday I'll get out the coconut oil and show you what I can do with my toys."

He'd twitched beneath her hand, giving her a look both hot and confused. She'd almost apologized for teasing him, but if he hadn't wanted to hear the details he shouldn't have asked.

"You are dressed far finer than I am, Captain," he'd said, steering the conversation into safer waters.

"Of course I am. If you're too well-dressed you'll draw notice. This way I will be the peacock in the party, drawing eyes to my sartorial splendor. That is not a criticism of you being an observer and not an actor, far from it. I value your fresh look at scenes all too familiar to me. You have an eye for detail and serve our purposes by being unremarkable."

He was dressed plainly, save for the striped waistcoat loaned him by Mattie. The brown and gold silk put him a step above the sailors in the tavern, but his own clean and mended shirt and trousers helped him fit in. He'd removed his coat and forgone neckwear, not yet acclimated to the tropical warmth.

She took a moment now in the tavern to admire his face and form as he stepped to the bar to refresh their drinks. If she was going to have random men foisted on her in island brothels, it didn't hurt that it was someone as good-looking as Oliver Woodruff.

She'd named him "Sunshine," but it was more than his bright hair that made her warm to him. His ready smile, his sense of humor, his untarnished soul—he was unlike the men and women with whom she spent her time. He listened to people, whether it was a newly liberated slave aboard the *Prodigal Son*, or an Irish sailor, or a barber. She knew few men of his class who could see beyond their own worlds of privilege and comfort.

Unlike the pair entering the tavern. Their voices were loud and their clothing new and expensive. Young bucks, pasty pale, callow, and freshly arrived from England was her guess. From their stumbling and loose gestures it was obvious they'd already been drinking heavily. She'd place money on them being relieved of their purses, at the very least, before the night was over.

Oliver stopped still when he saw them, and quietly faded back into the shadows. She looked at the duo with new interest. They sat and yelled for wine, then one took out a pair of dice, idly rolling them across the table.

"Dammit, where is the wine? These islanders are the laziest blacks I've ever seen. You there, boy," he said to a fisherman sitting at a nearby table. "Fetch me something to drink."

The man ignored him, but his companion looked murderous. Mattie watched as the tavern keeper finally brought over some wine and rough metal cups. It was a jug of the swill he kept on hand for customers he wasn't counting on for return business, either because they'd be discouraged by the offerings, or, in this case, were likely to wind up facedown in the gutter with a knife sticking out of some vital organ.

"This heat is helping me forget how dreary London is right now," the gamester said, reaching for his cup.

He removed his hat, wiping sweat off his brow with his handkerchief, stringy blonde hair plastered to his skull. "I'm in no hurry to get back there."

"It is better here than what we had in Georgia with that unexpected freeze, Lowry. You were fortunate your cousin sent one of his gals to warm your bed," said his companion, an overfed, soft-looking lad. He looked the sort kept around by sharper boys to bolster them in their activities and loan them money.

"She was a hot little thing, quite eager to please," Lowry said.

"It wasn't as if the wench had a choice, after all."

"Sissy had a choice, Wilson—my cock in her mouth, or getting sent back to the fields to pick cotton. She chose the better option, of course. I even left her a few pennies for her time and pleasure. And trust me, she was well pleasured by the time the sun was up."

Mattie picked up her mug and strolled over to the men, sitting without asking.

"Gentlemen. I couldn't help but overhear that you're newly arrived in the islands. Let me stand you a round to welcome you."

Without waiting for their reply, she snapped her fingers and the tavern keeper hurried over, bringing a far better bottle from his stock.

They finished their drinks and Mattie refilled their cups, raising her own. "To new experiences."

"Your servant, sir," Wilson said, and he seemed pleased he wasn't the one footing the bill. "I am Percy Wilson, and this is Nelson Lowry."

Lowry looked at her suspiciously, and she knew he was trying to slot her into his neat little files of how people were treated. He could see she was swarthier than they were, but her accent was polished and her clothes far finer than the others in the bar.

Without giving her own name, Mattie touched one of the dice, rolling it over onto its side, the two dots staring upward like accusing eyes.

"I see you play. Fancy a game of hazard?"

Lowry's eyes brightened and he drank from his own cup before thumping it on the table.

"Excellent idea. We'll roll for first cast."

The dice favored Lowry, and he rolled for the main. The play progressed amongst the two of them, and coins flowed back and forth, though the pile grew steadily in front of the visiting Englishman.

"First the wench favored you, now the dice do. I swear, you are the luckiest man I know, Lowry," Wilson said, his consonants loose with the wine he'd consumed.

There was a twitch at the corner of Lowry's eye, his high forehead shiny again with perspiration. He smiled as he cupped the dice, and said, "I've had good nights and bad, but the gods are favoring me tonight, friend. What did you say your name was, sir?"

"Captain St. Armand. I do a little trading in the islands."

The drinkers nearby snickered, but the Englishmen didn't notice, focused as they were on the cubes rolling along the table, the ivory catching the soft gleam of the lamplight.

Lowry threw again, and Wilson shook his head in wonder as Lowry nicked it.

"Damned bad luck, sir."

"One might say that, Mr. Wilson. Or, one might say, 'let's examine those bones,'" Mattie said.

Quick as a lizard darting after an insect, she clamped her hand down on Lowry's wrist before he could retrieve his dice. He tried to pull back, snarling at her, "How dare you accuse a gentleman of cheating, you nigger trash!"

Now the tavern was quiet as the grave, and Mattie saw Oliver stir in the shadows. She continued holding the Englishman's wrist and smiling, but it was the kind of smile that made the drinkers nearby move away from the gamblers.

"Mr. Fox, would you do the honors?"

A massive man with a shaven head and shoulders like granite stepped over to the table. He took a pewter mug and brought it down, smashing the cubes to dust. In the aftermath, the click of the lead ball rolling out of the loaded dice was quite distinct.

"Fox here is a blacksmith," Mattie said affably. "If he chose to take your head in his hands and squeeze, I wonder if we'd find it too is loaded with weights, instead of brains."

Wilson looked at Lowry in horror. "Loaded dice? You've been cheating with loaded dice all this time?"

He stood, his face grim, and bowed to St. Armand. "I am deeply mortified that I am in this…person's… company, Captain. Please accept my apologies, and be assured I was completely unaware of his habits."

Mattie inclined her head regally, and without another glance at his companion, Wilson turned and left.

"Percy, wait!" Lowry said, trying again to extract his wrist, but stopped with a gasp as she ground the bones together.

"Now, what shall we do with you?" Mattie mused.

"Keelhaul him, Captain!" one of the sailors said.

"I can show him the reef offshore," the fisherman offered. "Lots of sharks this time of year."

Lowry's eyes were wild as they tracked the men speaking. More suggestions were made, involving removing various body parts to mark him a cheat—an ear, a nose, fingers.

"All excellent suggestions, but we are, after all, trash. He's told us so. Who are we to show island justice to this fine white visitor?" she said.

"I didn't mean it! I apologize!"

"Tsk. Too late for that, friend. However, tempting as it is, your disappearance could bring unwanted attention to the men around me. Most of us prefer to keep a low profile, am I correct?"

The customers muttered angrily about him getting off easily but nodded in agreement. Many of them were adept at avoiding tariffs as they traveled through the islands, navigating through spots where they could avoid the Spanish *Costa Garda* or the British authorities.

Mattie released Lowry's wrist and he cradled it to his chest, his shoulders hunched.

"You will leave this island on the next tide, Lowry. There's a fishing boat or two that could drop you off somewhere if you offer enough gold. No, not that gold," she said as his eyes darted to the pile on the table. "That's your fine for being a cheating idiot. That plus, whatever's left in your purse. If you think to go to the authorities and complain you were robbed by island trash, consider how swiftly word can go to Governor Cockburn detailing your antics this evening."

He started to protest, but the blacksmith pinned his arms as Mattie leaned over and extracted his wallet from inside the coat, riffling through the notes and coins. Fox picked him up by the collar and quick marched the young man out the door, tossing him into the gutter.

"Drinks are on our fine English friend," Mattie said, throwing some money on the table as the tavern cheered. She knew they'd rehash this story for months, elaborating and expanding on how Captain St. Armand taught the Englishman a lesson about island life. By the time the storytellers were done there would be a knife fight or two added in, maybe an eye gouged out. Lowry had no idea how fortunate he was to escape with his life and limbs whole.

When Mattie sat with Lowry and Wilson, Oliver almost stepped forward to warn her, but instead she handled the situation as she always did, capably, efficiently, and with enough menace to ensure success.

His fantasies of having Mattie St. Armand in his bed seemed further away than ever. What could he possibly offer a woman like her? He thought himself as good as the next fellow, but he was no Casanova, no accomplished London rake. He was just, as Lowry had sneered at him in England, a "mill boy", even if his family owned the mill.

Yet, the way Mattie looked at him, the way she smiled at him and teased him these past days, it was different from how she looked at other men. He was certain of it. She would not be coy or play games as girls were wont to do in his circles. If she wanted him, she'd say so. If she didn't want him, she'd say that too. And if he persisted with unwelcome advances, she'd gut him like a trout.

Oddly enough, this honest, if bloody, behavior cheered him up. Wondering whether a woman you courted would slap you if you stole a kiss was all well and good, but wondering whether the woman would wear your guts for garters added an excitement to the day that he was beginning to appreciate. He wanted Mattie St. Armand, and while he thought about who she'd be if she was decked out as a woman, acting as a woman, it was Captain St. Armand who excited him tonight, the commander and warrior, the sharp-eyed pirate who saw through trickery. He sat back at their table, passing her a fresh mug of rum.

"Do you anticipate Lowry causing problems for you, Captain?"

"No. I'm not a fine gentleman, but I know something about the breed. They may run out on their rent, bugger a footman on the sly, neglect their tenants or forget to pay their tradesmen, but there are two things no one can get away with—not paying a debt of honor, and cheating. I have a cordial relationship with Sir Francis and that was no idle threat I made. All it would take is word to get back to England, and Lowry would be sunk."

"Will you do it?"

"Not unless I'm pushed into it. He'll be lucky if Wilson doesn't say anything, but I'm done with him. There's no need to draw attention to myself in that fashion."

She rose, leaving a generous amount of Lowry's money behind for the tavern keeper, and they stepped out into the soft, evening air.

A wisp of wind ruffled the branches and a nighthawk rasped out a call, and as they walked back on the sandy track to her house they were unmolested, enjoying the salt breeze after the tobacco and sweaty funk of the tavern.

"Lost in thought, Oliver?"

He stopped, his hand on her arm. "I've been thinking about what is worth risking one's life for, Captain. What rewards are worth the risk, what prizes may be won."

Her face was half in shadow, half in the filtering moonlight, and he couldn't make out her features. But when he put his hands alongside her face, he could feel the fine bones beneath the surface. He ran his finger alongside the scar at the corner of her mouth, the pucker drawing her lips up into a crooked smile he would always remember as uniquely hers.

No one else was on the road to see as he bent his head, his lips brushing hers. He pulled back and tried to gauge her expression, hoping it did not presage a knife in the guts.

There was no attack. Instead, she pulled his head back down, her lips soft against his as she explored his face in turn, running her fingers over his beard, lingering on his jaw, the pulse on his neck, the edge of his cheek, before gliding back down to his mouth.

Suddenly it didn't matter at all that she might be an inch or two taller than him. All it meant was they fit together perfectly as he angled his mouth across hers, their lips coming together as if they'd been made for this moment, for this place and time.

Oliver wrapped his arms around her and he could feel her beneath her coat, the firm muscles, the broad shoulders unlike any he'd ever experienced holding a woman. It piqued his desire, made him want to unwrap her from her garments, see what the mysterious Captain St. Armand was beneath her armor, her paint, the false face she showed the world to protect herself and her people.

For now, he was content to live in this moment,

especially when her moist lips opened beneath his and a purr of satisfaction rolled up from her chest. He parried her questing tongue with his own, taking his time, letting her kisses envelope his senses. Her body pressed close to his and her artificial cock rubbed against him, exciting him in a dark and dangerous way. He roamed his hands down to her cheeks, feeling the outline of her leather harness beneath her breeches.

He wanted to know more, to satisfy the edgy desire growing in him, to continue to feel that length pressing against him, rubbing against him, but he steeled himself and set her away from him. It was only a separation of a scant inch or two, but he was chilled in the tropical night, bereft and alone.

Her breathing was shallow and fast, and he saw the moisture gleaming on her mouth. She licked her lips, tasting him, and he nearly tossed his resolve into the ocean, ready to pull her back into his embrace.

"Why did you stop?"

Her voice was husky, strained, and he took a moment to frame his answer. He finally just shook his head.

"This is an important conversation to have, Captain St. Armand, but not in the middle of the road."

His answer seemed to mollify her and she gestured for him to move along the sandy track.

"As you wish, Woodruff, but never doubt, we will continue this conversation. You…surprise me."

"Is that a good thing?"

"Generally not. I don't like surprises. They usually involve bleeding."

The lights from the house guided them onward, and when they stepped into the foyer Mr. Nash was waiting for them.

"Captain, I've obtained most of what you requested, but I need to speak with you about some of the supplies."

He looked at Woodruff, frowned, then looked back at Captain St. Armand. Oliver hoped there wasn't another avuncular lecture in his future. He was inclined to believe further discussions would involve fists.

St. Armand looked over at him, then sighed.

"Off to bed with you, Sunshine. We leave in a few days and I want to get in as much training as possible."

"You let me carry a stiletto tonight."

"Carrying a knife and using it effectively are not the same thing, as you've learned." She waved her hand in dismissal. "Go scribble in your journal."

She was perceptive, knowing him well enough to understand he'd want to include tonight's adventures in his book, but she also gave him a clear warning look that he'd best be careful which parts of the story he included, and which he edited out. Writing about a tavern brawl would be tolerated, writing personal details about Captain St. Armand would not.

Not that he'd ever intended to include those kinds of details. Once he might have been tempted, because the market for titillating stories was always promising when one knew the right publishers. He couldn't do that though. He couldn't write about Mattie that way.

After he blew out his lamp he lay in bed, unable to sleep. He could hear the captain in the room next to his, the splash of water in her basin, and it was easy for his rich imagination to conjure up images of her removing her clothing, unbinding her breasts, peeling her smallclothes off to reveal the device she wore to simulate being a man.

What was her cock like? Was it a solid wood? Ivory? Alabaster?

Was the harness a soft deerskin so it wouldn't chafe, or was it sturdier leather for rough use? The thought of that implement rising between her legs, and how she might employ it for more than costuming, had him hard as the item in question and he stroked himself, imagining what she could do with it, what he could do with it if he had her beneath him.

Sweat broke out on his brow and his breathing became fast and harsh as he spread his thighs farther apart, pulling at his cock, envisioning her behind him, entering him, working him with her hand, moving within him in a rhythm echoing how he stroked himself now. Her breath would come faster as she made him take her, whispering dark words in his ears, and with a gasp he spent himself, frightened and delighted by his own imagination's workings.

It was a poor substitute for the real thing.

He pulled the sheet over his sticky body, his sweat cooling him as it dried in the night air. He needed to come up with an answer to explain his actions in stopping tonight, something to satisfy her, but for now he needed to worry most on surviving the next morning's exercises, or at least not embarrassing himself too badly.

CHAPTER 11

"WHEN A MAN'S HANDS ARE out of sight, it's not because he's going to surprise you with a kitten."

Oliver sputtered, angrily wiping sand from his eyes. "At this rate I'll be fortunate to live long enough to make it to Florida!"

"Oh, I think you'll survive the journey over. It's once we're there that worries me. Now, pick up that knife. It's not doing you a damned bit of good on the sand. Angle it like I showed you. When you're really good, meaning you've drilled every day since you were barely as high as a pirate's boot, you keep the edge of your blade from parrying a thrust. The edge is for cutting and needs to stay keen."

Oliver grasped the wooden knife, sweat running down his arms, sand clinging to the wet patches. He heard laughter from the side and scowled, knowing he looked ridiculous next to the captain. She was cool as a drink in the shade, composed, ready to humiliate him further.

The crewmembers who'd stopped by the house this morning lounged in the shade of the sea grapes and poinciana trees. Daniel Green stood there, with his arms crossed, shaking his head.

"Cap'n, if you don't put a real blade in that boy's hand he'll never know what it feels like to fight for his life."

"You're correct, Mr. Green. Perhaps you won't survive to make it to Florida, Woodruff. But never fear," she said cheerfully. "We'll give you a proper send-off with many a toast and jest to your memory."

"I like a fine and proper wake!" Daly shouted.

"Who doesn't, Daly? The trick is to make sure it's not your wake people are enjoying."

She thrust forward with her knife, but Oliver was prepared. She smiled when preparing to stab him—not a huge grin, but a slight tightening at the corners of her eyes. It was easy to let those lucent eyes distract him, but this time he was ready, bringing his own wooden blade under her guard and poking her in the upper arm. If it were a real blade he might have slashed open an artery, a potentially fatal blow.

But she'd been doing this far longer than he had. She tossed her knife to her "uninjured" hand and brought it hard into his belly, turning her hand at the last minute so it was her fist and not the blade that knocked the wind out of him.

"Even a wounded snake can bite. You might have killed me with that last one—and well done, you wiggled under my guard—but with my dying breath I would have taken you with me."

He could only nod, struggling to suck air back into his lungs. She cared enough about whether he lived or not that she invested her time and his energy in these daily sessions. Nonetheless, he'd be less than a man if he didn't want to make a positive impression on a pretty girl.

"Bring me pistols and I will show you what I can do," he coughed.

Oliver wiped his face on his shirtsleeve and caught his breath while a brace of pistols was fetched for him. He held one in his hand, admiring the balance. One could appreciate the beauty of a pair of Manton pistols, but form had to combine with function. The most beautifully inlaid pistol in the world was worse than a piece of tin if it misfired or threw his aim off because of poor craftsmanship.

As one would expect from the notorious Captain St. Armand, the pistols were every bit as lovingly crafted as the captain's wardrobe but weren't flashy. They didn't draw the eye like the massive blade at her thigh did. These were workmen's tools, cleaned and well maintained, with smooth action. Daly ambled down the beach to post a target on a palm tree bending out over the water, and the assembled layabouts called out mingled encouragement and insults at the distance.

"An American dollar says he never hits the target," one sailor said.

"Belay that," Green growled. "You know better than to wager silver with your shipmates."

"I'll wager a month's mending on the lad," Daly said.

His offer was quickly snapped up and countered, as he was nearly as skilled with a needle and thread as he was with threading a knife between a man's ribs.

"Show them how it's done," the captain said quietly.

Her steady encouragement after his poor performance with the blades made his back straighten as he eyed the distant paper. He knew he was good, he knew his life could depend on his skill with the weapon in his hand, but now he wanted to hit the target for an entirely different reason. He wanted to hear Mattie St. Armand say, "Well done, Oliver."

The breeze brushed his cheek as he went still, then squeezed the trigger. A moment later there were yells from the men, and some applause, but he was already reloading for a second shot now that he had the feel of the gun.

This one hit the target square in the center and silenced the pirates. They looked at him with new respect, and some awe.

From slightly behind he heard a contralto voice say, "Well done, Oliver."

A grinning Daly collected markers off his shipmates, saying, "Anyone could see Woodruff there could blow the balls off a squirrel. He's a dangerous man, our Oliver is."

The captain picked up the other pistol and took her shot, and they competed against one another until his hands were black from powder. He couldn't reload as fast as she could, but he edged her out in the number of times they hit the bull's-eye, and he might be forgiven if there was a swagger to his stride as his shipmates congratulated him.

His shipmates. The thought made him grin as they walked to the house. This rough band of seamen accepted him in their own fashion. He may not be able to reef the topsails yet or tie a perfect fisherman's bend, but he had skills they valued. If there were a fight, they'd have his back, confident he'd be there for them.

"I was impressed by your shooting today," Mattie told him over supper.

"Thank you. I'm glad I'm of more benefit to you than as a saleable corpse. Or than the ship's cat."

"Don't get carried away. The ship's cat has years of service on his record. Don't you, Roscoe?"

The bird looked up from the nut it was cracking, ignored her, and flew over to perch on Woodruff's shoulder, dropping the nut in his lap.

"I believe you've found an admirer."

"It's nice to be well thought of by one of the more valuable crew members." He scratched Roscoe's neck and the parrot purred with contentment. She could understand that. If Woodruff looked at her with those pretty eyes and rubbed her neck, she might purr with contentment as well.

She studied him now, remembering how he'd looked this morning when he removed his shirt during their shooting competition. She'd seen enough men stripped down to their breeches—or less—that she could generally ignore the sight, but there was something about his form that caught her eye and damaged her aim.

He'd been pretty before, but now it was a man's beauty—the corded strength that came from working, from testing one's limits. She admired his commitment to the rigorous training she'd put him through.

Despite all his gains, she knew this was not the life he was meant for and there could be nothing between them but a temporary dalliance. She could see herself retiring from her life at sea, but she could not see herself settling into life as the wife of a Manchester cotton merchant, gossiping with the other ladies, spending her days making rounds of calls drinking weak tea and conversing about the weather. She'd end up shooting herself, or one of them.

It was all ludicrous anyway. No one in that hidebound society would expect Oliver to have a woman of color by his side. She was fair-skinned enough to pass for Spanish or Italian or Greek, but she did not hide her origins unless it was to hoodwink the authorities. No, playing with her sunshine lad would be all she could have, but she would enjoy these moments while they lasted.

The next course arrived, a red snapper prepared with a peppered sauce ladled over the flaky fish. After Woodruff was served and the servants left, she poured some wine kept chilled in the cisterns behind the kitchens. She lingered over the fruity Spanish *verdejo*, twirling the goblet's stem in her fingers.

"You knew those men last night, at the tavern. That's why you were staying in the shadows."

He pushed his rice and pigeon peas around the plate, framing his answer for her.

"Lowry and Wilson were at school with me."

"Friends?"

"Not hardly. Lowry was the kind of bully who would take advantage of anyone he thinks he can cuff around. It was a school patronized by the offspring of those in trade and manufacturing. Some of the boys were the sons of peers sent down from more exclusive schools. Lowry was in that group. His father paid well for Templeton to keep him."

"And did he? Cuff you around?"

He shrugged. "Some, but he was no better and no worse than others there. I mostly stayed out of his way."

Her anger flared anew. She knew it was the way of boys, testing each other out, scuffling for primacy, but the image of a small, cowering blonde boy flashed into her head and— Good heavens! Was she feeling *maternal* over the idea of a young Oliver Woodruff?

She looked suspiciously down at her wine, but she'd barely started on it. "You did the right thing staying back in the shadows."

"I thought about coming forward, but you had the situation under control."

He likely didn't realize what those words meant to her, his confidence that she was capable of dealing with the situation. She knew she was capable, the men on her ship knew it, but anyone else who knew her as a woman first and Captain St. Armand second might have doubts about her abilities to deal with danger in a dockside tavern. This was one of the reasons she entertained thoughts about Oliver Woodruff which went disturbingly deeper than an hour of sport in his bed. None of the men who'd been her lovers had been able to get beyond their ideas of her role and her place. None. It was one of the reasons she'd found herself in another woman's arms so often. They saw her in a different fashion, accepted her as Captain St. Armand without her having to fight for that place.

"What they said about their visit to Georgia. It upset you."

She was about to dismiss this with a flippant remark one would expect from Captain St. Armand, but this was Oliver, and she could be honest with him.

"Yes. Hearing scum like that laughing over abusing a poor slave girl unable to say no disturbs me. I know my father, but I do not know who the white men were in my grandmother and great-grandmother's lives, whether those women were forced or willing. And how willing could that first ancestress from

Africa have been? Uprooted from her home, sold into slavery, she never had a choice.

"Teaching Lowry and Wilson a lesson couldn't help that girl Sissy in Georgia, but it gave me satisfaction. It also forced them to see free blacks like Mr. Fox as men to be reckoned with. I doubt it will change anything in their lives, but at least they had the lesson."

She looked down at her hands, and he knew this was a rare moment for Captain St. Armand, opening up and talking about herself and her motives. She knew her father, but did he despise her for being black, for being an island girl? Was it the real reason he'd pushed her away from England?

Oliver wanted to take her in his arms and tell her all would be well, that she didn't have to throw herself into harm's way to help others, but he couldn't. He didn't have the right. Today though, when she praised him on the sand, it became clearer why he couldn't simply take what she offered. He had to earn her respect, and it had to be more than the ability to shoot a target.

In the past, knights were sent on quests. They had to slay dragons and rescue maidens and solve riddles and fight mysterious foes. He had to slay a dragon for Mattie St. Armand to prove himself worthy. He had to go on a quest with her, not for her, and rescue those in need, and be her Sir Galahad.

She dismissed him when Mr. Nash was shown in, highlighting again the responsibilities this ship's captain carried on her slim shoulders. Later that night, after a frustrating bout of writing ending with many scratched up sheets of foolscap, he stepped out onto his balcony to clear his head, taking a deep breath of the rain-freshened air flavored with tobacco smoke. A dark outline on the balcony was silhouetted against the sky, the glowing tip of a cheroot bright in the dim light spilling out from her room. He stepped over and she passed it to him, and he took a lungful, enjoying the burn, the intimacy of sharing something that touched her lips.

"I am leading you into any number of bad habits, Sunshine."

"I would not follow your lead if I did not want to go there, Captain."

"I must say, you've surprised me. When I first took you aboard, I expected…"

"You expected a soft-handed, complacent Englishman."

"Which is what I received. At least the soft-handed part," she said, taking his hand in her own. She ran her fingers over his, tracing the roughness, the nicks and scrapes and new calluses. He shivered at her touch, but he wasn't cold. He was aware of all surrounding him, his senses alive in a way they had never been alive in the past. He'd lived his life going through predictable days—one dressed in a certain fashion, one ate certain foods at regular times, one read the same newspapers and books as the others in the same social circles. Even the conversations at the entertainments were the same. Pleasantries meaning nothing, compliments which were expected and empty.

It was only when he was angrily writing in his journal that he felt truly alive, able to express himself. But those were just words. Good words, words he might publish someday, but only words, not deeds.

"Not so soft now," she said.

"No." He threw the cheroot over the railing and lifted his hand, taking one of her curls between his fingers. When he released it, the hair coiled back as if it had a life of its own, gleaming in the lamplight spilling out from his room.

"But this is. Soft."

She was so full of life, even her hair looked alive, springing out all over. She still wore shirt and breeches, but her freshly washed hair was relaxed, not slicked back to look more mannish. She stood quiet beneath his hands as he toyed with her hair, lost in the silken texture, the fullness. Cocking her head to the side when he gently massaged her scalp with his hand, she purred as her eyes went half shut. He almost told her she looked like Roscoe, who'd preen while his head was scratched, purring and making small cooing noises. She was a creature of sensation, his captain, one who enjoyed life whether it was a fine meal, or a quality cheroot, or hands that touched her just so.

"You are so many contradictions, Mattie St. Armand. Strong and hard, but here, soft and touchable. So soft," he murmured, pulling her closer by inches, until his lips touched her forehead, a gentle caress before easing down to meet her moist mouth. It was a kiss that glided through him like warm honey, growing sweeter with each pass of his lips across hers, the feel of her velvet tongue seeking his.

She pushed against him, not to free herself, but steadying him against the rail as she leaned into his embrace, her arms going around his shoulders, running down his back, leaving shivers through him. He moved one hand from her head to her bottom to hold her against him, to feel her and hear her low noise of excitement as she felt his arousal against her. She was at home tonight and wore no padding, no binding, and it was without question a woman he held in his arms. Her breasts were not overly large, but he suspected if he caressed them they'd be just the right size, and he longed to do what he'd dreamed of, strip away her artifice and men's clothing and discover the woman.

But knowing whom he held gave him pause, and he reluctantly ended their kiss, pulling back from her. The tension thickened like the tropical air around them, heavy with promise.

"What?" she finally snapped.

"I'm thinking."

"I try not to overthink situations. Sometimes, you just throw a knife, see where it stabs and take it from there."

"Captain—Mattie—this isn't what I want."

She tried to smile, failed, and looked puzzled.

"It's not what you want? Hell, all the men I know would be delighted at any woman offering herself to them. What is wrong with you?"

"Nothing is wrong with me, but this isn't right."

"This isn't right? Are you going to quote morality tracts at me next? When I carried you off from a bawdy house I never thought I was carting a monk away with me." She threw up her hands. "I have never in my life known a man to turn down cunny when it's offered him."

He winced at her words.

"Does my language offend you?" She leaned in, drawing closer. "I am Captain St. Armand and I will goddamned say whatever the hell I want. Or are you offended by my *life*, Woodruff, the things I've done, the things I know? The *men* I have done and the men I've known?"

"No."

"No what?"

"No, Captain."

"That's not what I meant, you idiot," she snapped.

"No, I am not offended by the things you've done or the men you've done," he snapped back. "My blood runs as hot for you as any other man's. I could not want you so much if I did not know who you are. Does this feel like I don't want you?"

He yanked her back against his body and it was clear how much he wanted her. He ached with wanting her, but she needed to know.

"I want you, Mattie. Never doubt it!" he ground out, his own temper rising. "You are a beautiful and exciting woman, a lady and a warrior. I've never met anyone like you. But I will not be another of your faceless cabin boys, or toys to sport with in port, an evening's pleasure after a busy day fighting. When we are together, Mattie St. Armand, you will never, ever put me in that category again!"

They glared at each other and he would have worried she'd do violence to him until he realized someone was making kissing noises.

Some *thing* was making kissing noises.

"Who's a good boy? Who's a good boy?"

"Not you, you insufferable prig," Mattie muttered, under her breath. "Roscoe, come."

The bird flew into her room, and she turned to follow. She paused in the doorway, her back to him, fists clenched at her sides.

"I am not diseased."

"I know that," he said gently. "You would not

offer yourself to me if you were. You have too much honor."

She looked at him over her shoulder, her face half-shadow, half-light. "You think that about me? That I am an honorable person?"

"I hold your honor, and mine, very precious, Captain."

She said nothing more, but her back straightened a fraction as she left him in the dark.

CHAPTER 12

THE DAILY SESSIONS ON THE sand continued, but there was no laughter for the watching lay-abouts under the red flowers of the poinciana tree. She did not call him Sunshine but was serious and focused and the sailors wandered away, there being no enter-tainment anymore. Even Roscoe was more subdued, watching them from a branch while they sweated in the sand. He did not know if it was because he'd rejected her advances or because the time was growing short, or a combination of factors, but Oliver knew he'd never worked so hard in his life—a life that up until this point had been so staid and structured and stuffy he sometimes thought of it as a dream, someone else's life. Here, his life was a daily round of bruises and sweat.

When he graduated to real blades there was blood, an instant when he didn't move quickly enough, and pain snaked along the outside of his forearm. It wasn't the pain that made his heart stutter, but the flash of horror in Mattie's eyes. He dropped his knife and clamped his hand over the cut, and her horror was replaced with narrow-eyed anger.

"Pick that blade up, blast you. The only way that

knife should leave your hand is if someone's pried it from your cold, dead fingers."

"There's a lovely image!"

"Aye, and it's all too real," she snapped back. "For heaven's sake, stop. You'll only make it worse."

She whipped a handkerchief out of her pocket and wrapped it around his arm.

"There. I'll clean it back at the house, but for now you're going to keep at it, and you won't let that scratch stop you."

She called it a scratch, but his arm burned. He picked up his blade, not as long or heavy as her hunting knife, but a solid, serviceable weapon with a good grip and a brass hilt. He was rather proud of it, and if he couldn't throw it, he could at least hold it now without risking dismembering himself.

They continued sparring until Mattie called a halt, turning on her heel and walking up to the house.

He watched her as Roscoe flew over and perched on his shoulder.

"Poor baby, poor baby. Give Roscoe a kiss?"

He didn't kiss the bird, but scratched him on the head, and the animal made soft, happy sounds. At least one creature found him satisfactory. He sighed as he gathered the weapons and followed in Mattie's wake.

He'd written to his family to let them know he was alive and well (more or less), extending his visit to the islands. He mentioned the exotic food, the yellow shrubs beneath his window attracting butterflies and hummingbirds, the flamingos, the "boiling hole" near the house where pools of fresh water alternated with salt as it flowed in and out through an underground passage, and tales of a colorful parrot named Roscoe.

He did not mention Captain St. Armand, only saying that he was being hosted by an acquaintance he'd met aboard ship. A letter from his mother caught up with him, much crumpled and handled, but when he held it he was amazed at the strong feelings it evoked, even before he opened it. It was a connection, a link to what was his real life, this island sojourn being a bubble of sensation far removed from the factories and mills and winter of home.

She wrote him of the small instances of daily life, the meetings of the Altar Guild, harmless gossip, and some more serious.

"Miss Langley continues to shine at the area assemblies, attracting quite the following. She asks about you, my dearest Oliver, wanting to know when you will return. I believe she is pining for you, and it need not be stated that a lovely girl like her will not be available forever. When can I inform friends you will be returning to us?"

His mother had all the subtlety of an anvil dropping on one's head.

But at his core, Oliver *was* that person—the staid businessman who oversaw an industry expanding to create jobs and opportunities not existing before. In the islands he saw lush beauty, but also grinding poverty. Many of the former slaves had a subsistence life, and he could see that the captain too recognized how time and industry was leaving this paradise behind. Britain was at the forefront of building and business, Moffett Mills was a part of it, and his family was Moffett Mills.

Mattie found him on the balcony that night, thinking about England and the choices he'd made, and she walked over and took his arm.

"Go into your room. I need to change that bandage."

Roscoe was perched on the back of Oliver's chair, eating a dripping mango slice.

"Pretty boy. Give us a kiss. Give us a kiss."

"Ignore that animal, or you two will be playing kissy-face all night. Remove your shirt."

"Nice tits."

"Enough, Roscoe," Mattie said, going to her room and returning with a wooden case and rolled bandages.

He shooed the bird away and sat in the chair, and she leaned over him, delicately swabbing the wound, soothing it with a tingling ointment. The captain was as impersonal bandaging him as she would be patching up anyone else, maybe more so.

Nonetheless, her touch inflamed him. She smelled of sandalwood, a scent he'd always associated with men, but on her it was right. She warmed it, sweetened it, made it her own. Her head was bent while she worked at her task, and he could not help reaching over to touch her soft curls any more than he could not take his next breath.

She stilled, then looked up at him, her eyes glowing lapis in the lamplight.

"I will not be toyed with. Either you want me, or you do not."

He swallowed.

"That has never been in question. I've wanted you from the moment I realized you were a woman. Maybe sooner," he finished wryly.

"Then what is stopping you?"

"You are." At her look of puzzlement he went on, searching for words that wouldn't get him sliced open like a flounder, and yet anxious for her to understand how he felt.

"I know you are available to me," he said carefully, "but I care too much about you to let us simply use one another for relieving…momentary urges."

The scar at the corner of her mouth quirked up at his awkward phrasing, but then her eyebrows pulled together in a frown.

"Oliver, are you a virgin?"

"No. I mean, I don't think so."

"I know the evidence is generally clearer with a woman, but most men can tell whether they've lost that status."

"This is not amusing to me. It's complicated, Captain."

She looked at him, then said, "Wait here. I suspect this story will go better with rum." She returned with a bottle in one hand and a second chair in the other. She poured them each a dram, then flipped the chair around so she straddled it, her arms crossed over the back.

"Complicated, yes. Amusing, no. I understand," she said. "I have a deplorable sense of humor that I suspect comes from being in Roscoe's presence. Go on with your story."

He still feared she'd laugh at him. But he wasn't a coward, and he owed her some sort of explanation.

"I would say I am not technically in the state of being a virgin, but I wouldn't label myself experienced." He sighed. "There was a woman in town, when I went to school. The boys talked about her, said she'd tup you for tuppence. That was her name, 'Tuppence Sally.' It was a higher fee than that, but what mattered was she'd do it for money. Being at an age where I wanted to prove myself a man, I went to her. She seemed glad to see me, glad to open my breeches, glad to do whatever the nice gentleman wanted.

"Naturally, I found this extremely arousing, and being flush with money, and full of adolescent urges, I took advantage of the services she offered. It was delightful. Delightful, up until the point where a child began to cry behind a screen in her room.

"She told me to ignore the cry, the child would go back to sleep. When the babe began calling for her mother, I lost my desire, and my ability to continue, so I didn't finish the act. Regardless of the technicalities... Well, let's just say my first time wasn't what I'd expected."

Mattie leaned down, her chin resting on her arms.

"Was she angry at the child?"

"No, more resigned than angry. I realized Sally hadn't been with me because she wanted me. She was doing it because it was a task, another job done so she could earn coins to feed her child."

"Were you angry?"

"At a child crying for its mother?"

"No, you wouldn't have been angry, not at a crying child. You're not that man."

Her words flowed over him like the soothing ointment she'd put on his arm. Mattie St. Armand knew him as no one else did.

"No, I wasn't angry. I was saddened."

He had left all his available money on Sally's table, and it was a goodly amount. He'd never had to worry about money, never had to wonder where his next meal was coming from. It was an educational experience that night, but not the one he'd expected.

"I didn't want to be in a woman's arms because it was her job. Since that one, abortive event, I have not found anyone whom I wanted the way I need to want them. I need someone who wants me for myself. I could have hired women for the night, for an hour. It has to be…" he trailed off. "It has to be more. If that puts me out of step with other men, then so be it."

"You are a romantic, Oliver Woodruff. Other men would have said they paid for a whore and they expected to get their money's worth."

"Do you know, I've always fancied myself to be my own man, not other men? I didn't want that sad creature, earning coin the only way she knew how. I wanted a woman who would be in my arms because there was no place she'd rather be, no other man she wanted to be with."

He leaned on the table, watching her, the slight throb under the bandage reminding him of how this woman earned her money, and how dangerous she could be. Her gaze, every bit as potent a weapon as her blade, drifted down across his bare torso, and a shiver rode up his spine even though the night was warm. She rose from the chair, gathering her supplies. He watched her neatly put them away, and she stood with her back to him, staring into the case.

"Is that offer to join you in bed still open?" he dared.

She turned slowly, looking at him for a long moment. When she walked back to him, he offered her his hand and she took it in her own capable one, sun-browned, strong and clean. He raised it to his lips and placed a gentle kiss on the back, and her breath caught.

"Are you certain now, Oliver?"

"Yes, but I do have one request."

"Only one?" she said with her quirky smile.

"Put out the cat."

CHAPTER 13

MATTIE RETURNED TO HIS ROOM after set-tling the bird, closing the door behind her with a click and leaning against it.

Being in command came naturally to her. Some said it was in her blood. There were times she enjoyed reversing the role, but for tonight she wanted to see what her sunshine boy was made of. She crossed her arms, resting one booted foot on the door behind her.

"Take off your clothes."

He held her gaze with his, then began unfastening his trousers, the same rough cloth the sailors wore, but on him it was different. Maybe it was the way it hung low on his hips. The softness once there was replaced with muscle, firmed up since coming under her control, and she approved.

She approved even more as the cloth hit the floor and he stepped out of them, his feet bare, the rest of him bare now as well. Mattie took a moment to appreciate him in all his slender, sleek glory, his skin still milky white where it was covered, the rest of him bronzed and burnished from days on the beach and life aboard the *Prodigal Son*.

She liked his thighs. They were good thighs, solid, substantial, but not heavy. Long and lean. She knew some girls and some boys were entranced by a man's tight arse, but she noticed thighs first. Perhaps because they put things in perspective when framing a lovely cock-and-balls, like these did.

That was another thing she liked. While he shifted from foot to foot under her scrutiny, a rosy flush running through him, he clearly wanted her. He was special, her Oliver, not like the other men whose cocks came to attention in her presence. He had principles. She'd never considered principles an especially desirable accessory, but her attitude was changing, corrupted, one might even say, by being in the company of a good man.

Most men of her acquaintance would have been on top of her like barnacles on the hull, ready to let their cocks do their thinking for them. But no, Mr. Oliver "I have a conscience and a brain as well as a set of tackle" Woodruff wasn't like most men.

She was honest enough to acknowledge that was part of his attraction.

Now she walked over to him, taking her time, enjoying the moment. For wasn't that truly what a pirate's life was all about? Living for the moment, savoring the feel of firm flesh beneath her hand, the sensation of warmth from another's body so close to hers, the scent of clean sweat and the musk of an aroused lover? It was a glorious moment to be alive and she intended to show Oliver Woodruff just what that meant, glad his scruples were shelved for the night.

He was quiescent beneath her touch, letting her explore him at her leisure, but it wasn't easy for him. She could see that in the tension of his shoulders, the rippling flesh across his abdomen, the hands clenched at his sides.

"What changed your mind, now, tonight?" she asked.

She circled him like a shark, hungry not for blood but for sensation, sliding her hand down his spine to investigate the delightful hollows at his hip, the play of quivering flesh over strong bone.

"Mattie, is this the ti—"

"Answer me when I ask you a question, Mr. Woodruff."

He swallowed, shifting his legs wider. His gaze darted to the table where he'd left his glass of rum, and she thought for a moment he'd need to bolster his courage, but then he brought his eyes back to hers.

"When we were on the sand today and you cut me, I knew I could die."

She stopped moving, fisting her hand at her side.

"I won't apologize."

"I don't expect you to. You were teaching me, as you've taught me so much already. Under your tutelage I have learned to appreciate new experiences in the islands. With you, I have enjoyed new flavors, new sights, new people," he finished quietly. "I know you accuse me of over thinking everything, but this time, tonight, it was the right decision."

He caught his breath as her questing hand found a particularly sensitive spot, but he bravely continued.

"I realized, unlike that other time I spoke of, you and I are on more equal footing."

She circled back in front of him and raised her brows.

"Or you have the superior position, Captain. Heaven knows you're the better fighter, possibly stronger…"

"And smarter, don't forget that."

"I was going to say more experienced at life's vagaries."

Her lips curled up in a smile, something that didn't happen often enough when she was with a man. They were good for some things, some of them, but a man who made her smile when he was naked? That was a rarity.

"You are unlike any person I have ever met, Captain Mattie St. Armand. You are unlike any woman I am ever going to meet. All of you, your strengths, your experience, your beauty." He lifted his hand, running his knuckles down her cheek, over her scar. "It is who you are. I fancy myself a wordsmith, but sometimes my words escape me. All I know is, with you I have that 'more' I seek. Whatever we have together, this is the closest I can come to an interlude of equals, of two people. Mattie and Oliver. That's all."

His honesty brought a glow to her chest as she dropped her eyes before his heavy-lidded gaze. When was the last time she'd been with a man who hadn't tried to deceive her in some fashion, who hadn't strived to get the better of her, or use her for his own purposes?

Never.

Now she took a deep breath and rested her hand on his chest.

"Are you uncomfortable under my scrutiny?"

"I would be more comfortable if I wasn't the only one naked."

"Then do something about it."

"Aye, Captain," he murmured.

He started with her shirt, unbuttoning it until it gaped open, revealing the soft cotton strips binding her chest. He found the tie, his scribe's fingers careful and sure as he undid the knot, releasing her from her bondage as Captain St. Armand.

He paused when the cloth fell away, then slowly, reverently, he pushed the placket of her shirt open. "Beautiful," he whispered. "You are so very beautiful. All of you."

He fumbled now, lifting her shirt over her head, tousling her curls as he pulled it away and tossed it to the floor. She wore her breeches, but she stood still, her turn for quiescence as he learned her body with his hands, with his sensitive fingers. He explored her, feeling her ribs, frowning over the ropy scar snaking up from her waist, the groove of a pistol ball dimpling her left shoulder, and when he turned her to see her back, he laughed aloud.

"Weren't expecting that, were you?"

"Did he pose for this?"

"No, the artist was skilled enough to do it from a painting."

Oliver chuckled as he ran his fingers along the colorful parrot inked below her right shoulder blade.

"You constantly surprise me," he said, turning her back around. "And that is part of what I lo—part of what I enjoy about you so much."

His lips came down on hers before she could question what he'd started to say, but it didn't matter as much as his kiss in this moment, the feel of his lips opening up her heart and soul. There was nothing hesitant or shy about his kisses, and she knew he was a man who appreciated this intimacy, so rare for her. He was a man who savored what two people could bring to one another even when they were not in bed.

Now she shifted her legs wider as he wrapped his arms about her, one hand cradling her hair, the other pulling her against him. In his embrace she softened, even as he grew harder. He'd been right earlier. They complemented each other. When she needed to be firm, he was soft. When she was soft, he was firm.

His firm lips now demanded more from her, his tongue sweeping inside to conquer her mouth, the tug of response from her belly bringing the softness and moisture to her parched soul. His kisses moved her, and aroused her, as no other man's had. No other man who'd kissed her was Oliver. No other kiss that she'd had in her life was from his mouth, no other arms held her like his arms.

These were dangerous waters to swim in, waters where an unwary woman could lose her way. She pulled her head back, her breath coming short as she looked at him, grim now, the planes of his face taut with need.

"Are we done playing games?" he demanded.

She swallowed her flippant answer, nodding as she fumbled at her trouser flies, him brushing her hands aside as he deftly unfastened the buttons.

"Boots," he said, putting words to action, kneeling and yanking hers off while she steadied herself with a hand on his shoulder. She was not padded tonight and he pulled her trousers and drawers down, leaving her bare. She turned to walk to the bed, but a hand on her arm restrained her.

"My turn," he said, rising to his feet. No smiles now as he took his time, seeing the scars, the skin lighter where it had been covered by her clothes, but still darker than his, amber to his alabaster.

She gasped and arched her back as his hands slowly rose from her waist to her breasts, cupping them, the nipples rising up dark and engorged when his thumbs swept across them, tightening the tug inside her, the yearning for that more from him. His hands, tanned and scratched, callused in places they'd never been callused in his world, explored her body, her breasts, feeling their soft fullness, not large, but always so sensitive after being bound all day. His hands brought her pleasure as he learned her, and her body responded to his caresses, readying itself for him.

He swept her into his arms, and it was a testament to his labors aboard ship that he didn't stagger at her muscled heft as he carried her to the bed, laying her down as gently as a dove's feather floating to the sand.

The mosquito draperies shivered in the evening breeze, but she was on fire, fevered with wanting him as he stretched out atop her, his patience at an end, his kisses more urgent, more demanding. His bearded lips roamed down her neck and chest, the sensation of a man's kisses adding to her stimulation, the roughness of his face against the softness of her body. When he reached her breasts, he murmured "Beautiful" again before tentatively tonguing her areola.

He took her gasp as encouragement, and lavished attention on her, exploring her, knowing her. She responded in kind, the sensations growing as she twined her long legs about his muscled thighs.

Before she could issue more commands, he had her legs open and he thrust himself inside her. Her body bowed up at the sudden intrusion and she welcomed the slight burn, welcomed *him*, savoring the full length of this beautiful man. He wasn't hesitant now. There was no fumbling. He gave her a moment to adjust as she registered how very much he was filling her, then he moved, bracing himself on his forearms, sweat streaking his hair dark and he watched her responses as he worked himself in her.

She knew even before he did that he wouldn't be able to hold out, so she let him go, savoring his sounds, the hot rush of his seed inside her body. When he collapsed atop her she rolled them to their sides, and he struggled to get his breath back.

"That was amazing," he gasped.

She smiled tightly, for her pretty cabin boy still had lessons to learn.

"You're not done yet, Sunshine."

She took his hands and showed him how to touch her, and his eyes widened as he realized what she meant. He was an apt pupil, his long fingers finishing what they'd started, and when she hissed "Yessss…" in his ear she clutched his hand inside her, holding him as a miser holds gold, never wanting to let go of the treasure.

They both lay on the damp sheets, panting, then Mattie reached up and brushed his hair off his forehead, smiling at him in the lamplight.

"*Now* you're done."

He mumbled something into his pillow, and it sounded like "Aye, Captain."

They must have dozed, for when she opened her eyes again he had his head propped on one hand as he frowned down at her.

"What?"

"I released myself inside you. I meant to withdraw."

She rose and walked to the stand where a pitcher of lukewarm water and cloths sat. Dampening one, she ran it over her sweating neck and face, then rinsed it and brought it to him in the bed.

"You do not need to worry about my catching a babe from you. It is unlikely after one encounter."

"Yes, but—"

"I have herbs I take to ensure there are no consequences," she finished, ignoring his interruption, staring down at her hands. "It is not your problem."

He took her chin and turned her face.

"If you find yourself with child, I will take care of you, and the child," he said firmly. "It is my responsibility. This is not an area where I am yours to command."

It was so typical of him. Her knight, riding to the rescue even when there was no rescuing to be done. She'd take the tea later, as she always had since that long-ago talk with Mrs. Fletcher.

She'd been so young then, and so naïve. Hard to believe now, thinking back to that time when she'd given herself to the fumbling chandler's lad in Salem on a night when both of them had quaffed too much ale. After all she'd heard and read about the actual event, she'd been disappointed by the outcome. When she returned to the ship and unburdened herself to her bunkmate, Fanny Fletcher consoled her, then in the nights to follow the older girl showed her what lovemaking could be when one was with a skilled and knowledgeable partner. She smiled fondly in remembrance.

Mattie put her hand alongside Oliver's cheek, his beard silkier now than the early bristles, then stroking the sun-streaked hair fondly.

"You are a good man, Oliver Woodruff."

He said nothing in response, but pulled her head back down for a kiss, and she slipped beside him in the bed. There was a nagging voice in the back of her head saying doing this, now, with him was a foolish act by a foolish woman, but she would never have risen to where she was in life, with all of its scars and sorrows and joys, if she'd listened to the sensible voice in her head advising caution.

So, just as Marauding Mattie had done since she was a girl running headlong into danger, she threw herself into the temptation of lovemaking in Oliver's arms, seizing the moment, as a pirate does.

CHAPTER 14

"YOUR CLOTHING ARRIVED AND THE ship is ready. We leave on the morning tide."

Oliver looked up from his breakfast. He'd awoken alone. Did she ever spend the night? He didn't want to think about that. Didn't want to think about other lovers in her past.

"Is that sausage offending you, because I vow, Woodruff, you look as if you're ready to disembowel it."

She didn't look as if the night's events had changed her one iota. Fresh and bright-eyed, with a healthy appetite as she dug in to her meal, Captain Mattie St. Armand looked ready to take on the day, and her manner toward him had not changed either. The lovemaking was in the past. It was time for business.

He was the one whose world was turned upside down by the hours spent in her arms, the delights he experienced there. She was not shy about showing him how to enhance her pleasure, and his, and he brightened as he thought of their lessons continuing in Florida.

"I heard one of the men say we were going to Key West. Is that correct?"

"No, but I've been spreading that about. Gossip travels fast, and someone could inadvertently let slip where we're headed, alerting the American authorities."

That dimmed his appetite. He could never lose sight of their goal. It was an adventure to him, a job to her, but to the people they brought to the islands, it was life itself.

"Where will the ship be while we're in Florida?"

"Working. There are goods for trade along the coast and I make a tidy profit picking up cotton, tobacco, and wood."

He set down his fork and knife. "Those are all slave-grown products."

"Yes, they are. Just as the cotton your mills purchase is slave-grown. You'd be naïve to think you can distance yourself totally from the profits of slavery, for you cannot. Not in England, and not in America. It is the reality of the world we live in, Woodruff, and we cannot change that," she said, calmly buttering her bread.

"Then why do you bother?"

"You know the answer to that. I'm well paid for my efforts by the Anti-Slavery Society. And, if you can think about it beyond your little moralistic view, it would be highly suspicious for a merchant ship to be sailing around without doing business of some sort."

He sipped his coffee, mulling it over. Was everything in life morally flexible for her? They were so different, and surely the choices she made were shaped by the difficult life she'd led. She didn't talk about her life in England other than the glimpse he'd had when she'd said she'd run away from home. How could he judge her, the decisions she made?

At the same time, he knew part of what drove him on in this adventure was feeling he was finally doing something, instead of just talking about change. It had been so easy to be sanctimonious about slavery while sitting at his overloaded dinner table. She made him confront the harsh realities of his own life. The food on that table, the clothes on his back, the cotton sheeting on his bed—all were the products of slaves at their source, and he could not pretend he was not a part of the problem.

Mattie went to town, seeing to last-minute details with the ship and leaving Oliver at home. He sparred with Daly and the Irishman taught him some things about fighting he claimed even St. Armand didn't know.

"See, the captain, for all his ways, he didn't grow up on the mean streets of Dublin. When you're fighting for every scrap you put in your mouth, you learn a thing or two about being the one left standing at the end."

"Do you...do you ever think about the captain and how the *Prodigal Son* is different from other ships?"

Daly took a drink from the water flask on the table, his fair skin flushed and red from their exertions. He wiped his arm across his mouth and gave Oliver a steady look.

"It's best not to think too much about the captain or my shipmates," he said. "We're each of us a bit of flotsam and jetsam, aye? When I start to turn things over in my head, I remember what a good little berth I have and how much worse it can be. I know, for I've been there. Captain and Mr. Turnbull and Mr. Nash make it clear how the ship's to be run, and anyone who don't like it can ship out elsewhere. Me, I like my messmates and I like my pay. Rest of it don't matter to me, and it shouldn't to you, Woodruff."

Oliver was pensive as he stood next to his desk later that evening, looking at the clothing spread out on the bed.

"Only take what's needed for the journey, the rest can stay here," the captain said from behind him.

She was in the doorway, her hand propped up against the jamb, one of her quintessentially masculine poses. She left off and walked over to the bed, fingering the tobacco and gold waistcoat from her own wardrobe.

"You look good in this. It suits your coloring."

"I was just thinking we'd make a handsome pair of fellows in Florida."

"Mmmm…" She walked around the bed, caressing the bedpost, and a shiver ran down his spine.

"We'll be restricted there, once we enter into our roles." She leaned her shoulder against the post. "Here I have the freedom to be myself, to do as I wish. Most of the time."

She looked away from him, running her hand up and down the mahogany, the wood gleaming in the lamplight, and he swallowed, his mouth gone dry.

"What is it you wish?"

"What do I wish? What a dangerous question you ask, Oliver Woodruff. I wish for many things. Maybe…" She ran her hand up the bedpost again and his eyes followed it, the slim fingers caressing the wood, and when he looked back at her he saw how she watched him through heavy-lidded eyes, the heat in her gaze.

"Maybe what I wish is to tie you to the bedposts. Would you like that?" she asked in a low voice.

"I…I don't know."

"Of course you don't. You would have to trust me. Trust me completely. It's hard to put yourself in someone else's power that way."

She was still stroking the wood as she said this, and he grew hard watching her, imagining her stroking him.

"Have you—" He coughed, his mouth dry. "Have you ever been tied like that?"

"Not by a man," she murmured, and he may have moaned, for she smiled and strolled over to him, her hand on his chest. She could no doubt feel his heart beating fast beneath his shirt. She surely saw the sweat on his forehead as he imagined her activities with Mrs. Simpson in the brothel.

"Would you…would you strap on your implements?" he said hoarsely.

"There's only one way to find the answer to that, Sunshine." She ran her hand down his chest to his hip, caressing him. She propped her foot on his chair and slid a stiletto out of her boot, setting it on the table, then sat on his bed and leaned back on her arms, extending one boot-clad leg.

"Remove these."

"As your cabin boy?"

She just smiled.

He did not mind. Far from it, the idea of this woman ordering him to serve her—it made him feel needed and valued. There was a beauty in perfect service, in striving to do one's best to please one's partner.

She turned her head, her long neck bare. Her shirt was open slightly, and he saw the pulse at her neck, the warm skin covering the delicate collarbones. So strong, yet so fragile also. She was a bundle of contradictions, his captain, but he wouldn't have her any other way.

He came over and knelt at her feet, tugging off first one boot, then the other.

"We agreed to stay focused on our task until we were done in Florida," he said, dropping the boot on the floor. There was danger here, fear of the sensual unknown looming before him, tempting him to forget who he was, to give himself totally into the hands of a pirate.

"Did we?" she murmured, standing now as he knelt beside the bed, running a hand through his hair. "I don't recall agreeing to such a silly stipulation. Not when the moonlight is so lovely, the evening so soft, your sky colored eyes so very, very pretty."

"Moonlight or no —"

His words were cut off by one slender finger pressed against his lips, scented with the rich tobacco of her cheroot, and when he ran the tip of his tongue along its length, tasting of salt, and Mattie.

"You are not here to discuss tactics or plans. You are here to please me, and only that, and if you do a good job, you may be allowed to find your own release," she murmured. "Now, lie down here on the bed, on your belly."

He wanted to tell her no, he wanted to be on top of her, in her, but she was in command. She'd made that clear, he'd accepted it, so he followed her orders, the soft mattress pressing against his cock, which most assuredly accepted her commands. He hadn't been this hard this fast since his pimply adolescence.

He turned his head to watch her, a shiver rippling down his back when he saw her walk to the cedar chest that she'd carried in from her room. She pulled out a scarlet length of cloth and returned to his side, her eyes gleaming.

"Didn't I tell you the job came with special benefits, Sunshine?"

He thought she intended to tie him, but she took the cloth and wrapped it around his head, blocking the sight of her. He tensed beneath her touch, but when he moved to sit up her hand was on his shoulder, firmly pressing him back down.

"You are to stay here, only moving as I tell you to. I could tie you, but I don't have to, do I?"

She took his hands and placed them on the bedrail behind the pillows. "Hold fast to this and do not remove your hands."

He learned why when she rose and returned a moment later, and he felt cold steel at the back of his arm, stroking down to his hand and back.

"I have a blade in my hand. Do not move."

There was a tug and he heard the cloth tearing as she pulled the blade through his worn shirt, turning the linen to rags. But he didn't let go of the bedrail, not even when he heard the click of the knife being set on the table, and her sure hands unfastening his breeches and pulling them down past his bare feet.

"Captain—"

"Silence, cabin boy. I have more silk and it would be short work to gag you as well. But"—she leaned in and spoke softly in his ear—"if I did that I couldn't hear every whimper and groan I intend to wring from you tonight."

With his eyes covered he was blind, but he smelled her scent, the sandalwood hint she carried on her skin, blended with a fragrance uniquely hers, strength and woman and the sea all together.

She moved off the bed and her clothing rustled as it

slipped to the floor, then the mattress sagged beneath him as she straddled his hips, pressing him deeper into the bed.

"Don't jump," she said. "I'm not going to harm you. Now, you're going to feel something wet on your back. It's only oil."

The scent of sandalwood bloomed in the night as warm liquid trickled across his shoulders. After she'd set the bottle aside, she returned her hands to him, stroking his back, caressing him before she leaned in and began massaging, working the oil into his skin. He didn't realize how tense he'd been until he felt the muscles begin to relax, unknot beneath her skillful fingers. She adjusted herself, sitting astride him, and he thought he felt wet heat there too as she pressed into his bottom.

"Tell me, Oliver," her husky voice commanded, "when you were in school, did you play games with the other lads?"

"Football?"

A bite on his shoulder reminded him of who was in charge and nearly made him jump to the ceiling.

"No, not like football."

He swallowed as his mind dredged up memories made sharper by his closed eyes, the sensual stroking of the strong hands on his back, the rustle of the trees outside in the night.

"We all did that. It was what boys did."

"Did you toss-off each other? Give a hand? Tickle each other's trinkets?"

"Mmmhmmm," he agreed, lulled by her smoothing hands. Then her fingers quested lower, and suddenly he was focused again, every sense sharpened as her oiled fingers touched him lightly between his cheeks.

She left the bed and he could hear her walking around, thought she may have paused at her chest, and when she returned and straddled him again he smelled the tropical scent of coconut oil, and he knew.

"Captain—"

"Such smooth skin," she murmured, her lips next to his ear, her hand stroking down his back, massaging lightly, then harder, at his hip bone, at the muscles of his cheeks. "Was there one special boy? One with whom you did more? Tell me."

Sweat trickled down his neck and he swallowed, remembering. A miller's son, a rich miller who like Oliver's family wanted his boy to get a gentleman's education. Will had thick chestnut hair and freckles from his Irish mother and a smile too sweet for the brutal environment of boys tossed together with too little supervision.

"Yes. There was someone special."

"And did you enjoy it, what you did?"

"We shouldn't have done it—we knew—"

"I didn't ask you about 'should have,' I asked you if enjoyed it."

She punctuated this by running her oiled finger down the crack of his arse, gently pressing up against his opening.

"Answer me," she ordered.

"Yes," he whispered, the words wrung from his memories and his desire. "Yes, I enjoyed it."

At her nudge he lifted his hips, spreading himself, moving naturally into a position that felt right, here in the tropical night when he was far from the prying eyes of those who thought they knew him best.

But they did not know him. Not like Mattie St. Armand knew him. She put one arm around him, low at his hips, holding him, then pushed one finger inside him and he groaned at the sensation, the burn and the pleasure combined.

"Shhh… I will go carefully, sunshine boy. I won't allow you to be hurt."

She pulled her finger out and he sighed, but then the pressure was back, two oiled fingers inside him, filling him, making his cock jump in response, the sheets beneath him dampening with the fluid leaking from the head, from the dark pleasures he felt at those knowing hands.

"I won't hurt you," she said again, "but you must tell me if it's too much, if you want me to stop."

The air hung still between them, and he disobeyed orders and tore the silk off his eyes, looking over his shoulder at her. Mattie sat back on her heels, her hair plastered to her forehead, her golden skin sheened with sweat, her eyes black and wide and the pulse in her neck throbbed in rhythm with his heart, a syncopation of lust and desire. But what mesmerized him was the ivory dildo rising from the doeskin harness around her hips, gleaming pearl-like against her skin, cunningly carved to simulate a cock.

"I said I would show you my toys if you were very good, Oliver, but if you say no, I will stop."

"Don't," he said hoarsely, then tried again. "Don't stop."

She leaned forward then and holding his hair in her fist, kissed him, a slow exploration of his mouth as she pressed against him, the ivory warming against his skin. She broke the kiss, her eyes heavy-lidded and her lips swollen and gleaming as she reached across him to the small jar she'd placed on the bed and her fingers came back covered with the heavy oil. She stroked the slick ivory in her fist and his balls tightened in response. He thought he might spend right there. The silent air was filled with the scent of her oils, the musk of their combined sweat and the taste of her. He heard the ocean in the silence, the water moving in and out, and smelled the salt of the ocean or maybe it was the salt of their sweat or their blood throbbing together as she took his silence for assent and pushed his shoulder back onto the bed. Then she was pushing at him, inside him, the exquisite and unbearable intimacy of penetration wringing a moan from deep in his core. His harsh breathing hitched as she slowly pulled back, then pushed in him again, her dildo stroking sensitive nerve endings, burning him with delicate friction. She began to work him, one hand braced alongside his hip, the other underneath, fisting his cock in an oily grip that had him clenching the bedrail and holding on like his life depended on it.

He knew he wouldn't hold out much longer between the warm friction of her hand, the burn of her stroking inside him, the wet heat of her tongue on his neck. When he exploded with a cry wrung from his soul he knew why it was called *le petit mort*, for he was certain his heart stopped as he was overwhelmed by it all.

They were both breathing hard, like sails luffing in the wind, and she wrung a final gasp out of him as she carefully withdrew. He lay there, stunned by the sensations, wondering about Mattie's satisfaction, for she had seemed to climax along with him. He asked her while she took a wet cloth and cleaned him, wiping him down, removing sweat and oil and fluids from him with tender care.

"The dildo is double bladed and stimulates me

while I am using it," she explained in a husky voice punctuated with a kiss along his back. When he rolled over he didn't see the harness. She must have removed it when she fetched the cloth, and she looked so wonderfully feminine and tousled it was hard to believe she'd just fucked him like a man. As she climbed into bed with him he pulled her to him and all he felt in his arms as he rolled atop her, kissing her slowly and deeply, was Mattie, the woman he desired in all her guises.

Chapter 15

"SHAKE A LEG, WOODRUFF."

He'd awakened alone, again, and he looked over his shoulder at Captain St. Armand, dressed to return to her ship. Her freshly polished boots gleamed in the morning light and her newly trimmed hair was slicked back on her head. The masculine appearance was that of the lover who'd been inside his body, and he had to wonder how much was the role, and how much of what he was viewing now the reality.

They had pleasure and they had companionship. They did not have true intimacy. That was what he'd looked for, that was why he'd never wanted to take other women to his bed. He wanted all of her and she was holding herself back from him.

He walked over and before she could say anything, he grabbed her by her jacket lapels and had her mouth under his, her body pressed up against the closed door.

"The tide's not for hours yet. This time, now, is for us." He unfastened her belt as he spoke, undoing her breeches, thrusting his hand inside her drawers. She didn't say anything, but gasped when he put his fingers in her, testing her wet heat, undoing his clothing with his other hand.

She pushed against him, not struggling, but he wouldn't allow her to take charge, not this time. He placed himself at her entrance and thrust up, glad they were of a height. Shackling her wrists against the door with one hand, capturing her with his body, and his desire, he rode her. He wrapped her exquisitely long leg around his hip, trapping her in place as he marked her with his mouth, his teeth, his harsh words in her ear telling her she was his.

She gave herself up to him, accepting him into her slick embrace. The constraints of her partially undone clothing made her hold on him tighter, his thrusts shallower, but that contributed to him rubbing against her in a way that had her arching her back for more, tilting herself to give him access. They were only joined at their core as she ground herself against him, seeking greater sensation, and this time, he knew from her moans, from her labored breathing, they would finish this journey together.

He grinned fiercely, and when she was almost at her peak he took her earlobe where the gold ring dangled and nipped it in his sharp teeth. Her body arched as she tightened around him like a velvet fist and he exploded in her, because no matter what happened from this point onward, she was going to remember, remember him, and remember what it felt like as he made her his.

In the aftermath he heard her gasping breaths as he released her wrists, and released himself from her embrace, fastening his clothing as he silently watched her.

She ran a trembling hand across her swollen mouth, her heavy-lidded eyes on his while she straightened herself up, put her clothing in order, and took a deep breath.

"We leave in an hour. Be ready," was all she said as she slipped out the door, closing it behind her with a decisive click.

Mattie was still slightly dazed as she headed downstairs later. She prided herself on expecting the unexpected, but with Oliver Woodruff she was fast learning there were things... Well, he'd certainly surprised her. She licked her lips, relishing the swollen state of her mouth, the tang of added sensation from his kisses. There may be more pirate in the man than he suspected.

He was all that was proper now, standing at the door with his bags, chatting with Wellington.

"Goodbye! Goodbye, Sunshine!" Roscoe called from his perch in the entryway.

"Is the...cat...joining us?"

Mattie looked at her pet, upside down, gnawing on the coconut husk dangling from his rope. "Roscoe's an asset, but he's not suitable to the task we'll have in Florida. He's better off staying here, keeping an eye on the house."

Woodruff looked disappointed. The man and bird had formed a bond, which surprised her. Generally parrots were quite particular about to whom they offered their affections, and seeing how the bird responded to Woodruff, going to him for treats and "grooming" him, raised the Englishman in her estimation. There had been men in her life the bird wouldn't shit on, and she'd often wondered afterward if Roscoe wasn't a better judge of character than she was. He was less likely to be taken in by a pair of broad shoulders and twinkling eyes.

Mattie had plenty of opportunities in her life to regret rash decisions regarding whom she took to bed, but she couldn't regret her time with Oliver. She'd know more of the man's mettle in Florida, but she already knew he was a caring and capable lover.

"Kiss Roscoe?"

"Of course, Roscoe. You're a good boy, aren't you?" she said.

She went over to the bird and scratched him as she knew he liked, then waited as Roscoe demanded a kiss from Oliver, who looked bemused at the parting rituals of a piratical household but went along with the bird's demands.

Wellington received his final orders from the captain and Roscoe flew to his shoulder.

The bird and Wellington had a relationship where he treated the butler as his personal servant and the butler threatened to serve the bird up fricasseed with pepper sauce, but they did well enough together.

"Go with blessings, Captain."

"I will do my best, old friend," she said, and they mounted up for the ride into town. Rain had blown through earlier, freshening the air and even bringing a hint of coolness.

"It is winter back home," Oliver said to himself as he looked up at a black and red oriole winging overhead.

"Cold, rainy, and miserable. It's a wonder more Englishmen don't head out for better climates."

"It has its moments. When spring arrives, you feel it in your bones, in the land, even the city looks better for a bit of greenery."

"I'll grant you, June is tolerable, and you're less likely to succumb to a tropical fever there, but the islands…"

she paused, for there was no way to explain to a non-island born individual. Yes, it was a dangerous and miasmic environment, but it caught you up in its own rhythms. It didn't have the dramatic seasons, though hurricane time was its own excitement, but it was a place where she felt the tug of belonging. The soft lilting voices, the strongly seasoned food, the poor people who had music in their speech and in their step—as much as she fit in anywhere, she fit in here.

Oliver was only a visitor. She couldn't lose sight of that, couldn't daydream about what might be if they were different people in a different place. They weren't. They only had the reality of now, the reality of being Oliver Woodruff and Mattie St. Armand.

Captain Matt St. Armand. Someone with a mission, and a fat purse of gold at the end. The sooner she accomplished this task, the sooner she'd bid farewell to her Englishman and send him home with fond memories of the islands.

CHAPTER 16

The ship glowed in the lantern light below decks, for the crew was kept busy polishing and scraping and scrubbing in port until the schooner gleamed. The crew welcomed Oliver back with jokes about his improved fighting skills and his supposed laziness the rest of the time he was ashore. A mug of Mr. Holt's miserable but effective coffee was pressed into his hand. Even Daniel Green greeted him. Joe Carpenter, for the freed man had stayed aboard and taken on a new role, sat with the older sailor, the two of them carving bits of wood.

Oliver paused from where he was hanging his hammock.

"Is that a Jacob's Ladder?"

Joe nodded.

"Daniel here knows shopkeepers who'll buy these toys, along with some spoons and bowls. Earning a little extra is never a bad thing."

Oliver looked back at Daniel, whose sinewy dark hands cradled a wooden animal that looked like... *A camel*? He was about to praise the older man's skill when something about those hands caught his attention.

He was still smiling when he took a tray to the

captain with coffee and some fresh-baked cream cakes. She leaned over her table, examining charts by lantern's light, and she absently reached for her coffee.

He cleared his throat.

"I know at least one other woman who is on the *Prodigal Son.*"

"Do you now, you clever lad?" she said, not looking up, taking a sip of the bitter brew.

"Yes," he said, sounding smug even to his own ears. "It's Daniel Green. But Daly said he was a hero of the war against Napoleon. That can't be right, him being in the navy."

She looked up at him over her cup rim and only smiled.

He let that smile sink in, then cleared his throat again, this time from embarrassment.

"I'm wrong again, aren't I?"

"About which part?"

"I'm almost certain Daniel's a woman. I'm wrong about her—him not being in the navy. But how is that possible?"

She straightened, and sat on the edge of the table, swinging one shapely, breech-clad leg. It nearly distracted him from her answer.

"Let us suppose you're a frigate captain during the war, with an experienced topman. Turns out your valued sailor sits instead of stands to piss but is someone you can count on in battle or in a gale. Now, are you going to throw that sailor off the ship to be replaced by some cobbler hauled in by a press-gang?

"Everything Daly said about Daniel is true. Even after his true identity was uncovered, he continued to serve his king and country. You should be grateful. And he's not the only one of his kind to serve honorably."

"Will I ever stop making assumptions about people based on what I see on the surface?"

"If you do, you'll be an exceptional man."

He let that sink in while the sounds of the ship at night, never fully quiet, hummed outside the cabin door.

"Let me stay tonight."

She rolled up the chart, putting it back in its proper place. When she turned to look at him, her face was calm.

"People believe the captain of a ship has absolute power, especially aboard a vessel like the *Prodigal Son*."

"A pirate vessel?"

"I shall pretend you did not say that. No, what I mean is, that while I have the power of life and death, in many ways I'm also completely powerless."

"And here I would have thought the captain of a pir—of a vessel such as yours has complete freedom."

She smiled ruefully.

"In some things, yes. But I must have the respect of the men to function. I have seen captains lose their men's respect. It never ends well. On land, what I do is one thing, at sea, another." She waved him to the door. "Good night, Mr. Woodruff."

"Will it be different in Florida?"

"Many things will be different in Florida."

The air was heavy with rain when they dropped anchor at Amelia Island. The sullen skies matched the look of the town, ramshackle wooden buildings and hogs running through Fernandina's dirt streets, but the harbor was full of ships.

"Lots of money to be made here on the edge of the United States," Nash said to him as they prepared to disembark. "Sneaking contraband past the Revenue Marine keeps this town flowing with commerce, and the officials up in Georgia are happy to look the other way and make their own profits.

"Cap'n said you're to enter port as a sailor off ship, not as Mr. Woodruff. Your gear's been sent ahead."

He took an oar as they rowed in, and Nash whistled to a boy wearing only a ragged pair of cotton trousers held up by a rope. The lad ran over and the sailor flipped him a coin, saying, "Take him to the Ortega house on White Street.

"Remember your promise, Woodruff."

"I will guard the captain and protect her, Mr. Nash. You have my word."

The old pirate looked at him through his spectacles, then grunted. "Godspeed to you, lad."

"Fair winds and following seas," he replied, bringing a small smile to the weathered face as they shook hands.

Oliver hoisted his small trunk, trailing the boy. The town did not improve on closer appearance. It may have been prosperous at one time, but now whatever money was spent went into the grog shops and to women lurking in doorways to entice men with too much silver and too little sense.

The wooden house on White Street was a modest affair, two stories with a balcony, a far cry from the pink residence in the Bahamas. A maidservant let him in, taking his hat and murmuring a few words in Spanish that he assumed was a welcome. He set his case down, looking around. The house was tidy, with a central staircase going to the upper level, and enticing smells from the kitchen in the back.

"Come upstairs," a familiar voice said.

He followed the sounds to a bedroom, barely registering that it was small, with a single bed, before strong hands grabbed him by the lapels. He reacted automatically, breaking the hold and shifting his weight so his opponent ended up against the wall with an "Oof!" and one hard arm braced across his throat.

Her throat.

"Now, that's what I like," Captain St. Armand murmured hoarsely. "A man of action!"

"For pity's sake, Mattie, I could have hurt you!"

He felt a hard nudge in a sensitive area and looked down. There was a dagger pressed against his inner thigh.

"One slice and you'd be bleeding out like a fountain."

She reached up with her free hand and ran her knuckles down his face, over his bearded chin. He grabbed her wrist, pinning it to the wall.

"Drop the knife."

"What have I told you about giving up your weapon?"

"That's the blade I see, not the only blade on you."

"You *have* been paying attention." The knife clattered to the floor as she leaned in and brought her lips to his, showing him other weapons in her arsenal capable of disarming the strongest of men. He surrendered, releasing her hand so he could wrap his around her nape, holding her still as he explored her mouth.

Their time apart had been brief, but when he held her in his arms again it was as if his senses had hibernated, waiting for her, anticipating her, now coming alive. He inhaled the fragrance of sandalwood and the coconut oil taming her curls, stirring memories of the oil's other uses. Even with the binding on her soft breasts and the false padding in her trousers, he wondered how he'd ever thought Captain St. Armand anything but a woman. The most desirable and beautiful woman he'd ever known.

Holding her in his arms again after their time apart was like a cool drink on a sweltering day, and he wanted to capture this moment like honey in the comb, sweetness to be savored long after its creation.

Mattie broke her kiss, her eyes slumberous as she ran her knuckles over his bearded face again.

"I believe I'll miss this, Mr. Woodruff."

A knock at the door brought them apart, and it was followed by a maidservant carrying a can of steaming water. Mattie said a few words in Spanish to the girl, who nodded and left.

"Estela and her mother keep the house, which I'm leasing from an acquaintance. They'll see to our meals and our needs."

She walked to the door and locked it, then turned to him with a smile.

"Time to lose that fur, Sunshine."

"I'm not going to the barber?"

"Do you trust me, Oliver?" She reached over to the chest of drawers and pulled a razor off the top, holding the glinting steel in her hand.

"I trust you," he said without hesitation. "You will not harm me. At least, not with a knife."

She looked surprised at his response, but only said, "Take off your shirt and sit over by the window."

He moved the chair so she could take advantage

of the afternoon light pouring in, then pulled his sailor's shirt over his head. He wore no smallclothes and shivered in the cool air. Florida in the winter was colder than the Bahamas, as she'd warned.

Mattie built up the fire and brought him a piece of toweling. She paused before draping it over his chest.

"I can shave that fur off as well," she offered.

He glanced down at his chest hair.

"Why would I want to do that?"

"Increases sensitivity. And you might find the scrape of the razor exciting. Many men do. No matter where they're shaved."

She had a wicked smile to accompany this statement, but he shook his head.

"No, thank you, Captain. Having my face clean will be enough for me."

"Pity. You could also have this pierced, you know."

He yelped as she tweaked his nipple, and when she went to do the other one, he grabbed her wrist. She didn't try to pull out of his grasp, but leaned down and bit him, and he jumped and released her.

"You see? Sometimes a little pain in a sensitive area can be exhilarating."

To illustrate this, she reached down and cradled him in her palm, and he didn't need her hand on his cock to tell him he was aroused by her actions. Just being in the same room with her was enough to get him hard, but when she did things to him that made his senses come alive, it was a dangerous and glorious combination.

She looked over at the can of steaming water sitting near the low fire while he thought back to conversations belowdecks, and while he knew the sailors exaggerated their exploits in love and war, certain stories stayed with him. He pulled her into his lap, a move that surprised her.

"Now I'm not in such a hurry to be shaved."

He began unfastening her buttons, first on her waistcoat, and then her shirt. He eased the razor out of her hand and held it up to the sunlight, where it gleamed with menace.

"You've already stropped it."

"I wanted to be ready for you," she said, running one finger down his bare chest, over the furring of hair he had there.

"Hold still."

She paused and her breath caught as he eased the blade next to her skin, slicing through her bindings. She took a deep breath as the fabric fell away, and he folded the razor and set it aside for later.

"Poor little lambs," he said, placing a soft kiss on first one breast, then the other. "Stifled and confined all day with no one to play with them."

"They do enjoy a good romp in the fresh air."

He chuckled against her skin, here where she was so soft, so fragrant. When she moved to unfasten his trousers he stopped her.

"Are you certain you want to shave me? I won't be able to do this," he said, angling his chin so the beard bristles brushed over her nipple. She shivered in his arms and he tightened his hold, raking his face down her throat, bending her back so he could open more of her clothing to his gaze. His beard left a slight redness in its wake and he looked on it with satisfaction, his mark on her skin.

"Up," he commanded.

She raised an eyebrow at his peremptory tone but stood in front of him and he undressed her like a doll, pushing her jacket off, then her waistcoat, pulling her shirt over her head. She was still, letting him handle her, manipulate her, and he wondered if this was something special he brought to her, the ability to give up some control, to not be the one directing all the movements. His hands spanned her waist, so slender to be supporting so much muscle in her back and arms. She raised her hands over her head, stretching in front of him and he knew he'd never see another woman like her, one whose form embodied so much power in its shapely frame. The definition of her sinews and muscles beneath her skin should have looked masculine and off-putting, but he found it arousing. It was part of the totality of Mattie St. Armand, the strength and the softness, the hardness and the yielding.

He smoothed his hands up over her skin, stopping when he reached her breasts, exploring the pert nipples with his thumbs as she caught her breath, letting him take his time and have his fill.

"This will be more enjoyable for you if you let me reciprocate," she said huskily.

"I am enjoying myself tremendously, thank you. You keep your hands where they are," he ordered, moving his fingers down to the placket of her trousers while he continued to toy with her. If there were sounds from the street he didn't hear them as he unfastened her, the air so heavy and still he could hear the rasp of the buttons being freed, their breathing the only other sound in the quiet room.

The leather of her harness caressed his fingers as he slowly lowered her trousers, past the padding she wore to complete her costume. Even that was arousing. He unfastened the harness and let it all fall away, baring her to his scrutiny.

"Lovely," he said huskily, leaning forward to give her mound a kiss. She gasped and shifted, and he looked up. "Do not move. If it is easier, stand at rest with your hands at your back."

Her gaze was mutinous, but she did as ordered, though he suspected she'd turn the tables on him at some point. That thought too was exciting, but not as exciting as having her here like this, in front of him. He pushed her trousers down, then helped her out of her boots. Another knife clattered to the wood floor.

Now she stood naked before him and he seated himself, watching the play of sensation over her face as he used his hands to explore her. The dusky blush in her cheeks was echoed in the dark, rosy nipples, and her firm belly was golden in the afternoon light.

She was a hard woman, his captain, but not everywhere. Not here, at the top of her thigh, where the skin inside was soft, so soft as he placed his bearded lips there, the pulse of life flowing through her. That skin untouched by sea air or sun, but still warm, and he took his time, savoring the feel of it beneath his mouth, feeling the quiver of her strong muscles as he tasted her.

He took his thumbs and gently spread her, opening her to his gaze like a hidden treasure of the sea, one with a pearl concealed in its folds. Strong as she was, she nonetheless had to brace herself on his shoulders with a moan when he took that pearl between his lips, his tongue exploring her, knowing her.

He learned what made her gasp, and he learned what brought pleasurable cries to her lips as he stroked her with his tongue and drank in her desire. He supported her when she would have collapsed, and he was thankful for every aching muscle, bruise and sprain he'd suffered if it made him stronger for this moment, for her.

She came apart in his arms, tightening like a bowstring before her release, and he supported her as her body slid down his, her legs straddling him and her loose form draped over him as he held her, stroking her sweat-slick back, wanting to cherish this moment.

It didn't matter what men she'd known in the past. What mattered was that he was the man who held her now, who heard the rasp of her breathing in his ear, who felt the soft kisses she placed on his neck. He did not know how long she would be attracted to him, but if he rushed his fences he could end up with a brief glimpse of heaven, a taste, when what he wanted was a feast.

She pulled back in his arms, her eyes dark and heavy-lidded. Then she grasped his jaw and kissed him, a slow, soft kiss containing a promise of more. She leaned back, running her knuckles down his cheek.

"You're correct, Sunshine. Some things just aren't the same after a shave."

She rose off his lap and glanced down at him.

"We'll take care of that for you later, but for now let me shave you while the water's hot."

She pulled her rumpled shirt back over her head, the white linen contrasting with her tan skin and displaying the long legs to perfection.

"Leave it open," he commanded, somewhat amazed at his own audacity.

"What have you been learning under my command, Mr. Woodruff?" she murmured, but then added, "As you wish."

She set a towel near the hot water, then picked up small shears from the chest.

"First a trim, then the shave."

"You've done this before?"

"You'll find out, won't you?"

He expected her to lean over him, but instead she straddled him again, her soft mound resting against his erection, and he caught his breath.

"Is this a good idea, with you holding those shears?"

"Sunshine, we haven't even moved on to the razor yet. Just relax and think of something soothing. Think of England."

Impossible, when he could feel her against him, her lush moistness dampening his trousers and heightening the sensation of heat and friction against him.

"Tsk. I'm going to have to do something to keep you from squirming."

She climbed off him and he breathed a sigh of relief, until he saw her pick up her cravat from where she'd tossed it earlier, the black silk gleaming in the lamplight.

"Stay there," she commanded, walking behind him. She took his wrists and crossed them behind the chair, looping the fabric around them, securing them to the slats of the chairback.

"Mattie—"

"Too tight?"

"No, but I have to ask again… Is this a good idea?"

She brushed her lips next to his ear. "By the time I finish with you, you are going to think this is the best idea anyone's ever had in the history of ideas."

He wasn't certain, but parts of his anatomy were in full agreement. He was hard as a brick, and when she straddled him again he pulled against his bonds, but she was an expert sailor and there was no give in her knots.

Oddly enough, that only made him harder.

"Now, where were we? Oh yes, the beard."

Her open shirt moved with her as she trimmed away at his hair, holding him steady under her careful hands.

Clumps of blonde hair fell to the floor, tickling his neck and chest, and when she was satisfied, she warmed a towel in the hot water, wrapping it about his face.

"Relax," she said.

Relax? The combination of being bound to the chair, his eyes covered by the hot towel—he couldn't relax. His senses were heightened by his bondage, and the scrape of the razor over the strop sent a shiver down his spine having nothing to do with the air ruffling in through the curtains. Thunder rumbled far off, and the street outside quieted as the sun set. He heard the soft pad of Mattie's bare feet as she returned, then blinked when she uncovered his face. She'd lit another lamp, and her smile was warm as the light, her deft hands lathering his shaving brush with her own sandalwood soap.

"I'll smell like you," he murmured.

"Is that a bad thing?"

"No," he inhaled. "Every time I catch the scent I will be happy, because it will remind me of you."

She paused, looking at him. Was she not used to men paying her compliments, compliments beyond her renowned fighting skills or piratical cunning? Warmth spread through his chest. Other men were an amusement. He was her lover.

She spread the lather over his face.

"It is an odd thing, but I have noticed that even when men and women wear the same scent, it can smell different. I wonder why that is?"

"No matter how you disguise them, men and women are not the same creatures."

She paused, the steel gripped in her hand.

"Perhaps. The important thing is we convince people to see what we need them to see. To that end... Hold still, Oliver."

She took his face and stroked the razor down, watching him carefully as she scraped away the remaining hair. It didn't take long, and he did relax, even though she was still straddling him. Yes, it was arousing, but it was also extremely intimate, and he realized he enjoyed the pleasure of simply having her close to him as much as he enjoyed the stronger sensation of having sex with her.

His mind flashed to a point many years from now, when they might be two old people, sharing a quiet moment together before the fire. The problem was, he could only envision her in breeches as she sat beside him.

"Ouch!"

"That's on you," she said without sympathy. "Do not smile while you're being shaved. Here, it's only a drop."

She dabbed at the tiny nick, then finished up at his neck, pulling the razor expertly around his Adam's apple, and he was careful not to move until she wiped off the remaining soap.

"Will you untie me now?"

Ignoring his request, she fetched her mirror. The face looking back at him as she angled it was one he recognized. It was not the pirate-in-training but rather the Manchester businessman—sober, careful.

Boring.

Mattie smiled down at him, then sat on his lap again and ran her hands up his chest to his bare face, stroking him with a purr of satisfaction, leaning in to kiss him. She shifted against him, her softness against his hardness, and he caught his breath.

Perhaps not so boring anymore.

"Now will you untie me?"

"So impatient," she whispered, placing small kisses around his face, his chin, his neck as he arched his head back, moving her hands down to run over his ribs, his belly, and lower.

She raised herself up and he strained against his bonds, but she wasn't leaving him. She unfastened his trousers and released him, and with an agonizingly controlled slide she lowered herself atop him until he was all the way in.

"Bloody hell, woman, you're going to be the death of me! Untie me!"

Instead of obeying his command she leaned back, hands braced on the chair, and repeated her maneuver, raising and lowering herself by inches.

His feet weren't tied and he set them, trying to thrust up as she held him down. The seductress laughed, her eyes narrowed into slits of sensual evil as she bit his neck.

"Accept it, Oliver. You will not spend until I allow it."

Words came out of his mouth that he'd never said to a woman, never said in his life, but she only continued her slow torture, the muscles in his back tightening, his balls tightening, until finally she lowered herself one final time, and said, "Now!" as she gripped around him like a vise. He shoved up and the explosive release shuddered through his entire frame, the intensity stealing his breath.

As he came back to himself, sweat pouring off him, she relaxed against him, then walked behind him to undo his bindings. He rubbed his aching wrists, restoring full feeling to them as she gathered up the debris from his shave. She always looked so calm and collected after these moments that changed his world. Would he ever affect her as she affected him?

Mattie kept her back to Oliver so he wouldn't see her trembling hands. She couldn't let him know how much their lovemaking meant to her. She'd desired men in her life, she'd enjoyed men and women, but she'd never felt like this.

She hungered for him. She needed to consume him, to pull him inside her, to become one with him. It burned her like no other desire she'd ever had, no other longing. This was what she'd been missing in her other encounters—the passion that the poets extolled, the desire that led smart women to make foolish choices. She knew though, someday he'd be gone from her life.

That thought brought her up short.

Regret. There was a new sensation for her. Normally, she was glad when she left her lovers. They'd start clinging, sometimes whining about staying with her, but she always left for a new port, a new man or woman, a new sensation with a new partner.

They were both quiet and she heard him getting dressed, gathering his things. He walked over to the chest of drawers and draped the black silk over it and she reached out, stroking one finger down the fabric, cloth that was soft, but so very strong. He covered her hand with his as he stood behind her and placed a kiss on her neck.

She raised her eyes to see their joined reflection in the mirror, both of them sober and still, his other hand resting on her shoulder. He looked appropriate there, at her back, as if that was where he belonged, guarding her, serving her in all ways.

It was a concept that warmed her heart and she reached up and covered his hand with her other one, squeezing it.

"This is—it's not what I expected," he said.

Mattie nodded. He didn't need to explain. She knew what he meant. Neither of them had expected this. Neither of them was ready for it.

But there was more at stake here than the two of them figuring out their own lives, and she stepped away from him, feeling the cold at her back when he was no longer there. The air was heavy and thunder rumbled outside the window, nearer now.

"Storm's coming. It'll be cooler tomorrow."

CHAPTER 17

DAWN FILTERED THROUGH THE WINDOW
and Oliver reached out sleepily to pull up the
covers, then realized the bed was cold because it was
empty. He put his hands behind his head as he stared at
a crack in the ceiling, trying to ignore his erection. He
wanted more. He wanted to wake up beside her, not
just have her pop in and out of his bed. He wanted to
hear her soft breathing during the night, to wake up to
her kisses, to her embrace.

He wanted *her*. Not for an island adventure. He
wanted her for always. He could no longer imagine
marrying a girl back home, someone who would be
suitable in all ways save one. She wouldn't be Captain
Mattie St. Armand.

But that wouldn't happen today, so he pulled on
his trousers and the shirt he'd tossed over a chair and
followed the scent of coffee downstairs.

There was a maid in the kitchen wearing a worn
calico dress and rough brogans on her feet, a different
girl than yesterday. Her hair was wrapped in a red rag,
faded from many washings, and she bent over a pot at
the fire, stirring its contents.

"Good morning. Do you know where I can find

the mistress?"

The girl rose and even before she turned Oliver knew he'd made a serious mistake. But how could he not? This woman bore almost no resemblance to the pirate St. Armand. Her curly hair was scraped back and hidden under her head wrap, her gown was loose and ragged at the hem, her shoes scuffed and worn. She wore a white apron over it all, standing with her hand on one hip, a wooden spoon in the other hand.

At least it's not a knife.

"The 'mistress'?"

"As in 'mistress of the house,' not 'mistress' like a slav—I should stop talking now, shouldn't I?"

"That's a prudent move, Sunshine."

She fetched a plate and dished up his breakfast.

"I should be doing that for you," he protested.

"Sit. I'll serve you. It helps me... I'm 'Maybelle,' and you're not my cabin boy, you're my master, and it helps me move into the role, acting it out this way."

He sat, and she brought him a cup, pouring coffee for him. His plate was filled with fried eggs, sliced ham, and a white paste she told him was grits. He looked at it suspiciously, but when he added the red-eye gravy and plenty of pepper he found it edible, a bit like porridge but creamier.

She did sit at his insistence, and he gave his meal its full due.

"Where's the cook?"

"She doesn't come in until mid-morning."

"You made this?"

"Don't look so stunned. Everyone should know how to prepare food to feed themselves. I can also skin a rabbit and cook fish over a campfire. Can you cook?"

"Where would I have learned? The only reason I visited the kitchen as a child was to cozen a piece of cake from our cook. The work I did for Mr. Holt was my first experience in anything approaching a kitchen, and he didn't teach me much besides chopping and stirring."

"See, now if I had a son, I'd teach him to cook."

The words hung in the air as they both considered what it would mean for Mattie to be bearing a child.

His child.

"But that's unlikely to happen," she said briskly, and rose from the table to put the dishes in a pan for cleaning later. "It's time for us to head into town, learn what we can."

"Are you worried about the cook seeing you like this?"

"No. I helped her sister and her husband—a free man of color—relocate from Florida to Havana, and the family's grateful. She won't say anything."

Mattie went to her room to prepare herself further while Oliver shaved and dressed in clothing Digby had made for his role in this affair. The man reflecting from his mirror was a different man than the one who'd boarded ship for the islands. He could see the physical differences, the harder lines of his face, a firmness to his body missing from his previous life. He held his hands in front of him, seeing the sinews and calluses, some from writing, most from learning skills he'd never thought to learn.

He sharpened his pencil, tucking it into his coat pocket along with his journal. Capturing the local color in his writing had improved in the islands and aboard the *Prodigal Son*, and he wanted to keep these moments alive, either to share through publication, or to savor for himself later.

Someone reading his account one hundred years hence would see a description of a blue-eyed mulatto rogue, probably a pirate, quick-witted, and even quicker with a blade. What he wanted to write was, "Look, you people who think everyone should have their place in society, women in the parlor, men in the mill offices, white people over black people. Look at Mattie St. Armand! Look at this woman who's bold and beautiful and makes useless scribblers and dreamers fall in love—"

He caught his breath, staring at his reflection. He couldn't tell her, now was not the time, but if he fancied himself someone who could say something meaningful, if that was why he kept writing, he had to convince himself he could use his words to convince her. He didn't know how, but he knew he had to. Once, his future depended on Mattie not slicing him up for chum or selling him to the anatomists. Now, his future depended on her being with him, forever. He did not know if she loved him. She'd certainly never said anything. It would fall on him to take the risk, and to use the words first.

They exited into a day clear and brisk. Mattie had been correct that it was colder than in the islands, and he was glad he had an outer coat and scarf.

She wore a brown shawl and carried a basket over her arm. He couldn't get over the difference in her. It wasn't just what she wore, it was how she held herself, how she moved her hands. Her shoulders were slumped and her eyes cast down, and there was a stillness to her, an effort at effacement to draw the eye away. Instead of being a bold statement about a brash young man, her demeanor and attire said, "Look away. I'm only part of the furnishings."

She'd even dulled her skin and used her paints to make her eyes shadowed and muddied. The shapeless dress was fastened to appear thicker through the waist and her walk was more of a shuffle than the firm step he knew so well.

When they reached the town center, the narrow wooden walks in front of the businesses only allowed pedestrians to walk in single file, and when a rough-dressed man with a bush of red beard pushed past her, Mattie stepped into the filth of the gutter to give him room. Oliver had to clamp his teeth together to stop from saying anything, for he'd seen the same behavior from the slaves in town.

They bought some greens and pecans, and his servant waited patiently in the shadows while he inspected hats in a storefront. He'd been well coached by Mattie, and he looked for the praline seller at the docks. It was hard to spot her at first, but the burnt sugar smell led him to a toothless old woman mumbling a song to herself as she sat and rocked.

"Fresh pralines, bes' pralines, fines' pralines for you, sah," she said when he stopped in front of her. "I got fresh pralines with pecans from my own tree, yessah."

"You say they're the best?"

"They the bes', yessah," she said.

"What about persimmons, auntie?" Mattie asked in a soft voice. "You got persimmons today? Persimmons that won't cause a belly-ache?"

The woman paused from folding the paper with the still warm pralines, looked up with suddenly sharp eyes at Mattie, then skewed her glance over to Oliver, who did his best to look stupid and harmless.

"Persimmons ain't ripe, gal. Used to get persimmons

at the Stilwell home, but it burnt down, mmmm, mmm," she muttered. "Sad times there. Now I got to go far to get persimmons, but they ain't ripe yet."

"Massa Oliver, you say, 'remind you to get lemon drops,'" Mattie said with a nod at the apothecary across the street.

"I di—yes, I did, didn't I?"

He almost said thank you, but then remembered one didn't thank a slave, so he took himself to the shop across the road when Mattie said, "Four pralines, auntie."

He returned as Mattie passed some pennies over to the old woman and they took the confections with them, but when Oliver went to eat one, Mattie shoved them to the bottom of the basket under the greens. They were heading back to the house when two young men stumbled out of a tavern. They wore the rough clothes of drovers and one gave a low whistle.

"Dang if that ain't one fine-looking wench," he told his companion, elbowing him in the side.

The other one spat tobacco to the side and gave Mattie a lewd perusal from the top of her head to the ground.

"Hey, friend, you hire that gal out? I got some mending I need done. Even got my own needle." He snickered, rubbing the front of his dirty trousers.

"You boys move along," Oliver said through his teeth, taking Mattie by the arm and pulling her behind him.

"Is there a problem here?" said a deep voice from behind Oliver.

The two drovers' eyes widened, and the second one said, "Nossir, Marshal. We're heading back out to the cattle."

"See that you do," the man said, and Oliver watched them leave before turning around.

"Thank you for your assistance."

"I'm Marshal Torres. I don't recall seeing you about Fernandina. What brings you to the Territory, friend?" he asked bluntly.

The marshal had a square frame and heavy mustaches dangling down alongside his mouth, and side-whiskers down to his jaw. His hazel eyes under a battered leather hat were keen as he assessed Oliver in one glance—his attire, his demeanor, his worth.

"I'm Oliver Woodruff. Just passing through on my way to Georgia." He waved at Mattie, behind him. "My mother's maid took sick, so she asked me to get a girl to serve her while she's in Savannah."

"Where you from, gal? Speak up. You're not in trouble," the marshal said, not unkindly.

"Key West, sir."

The marshal gave Oliver a sharp look. "You brought a girl all the way from Key West?"

He shrugged. "She was available for sale and was experienced as a maid. I've no use for a colored girl in England, and that's where I'm headed after my business here is done."

"That business being?"

"Cotton, Marshal. I'm interested in some property in Middle Florida for cotton for our mills, then I'm off to St. Simons to look at sea island cotton. It'll fetch twice the amount of upland cotton in Liverpool, if I can ship it."

The marshal relaxed his stance at hearing Oliver was a mill owner.

"Good cotton country west of here."

"So I've heard," Oliver said, touching his hat.

"Good day to you, Marshal."

They returned to the house, but Oliver felt the marshal's eyes on him as he left. Part of the attraction of Florida as a haven for pirates and smugglers was the lack of clear law enforcement jurisdiction in the Territory, but Mattie had warned him that no one wanted run-ins with the U.S. Marshals.

She was quiet beside him as they entered the house, but he couldn't contain himself any longer.

"How do you stand it?"

Mattie straightened and looked him in the eye.

"How do *I* stand it? How do the people out there stand it?" she said, pointing at the door. "I can board my ship and sail away. They have to live with this horror day in and out. Bloody hell, it's a wonder we don't have St. Domingue all over again, with slaves rising up one fine day and slaughtering their masters in their beds! Now you understand why I needed you for this expedition. As 'Matt St. Armand' I'm recognizable and wanted by the law. With a white man in charge of me though, then I can go anywhere," she said bitterly.

"Some slaves do revolt. I've read it in the newspapers."

"There have been revolts, Vesey and others, but the consequences are devastating. They won't succeed while the slaves have ties to the whites, ties of blood in many cases. And all their loved ones are hostages to fortune. For some of them, the hell they know is better than the unknown. I can only help the ones who are so desperate they'll risk everything for freedom."

He reached forward, placing his hand alongside her jaw in a gentle caress.

"I suspect the preacher in New Providence would be surprised to hear you say such things, Mattie St.

Armand. Hardly the words of someone who's only here for the money."

She moved out of his reach and took the pralines, unwrapping them and passing Oliver one.

"Don't you damage my hard-won reputation, Oliver Woodruff."

Instead of telling her how fortunate he felt to know the real her, he took the praline, enjoying the crunch of the pecans and sugar dissolving on his tongue.

"Look." She showed him the scrap of newsprint wrapping the pralines. Two small black seeds sat there, easy to overlook.

"Two nights, maybe three, and our packages will be waiting for us at the Stilwell farm."

"Do you know where it is?"

She nodded. "Out on Lanceford Creek. One of the homesteads burned by the Indians a couple winters back. The Stilwells were lucky, they survived, but their farm is gone and I heard they moved out to Texas to start over."

She moved briskly into the kitchen, putting up the purchases from the market. "I'm unhappy the marshal met us, but you handled yourself well, Oliver."

"Yes, I am concerned how facile I'm becoming at bending the truth."

She grinned at him over her shoulder. "'Bending the truth'? Those were outright lies, you rascal!"

"Not so," he protested as he followed her, hating it that she grinned harder as the blood warmed his cheeks. "I am a mill owner, and I could use sea island cotton."

"And your pretend mother needing a slave?"

"Very well. You're correct and I'm a pirate, just like you."

She stepped over to him and put her hands alongside his face. "No, Oliver. Larceny comes naturally to me. I learned it at my father's knee. You had to be pulled into our criminal enterprises. You are a good man."

She leaned in and gave him a kiss, and he would have wrapped her in his arms to continue, but she slipped away, saying it wouldn't do for the cook to catch them kissing, either as the slave girl or as Captain St. Armand.

After luncheon, she went over maps with him.

"We need to be waiting for them, here. This time of year, some slaves have more freedom to be on the roads visiting kin at neighboring farms, but the patrollers will also be out so we have to be ready."

A whistle from the back door brought her head up.

"I do believe those are our supplies."

Out in the yard an Indian sat atop a two-wheeled cart pulled by a mule, and when he saw Oliver his hand casually moved to the pistol at his waist.

"Good day to you, Ezekiel. You can relax. Woodruff here is my cabin boy."

"I am not your cabin boy when we're on dry land."

"Semantics," she said, waving her hand, and the young man grinned as he climbed down. When he turned, Oliver saw the kinky black hair draped beneath his turban and knew him for one of the black Seminoles he'd heard of, and his hand itched to write in his journal.

"Oliver Woodruff, meet Zeke Factor."

Factor stuck out his hand and Oliver shook it, knowing he was been assessed every bit as thoroughly as the marshal had assessed him.

"Is that one of Mr. Colt's revolvers?"

The Indian preened and touched the weapon lightly.

"I got it off an army officer. He no longer had a need for it."

Oliver let that remark go as Mattie added, "I won't use one. Those things are likely to misfire and I can load and fire faster with what I'm used to. Good range, but too prone to mishaps."

"Texans like them," Factor said.

"Texans are insane. That's hardly a reliable recommendation," she said.

Factor laughed, and his silver earrings jangled. He wore a red calico shirt, leather leggings, and tall boots.

"You're looking mighty fine, Ezekiel."

"Haven't you heard, 'Maybelle'? I'm an interpreter for the Army now."

"We'll talk inside," she said, and Oliver followed her while Factor saw to the mule.

When they were settled around the kitchen table with coffee, Mattie reviewed the maps, then shook hands with the Indian and gave him a bag of coins.

"Mr. Nash is expecting to hear from you, and you can give him direction to our rendezvous point. You take care of yourself, Zeke. Don't get on the wrong side of the soldiers."

His face was shadowed as he looked at her grimly and shook his head.

"You've heard the talk, Captain. Soon Florida will be nothing but cotton, slaves, and cattle, and then it will be part of the United States. Only place left for us will be down in the swamps and the sawgrass where no white man's willing to go."

He left on foot, and Oliver turned to Mattie.

"You trust him?"

"I have to. I don't know the land like he does. But he'd give me up if he was caught helping us. He has to think of his people, both the Indian and the colored."

"Then we'd best be ready for your packages."

She nodded and looked out the window.

"It's getting late. Help load the supplies."

The air chilled quickly as the sun lowered, and Mattie put extra quilts and some food in the cart along with their bags.

"We won't be returning," she explained. "We'll rendezvous with a boat up on the river and leave from there for the *Prodigal Son*. Don't look so serious. In a week's time we'll be back in New Providence, relaxing in the sunshine."

They ate in the kitchen, the room still warm while the rest of the house was cooling down fast. Oliver laid a fire in the bedroom as Mattie packed her bags.

"Is there a tub for bathing here? I'd like a wash and a shave before we leave for the back country."

She set down the box of bullets she'd been counting.

"You are full of good ideas, Oliver."

They returned to the kitchen, and under Mattie's direction he fetched the tub and filled it with hot water.

He walked over to her and ran his knuckles down her cheek, lingering over the scar at her full lips. "You are so caught up in taking care of others, seeing to your crew, to the people we help, even to keeping me from getting hurt. Everyone needs someone, and you strike me as being too alone. Who takes care of you, Mattie St. Armand?"

She sighed, and something flickered in her gaze.

"There are people who care for me."

"They are not here. I am. Tonight, let someone take care of you for a change. Let me serve you, as a good cabin boy should," he finished with a smile for her alone.

She dipped her head and he undressed her, taking his time over the simple garments, rough cloth and scuffed leather, not what he was used to with this woman.

"You should always be dressed in satins and velvets, Captain," he said softly. "Silks to remind you of the woman beneath the disguise, softest cashmere to warm you in the winter."

He pulled her plain shift over her head and she was bare now, save for the deerskin sheath strapped to her leg, the one holding her hunting knife.

He knelt at her feet, undoing the knots, leaning forward to kiss her inner thigh, reddened from the straps. Her skin glowed deep gold in the firelight, warmed from within by the fire that burned in her. He knew her now, as he never could have before. She could not sit by while others suffered, no matter what face she put on it. He might not always approve of her methods, but she had a passion for justice. It inspired him, drawing him to her service, wishing to fulfill a quest for his lady's approbation, to kneel at her feet and carry her token into battle.

"My sunshine," she murmured, her hand threading through his hair.

"Into the tub, my lady," he said, giving her his hand as she stepped into the water, slowly lowering herself into its heat with a purr of satisfaction. She reached for the soap, but he said, "Wait."

She did, watching him through half-lidded eyes. He took his time, getting his fill of looking at her, the muscles cording her upper arms and defining her sleek shoulders, the breasts with their dark nipples, hard from the cool air, and from arousal. He felt an answering sensitivity as the linen rasped across his chest when he pulled the studs from his shirt, letting her get her fill of him as he drew the cloth over his head. Her gaze followed his movements, and her hand dipped into the water, down between her legs as he set the shirt aside on the chair. His trousers strained at the front as he watched her toy with herself, the small movements rippling the surface of the water. He licked his lips, then picked up her soap and lathered a cloth.

"Keep touching yourself," he whispered. "I want to watch you."

Mattie leaned back in the tub, eyes half closed. Oliver knelt behind her and stroked the cloth down her arms, across her neck and chest. He treated her like she was soft, but it was not an insult, not an attempt to lord it over her. He did it because he cherished her.

She thought she knew all about men and women. Women to her were the sea, each one redolent of salt and the rhythm of the waves, changing with the moon's pull, just as her desire for those of her own sex waxed and waned.

Men were the ship—solid, substantial, oak and pine, shoulders like yardarms and cocks like masts. When she cradled a man's rod in her hands, the steely heat surrounded by soft flesh, each one felt different, yet the same, and each loved to be petted and stroked and admired.

Oliver was all of that, but more. He was substantial and he could be soft. His kisses were unlike any she'd had, from men or women, and she couldn't explain why at first, but then she realized the difference. There was a sweetness to him, with an underlying spice. All her other partners had been rakes and rogues, adventuresses and women who made a living with their bodies. Oliver's kisses took her back to a time when she was young and full of hope. Being with him was its own reward, the sunshine of his smiles, the saltiness of his responses to her, the comfort of being held in his arms, cherished.

It was all new and different for a woman who'd only sought physical release from her partners, and it frightened her as she'd never been frightened staring down an enemy's guns.

Neither of them spoke of what would happen once Mattie's task in Florida was completed, but that night when they retired to his bed, he made love to her tenderly, using his body, his hands, his newfound skills to bring her to climax, and she found contentment as she melted in his arms.

Mattie eased herself out of bed, leaving him to sleep while she returned to her room. She pulled on her wrapper and a moth flew in the open window, drawn by the light. As it immolated itself in the lamp, she wondered if it was worth it to the moth, that moment of brilliant intensity before the inevitable destruction.

CHAPTER 18

A HEAVY FOG COVERED THE GROUND as they hitched up the mule and headed north. Other early risers were out—fishermen headed to the docks, a bakery where Oliver stopped to buy a fresh loaf. He passed it back to Mattie, who sat in the cart with the bags of goods, some clothes, cornmeal, lard, and coffee. Today she wore a droopy cloth bonnet with frayed strings, and it shaded her face. In her rags and cheap cotton she looked almost like a large parcel herself.

"We can't take too much and raise suspicions, but we can bring some for ourselves on the road and for the folks when we find them. They're liable to be hungry at the very least," she'd told him.

Oliver remembered how the slaves they'd snatched had fallen on the food served them after starving belowdecks.

Marshal Torres passed them on the road. He looked weary, as if he'd been in the saddle all night, but he pulled up his horse to greet them.

"You have papers for Maybelle, Mr. Woodruff?"

"I do, from when I purchased her."

The marshal grunted. "You may come past patrollers while you're traveling. Those boys can be rough sorts, but if you've got papers you should be set. Maybelle, you be a good girl for your master now. I don't want to hear of any trouble."

"Nossir, Marshal."

He grunted again and waved them along down the sandy road.

When they were clear of town Oliver followed Mattie's instructions, doubling back and heading for the creek.

Once they were away from town they didn't pass any travelers. The area was still subject to Indian attacks, though most had been driven south into the swamps or rounded up and moved west. Had they not been on a dangerous mission, he might have enjoyed the day more. The sky was a vivid clear blue when the fog burned off, and the crisp air was full of birdsong as they traveled through the scrub and pines. They passed some wild orange trees next to the rough outline of a building's foundation. The fruit was ripe and they took time to pick a basket full.

"It's like paradise," Oliver said, "oranges for the picking, a beautiful day even though it's December."

Mattie sat beside him now that they were away from town, and she spat an orange pip to the side.

"Don't be fooled by one or two pleasant days," she said. "When it's fever season in the summer this place is hell, not heaven. That's not even factoring in the hurricanes and mosquitoes. I've seen men risk deadly nights in a boat on the water instead of sleeping on land and being eaten alive by the insects."

They removed layers of outer clothing as the day warmed. Late in the afternoon, Mattie looked at her map, then at the trees around them,

"Turn off here, this track next to the fallen oak."

After a short stretch the path became too overgrown with vines and saplings for them to proceed easily. They abandoned the cart and loaded the supplies on the mule.

Mattie passed Oliver the rifle. "You're the better shot, and I can't take a chance being seen with a firearm."

"Am I looking for anything in particular?"

"Nothing four-footed is likely to bother us."

The mule perked up when it smelled the water, and after navigating through a patch of tickweed and palmettos, they came to an open area. A burned-out farmstead sat on a rise, a brick fireplace with a broken chimney all that remained.

Mattie shaded her eyes and looked west to where the low sun glinted off the water.

"Is that a boat?" she said.

After securing the mule they took a bucket down to the creek, where the boat was pulled up on shore. There were vines creeping over it, but it appeared whole and unbroken. Mattie poked around it with a long stick to chase out any snakes, and sure enough, a black racer slithered away for a quieter site.

"How did a boat get here?"

Mattie shook her head.

"No idea. Could be the Revenue Marine was here and had to abandon it. They've cutters down here, and men fighting the Indians."

While Oliver took care of the mule, Mattie built a small fire in the fireplace. She had him cut palmettos for a rough shelter—a lean-to to give them protection from the night mist. Supper was cornmeal hoe cakes in an iron skillet, with coffee and sliced ham, and Oliver told her it was one of the best meals he'd ever eaten.

"You're the first man to ever compliment me for my cooking skills." Mattie smiled.

"I imagine most of your—" *Lovers* stuck in his throat like a fishbone. He did not want to talk about, or think about, the other men in Mattie's life, the men who'd preceded him. He only wanted to look forward, not back.

"Most of your associates never had the opportunity to get to know you this way."

"No," she said softly, drawing up her knees as she stared into the low flames. "You are the only—you know me—"

She stopped and looked up at him. Her form was half-lit, half-shadowed in the night.

"Come here," he said softly. "Let me warm you."

She came to him and he held her in the shelter of his arms. They sat, listening to the night sounds, a hunting owl, the final squeak of its supper, a fish jumping in the creek burbling nearby. It was easy to pretend, just for a moment, it was only the two of them, one man and one woman in paradise.

They made love in the dark, silently, tenderly, only unfastening and then rearranging their clothing as the night was chill. After, he lay with her head pillowed on his shoulder, and she stroked his arm.

"I am expected to marry when I return to England."

She stopped stroking him.

"Isn't that what men like you do? Marry? Settle down, leave your wife to raise a house full of children while you toddle off to your mills and your clubs and your mistress?"

"I would not betray my marriage vows."

"Please." She snickered. "The island brothels are

filled with men who thought they'd be true to their vows until the nuptial bliss was replaced by the ennui of the same face every day, the same body every night."

"Not always. I know men who are faithful."

She was silent for a long moment.

"So do I. But it is a rare commodity."

"I would not betray my vows," he said again.

She raised her head, and he couldn't see her face, only the outline of her form.

"I believe you," she said simply, and kissed him. "But you will return to that life, and you will marry, and you will do all the things demanded of you because that is the kind of man you are, Oliver Woodruff. A good man.

"Now, go to sleep, Sunshine. The sooner we take care of this business, the sooner you can return to that world of yours," she said briskly, but it was a long time before he fell asleep.

CHAPTER 19

THE NEXT DAY HE FISHED while Mattie examined the boat and cleaned it out. The chamomile scent of dog fennel filled the air and bees hovered around overripe persimmons fallen to the ground. It would have been idyllic if not for the tension in the air, the expectation that their "packages" would arrive and events would move quickly.

Mattie changed back into her men's clothing.

"I know I'm taking a chance, but the two of us traveling together with a couple of slaves won't look as suspicious as you traveling with a group of slaves by yourself."

He suspected part of her rationale was the ease of movement in her men's garb, and how it changed her. She was so used to playing the man it affected her walk, her stance, and her fighting readiness.

Mattie retrieved some of the bright orange persimmons, which had a pulpy, fleshy center like a plum. They were sweet and fibrous, but she warned him away from the unripe fruit, which she pronounced astringent and "mouth puckering." She also showed him a pecan tree and he gathered the fallen nuts the squirrels hadn't retrieved. She'd pause frequently and look toward the west, her hand moving to her hip and the knife sheathed there.

She took the catfish he'd cleaned—one of his new skills picked up under Cicero's tutelage—and dipped them in the cornmeal, frying them up with fritters called "hush puppies" sizzling in the lard to accompany them. Just as they were about to eat, Mattie put her hand on his arm, motioning him to silence.

She started singing in a low voice as she stirred the food around, "Run to Jesus and shun the danger, I don't expect to stay much longer here…"

A woman stumbled out of the brush, dragging a little girl behind her. A red rag was clutched in her hand and she stopped cold when she saw Mattie and Oliver, fear warring with hope in her eyes.

"Do not be afraid," Mattie asked in a low voice. "You were told people would meet you at the Stilwell place."

"Told to look for the rag roun' the persimmon tree," the woman gasped out. "I might hear 'Run to Jesus.'"

"You've come to the right place, sister. We were expecting you. Come, eat with us," she said, waving at the food.

Oliver took a tin plate and filled it with fish and hush puppies, and sliced two persimmons. He held the plate out to the little girl clutching the woman's skirts. The woman looked at him as if she'd never seen such a thing before, and it was likely she hadn't, a white man giving her his food.

"Stay here, child," she said, and inched forward, reaching for the plate. She took it cautiously from Oliver's hand, watching his face, her gaze darting to Mattie as if trying to figure them out. When she passed the plate to the child the girl fell on it, shoveling it into her mouth as quickly as she could.

"Slow down, girl. You'll make yourself sick," Mattie said, but there was more concern than harshness in her tone. She filled a second plate and gave it to the woman, and only then did the two of them take the little that remained.

"I was not certain you'd be here before tomorrow." The woman stopped eating for a moment, exhaustion pulling down her face. She wore a twist of cloth around her head, and a dress better tailored and less ragged than Mattie's, which surprised him. The child, however, wore only a tow linen shift exposing her knobby knees. She had large eyes with a hazel cast to them, and her skin was a substantially lighter shade.

"Couldn't wait," the woman said, in a low voice. "Ol' massa pass. I hear young massa say since sister pass of the fever, he put her baby girl in his pocket and sell her downriver to N'awlins. Ain't gonna let them sell my Liza's baby."

Oliver's hands grew icy as he looked at the child, who couldn't have been more than eight or nine years old. He remembered what Mattie said about the demand for light-skinned girls in the brothels and markets of New Orleans.

"Is she his?" Mattie asked, and Oliver was puzzled for a moment until he realized she didn't mean, did he own her, but was asking if he'd fathered her.

"No. Ol' massa, his daddy. He the one."

"Dear heaven," Oliver murmured.

"Hear him talking with mistress, Mistress tell him not to sell Daisy 'til after Christmas. I'm too good a cook, she say. If I'm fretting over the child, who'll make the Christmas turkey with oyster stuffing the way she like it?" she said bitterly.

She looked fiercely at him while she said this, and a fleeting smile touched Mattie's mouth.

"You needn't fret over Mr. Woodruff here…"

"Ella, that's my name."

"Ella. He's come all the way from England to help you."

Ella continued to eye him suspiciously, and Oliver swallowed. She may be a fine cook, but he'd let Mattie take care of their needs for the near future.

"I'm Captain St. Armand, and you've likely heard of me."

The woman's face brightened as Mattie introduced herself.

"Indians trust you, and they's who told me about the rag and the tree here."

The little girl finished eating, and leaned against her aunt, her eyes drooping down.

"We'll hide out here for the day, travel tonight after the sun's set," Mattie said. "You get some rest now, while you can."

Ella nodded wearily. "Paddyrollers is out. Always are at Christmastime."

Oliver looked at Mattie.

"Patrollers. The men who earn coin bringing escaped slaves back to their owners," she explained.

Daisy blinked and looked around at their surroundings, and Oliver remembered his shopping trip in Fernandina. He retrieved the bag of lemon drops and held them out to the child.

"Here, have a sweet."

The little girl looked at her aunt, who watched Oliver carefully, but then gave a nod.

The child put the lemon drop in her mouth, her eyes closing in delight as she sucked on it. She tugged on Ella's apron.

"Is it Christmas, Auntie?"

Ella looked around at the campsite, the food, and the mule that would carry them to freedom. A smile broke over her face, rendering it achingly lovely.

"It surely is, baby girl. It surely is."

Ella and Daisy stretched out on the ground where they sat, and soon both were fast asleep. Oliver fetched the blankets from their bedrolls and covered them. Ella's broad face was seamed with care and fear, but now in sleep she looked younger. He realized she was little more than a child herself, but her arm was wrapped around her niece, protecting her even as she slept.

The sun sent shafts of golden afternoon light through the trees when Mattie shook the woman awake. Ella and Mattie packed up the camp while Oliver wrote up the day's events in his journal. Daisy watched him write, her finger in her mouth. He stopped and said, "Can you read and write, Daisy?"

The child's eyes grew large. "I get a whippin' if I try to read, mister. Auntie say so."

"When you're away from here there will be schools for you and books to read."

He found a blank page in the journal, and printed "Daisy" in block letters, putting a daisy over the *i*. Then he carefully ripped it from the binding and passed it to her.

"See here? This is your name, Daisy. D-A-I-S-Y. You can practice writing it, and that will be your first reading lesson."

He gave her one of his pencils, and showed her how to form the letters, and finally she tried on her own. The "S" was shaky, but she managed.

"Look, Auntie! I can write!"
"Child, you know you ain't—"
"Quiet!"
They all looked at Mattie, who stared west.
Hounds bayed in the distance.

CHAPTER 20

MATTIE WHIPPED HER HEAD AROUND to look at Oliver, who jumped to his feet.

"Take the boat. Take them and go," he said abruptly. "I'll take the mule and let them chase me through the woods."

"No, I can—"

"Listen to me, Mattie!" He grabbed her upper arms. "Can you row? Of course you can. All I can do is scribble. And wait."

He wasn't bitter as he said this. On the contrary, when he released her, his shoulders straightened and he looked taller, stronger.

"Row them to safety, take them down the river. This is why you brought me! I'll take the mule and distract them. They'll come after me."

She stared at him, stunned into silence. The child whimpered, the distant dogs baying again, and she shook her head. "Come with us, the boat will hold you!"

"I will slow you down. You can't row four as quickly as you can row three, one of them a child. I'm a white man. Isn't that why you wanted me with you? You know as well as I that whatever awaits me, your fate is a thousand times worse. Go, Mattie, do what you came to do! Do good. I will meet you in New Providence, and we will drink rum, and feed nuts to Roscoe, and we will laugh. Go now, before it's too late."

He leaned forward and pressed his lips to her forehead, and when he drew back, his face was alit with purpose.

"I can do this, Mattie. I can buy you time to get away. I gave my oath to Turnbull and Nash that I would do everything in my power to see you safe. I will not forswear myself. We all have our tasks. We all have promises to fulfill. Let me fulfill mine."

He was her own Galahad, her knight, not in shining armor, but in rumpled clothing and a shining smile, and he was more dear to her in that moment than anyone had ever been in her entire misspent life.

"Cap'n, what do we do?" Ella asked in fright.

"Take off the girl's dress, then you two get in the boat. Oliver, give her your spare shirt."

He rummaged through his pack, passing the shirt and turning his back as the little girl changed. Mattie pressed the ragged cloth into his hands.

"Keep this with your gear. It will…" she swallowed. "It will bring the hounds to you. They won't be able to track us on the water."

He held the cloth to his chest like he was riding into battle with his lady's favor on his arm. She wanted to shake him, tell him it wasn't like the damned stories he enjoyed. This was real and dangerous.

But he knew that. He'd learned under her tutelage and it was his time now. Time for him to be the person he was meant to be, the hero of his story, and of hers.

Mattie knew what she had to do. She'd known her

purpose from the day Captain Fletcher took her to a slave auction so she would be a witness to the evil and know that what they did mattered. Oliver was correct. He might survive capture. Her odds were far worse.

And hadn't she always gone with the best odds?

He pulled her head to his and kissed her, and she held him safe in her arms for a moment longer, a moment she would have frozen in time forever if she could.

But that was not to be, not today. He reached into his coat and pulled out his journal, pressing it into her hands.

"Take this. Keep it safe for me."

"You know how to make your way back after you get away?"

"I follow the trail we took here," he said simply. "And I remember Florida is a peninsula. If I go east, eventually I'll hit water."

She tried to smile but it wobbled and her sight was blurred. She swiped her arm across her face, and he kissed her on the forehead again, tenderly. She pulled him into her arms, hugging him fiercely.

"I will come back for you, Oliver Woodruff. No matter what happens, I will not abandon you."

"Of course you will return for me. You need your cabin boy. Go now."

She climbed into the boat and watched him as he took the mule and disappeared into the trees, watching the empty space where he'd been until a curve in the creek took her away. Then she focused on rowing to safety, to the friends who waited to help them.

They were getting nearer, the sound of the dogs, louder, closer. He used the crop on the mule, but when he heard hoofbeats and the shouts behind him, he loaded his pistols, and pulled off to a clearing in the brush.

The hounds burst through the trees baying and barking. They were on long leads, and his guns were ready in case they attacked, but the men storming through behind them brought them to order. The mule shied, and he controlled it while the men pulled back the dogs at the marshal's sharp command. There were two of them with him, a father and son from their faces, and they didn't look happy about Marshal Torres giving them orders.

Seeing the marshal with the patrollers changed everything, but he straightened up to face them. He hoped to talk his way out of the situation and almost smiled, for lying to the authorities was something he'd never have considered before he fell in with pirates.

"You seem to have lost your way, Mr. Woodruff," Torres said, pushing his hat back off his forehead.

"Isn't this the road to Callahan?"

"No sir, it is not. Where's that gal of yours?"

The younger patroller spit tobacco to the side, too close to the marshal's horse, and Torres gave him an irritated look.

Oliver scratched his chin, screwing up his face in concentration. "She ran off during the night, Marshal. It was most unexpected."

Torres just looked at him in disappointment.

"That a fact? Don't suppose you know anything about a colored woman named Ella and a little girl who ran off from the Chase farm?"

"No, I wouldn't know anything about that."

"The more I thought on it, the more I thought about your gal Maybelle, and then I remembered this."

He pulled out a folded piece of paper from inside his coat and shook out the creases. Oliver knew what it said even before he read it aloud.

"'Wanted for stealing three slaves in Pensacola: About 25 years old, five feet ten or eleven inches, dark haired, light eyes, downcast, sly look, may be a mulatto.'

"Thought your slave looked awfully tall for a gal. Easy enough to disguise a man as a woman in a bonnet."

"I think I'd know if the slave I bought was a man. I can assure you that she's a woman."

"Damn it, Marshal," the older man said angrily. "You know he's a lyin' thief and we know he's a lyin' thief. Those damned hounds know he's a lyin' thief! I say we make him tell us where those niggers ran off to, then we string him up here and now!"

"That's not going to happen, Bisbee," Torres said. "However, we'd like to have a look at your gear, Woodruff. These dogs seem mighty interested in it. Now, get down from that mule, slow like."

Oliver knew he'd stalled as long as he could. The thought of shooting them never occurred to him. He could have shot the dogs, with regret, but he wasn't prepared to gun down men in the woods solely so he could make his escape.

Apparently he wasn't as much of a pirate as Mattie hoped he'd be.

He dismounted, standing by the mule's head. Torres motioned to the younger man, who took his bag off the mule and dumped it out onto the ground. Immediately the dogs rushed to Daisy's shift, grabbing it and tearing it to shreds with their teeth and claws.

At that moment Oliver was more glad than anything else that the little girl was in a boat, somewhere far from here. The vision of the child being mauled by hounds made his gut churn and steeled his resolve. Dusk was coming on, and the longer he could keep them away from their quarry, the better their chances for freedom.

"Told you he was a lyin' son of a bitch," older man said. "That's the little one's dress. He's a slave stealer, likely stirring up insurrection too. I say we make him talk, then string him up!"

Torres moved his coat aside and put his hand on his pistol.

"We're taking him to Fernandina and doing things proper and legal in a courtroom. Mr. Woodruff, you're under arrest for the crime of slave stealing and fomenting insurrection. Bisbee, if I see your hand move any closer to that pepperbox in your coat I'm going to blow your head off and let the judge sort it out."

"You have no right to talk like that to me!"

"Until things change in Florida Territory, I have every right." He dismounted, pulling a pair of shackles from his saddlebag, and patted Oliver down, removing the pistols and unloading them.

"You're carrying a lot of hardware, Woodruff."

"I heard there were desperadoes in the woods, Marshal."

"Yeah, I hear that too," Torres said laconically, fastening the shackles to Oliver's wrists. "Johnny Bisbee, you leave that money back in the man's bags. It ain't yours to take, and I only brought one set of shackles with me. And don't you even think of trying to shoot it out, 'cause I've seen you, and I know I can bring you down first."

The two patrollers looked mutinous, and from their rough clothing and speech, Oliver suspected taking his money would only be seen as their just reward for chasing him through the woods. They were feeling especially cheated when they learned from the marshal there was a two-hundred-dollar reward for the mulatto slave stealer.

"Chase won't pay us if we don't fetch his niggers back."

"That's your problem," Torres said. "My job is to get this man to trial."

After conferring, the Bisbees decided to let the marshal take Oliver in on his own, and they'd continue looking for the runaways. Oliver sent up a silent prayer that Mattie, Ella, and Daisy would get away, but he knew he could not have made any other choice. He served his captain and his lady, and as he rode beside the silent marshal, he did not regret any of his choices.

They rode without speaking, surrounded by the night sounds of an owl calling to its mate, and the ever-present chorus of frogs from the creek. A mama opossum skittered across the path, her young close behind.

"I don't suppose you want to tell me where they are?" the marshal said, breaking the silence. The moon was full, providing enough light for them to follow the road back.

"I have no idea what you are referring to. My girl ran off. That is all I know."

Torres sighed. "Folks 'round here have long memories and short tempers, Woodruff. An Englishman like you might make it easier on yourself by talking."

"Marshal, you seem like a reasonable man—"

"Mister, don't you talk to me about reasonable. A reasonable man doesn't take what doesn't belong to him. You're charged with slave stealing—a serious crime in this territory."

Oliver shut up, but he was still sanguine about the outcome of events. There had to be other reasonable men in East Florida.

CHAPTER 21

IF THERE WERE REASONABLE PEOPLE willing to discuss the rights of man, they weren't in Nassau County. The jail had nothing to recommend it, but Oliver considered himself somewhat fortunate to be incarcerated after he saw the crowd gathered outside its doors when Marshal Torres brought him in. They made it clear they'd just as soon string Oliver up from the nearest live oak and save the county the cost of judging him.

Torres held firm, telling the crowd, "You mess with my prisoner and soldiers will pour out of Fort Marion like you kicked an anthill."

Torres even argued with Ruskin, the jailer, who insisted the prisoner be shackled inside his cell, but once he handed Oliver off it was out of his hands and the shackle went on, five pounds of iron attached to a log chain. Clearly they thought him much more of a desperado than the crew of the *Prodigal Son* ever had. Within a day of being shackled he'd torn off his shirtsleeves to wrap around his ankle and protect it from the chafing of the iron.

It was hard to not give in to desperation. Each morning he'd wake thinking, "Today's the day.

Mattie's coming for me," and each night he fell onto his pallet thinking, "Tomorrow she'll come."

His leg was swollen from the shackle, but he still dragged himself back and forth across his cell, because if he stopped moving he'd lie on his pallet and give in to the despair that oozed through the jail like a miasmic fog. Runaway slaves were kept in the room next to his and he could hear their punishments, fifty blows with a paddle, or a cowhide strap, or both, men and women alike. Part of what kept him moving was the fierce happiness that Ella would never suffer that degradation again, that she was living free in the Bahamas, that Daisy would never know what it felt like to be trussed like an animal, doubled over and helpless while she was whipped.

He ate the disgusting food, even after he saw the dogs in the yard lick the cooking utensils "clean." He'd never complain again about scrubbing a pot. He had to keep his strength up. Mattie was coming for him. He knew it. She would not abandon him here, in jail, risking death or imprisonment in Florida Territory. When she rescued him he would write it all down, he would tell the world. It was this, and his belief in Mattie's return, keeping him sane. Even his attorney recommended he plead guilty and throw himself on the mercy of the court.

"Not that I expect much mercy for you, Woodruff, but I'm guessing it might help your situation."

Cyrus Hamilton was sent by the court to represent him, but he'd made it clear from the outset he was only taking this case because no one else would.

"You're fortunate Judge Prine is in the area, because if he was out riding the circuit you'd be here even longer," he said, looking with distaste at Oliver's bare feet and the heavy shackle around his ankle.

"What did you learn about my bail?"

Hamilton looked at him cynically. "Do you have ten thousand dollars on you?"

"What? That is an outrageous sum!"

"You are not exactly a popular person around here. I'm going to do my best to get a jury that won't convict you without hearing the evidence, but it's not looking good. Are you sure you don't want to plead now and save us all the trouble?"

"I thought you were my advocate."

"I'm a realist first, but it's your choice." Hamilton looked down at the dirt floor and frowned.

"You'll need your boots for the trial."

"They have gone missing," Oliver said, though he knew exactly where they'd gone. He bribed Jim, the slave who emptied the slops in the morning, giving him his boots in exchange for a pencil and some old papers retrieved from the trash. Without a knife the only way he could sharpen the pencil was by rubbing it against a rough sliver of metal on his chain, but he kept notes, tucked up next to his heart.

His attorney sighed.

"I'll hunt up a shirt and a pair of boots for you and add it to my fees. Not that I expect to get paid. I'll be lucky if they don't string me up too for this."

Hamilton gathered his papers and stood.

"Trial's set for day after tomorrow. Try to get some rest, and if you're a praying man, now's the time."

Oliver rose as well, wincing at the soreness from the chain.

"I do appreciate your efforts, Mr. Hamilton."

"Yeah, well even slave-stealing scum are entitled to a day in court."

"Your faith in me warms my heart."

"Do not try that bullshit in the courtroom, mister. Judge Prine—" He shook his head. "I'll see you in a couple days."

He sat at the rough table now, writing notes about today's whipping of the cook. Rain poured down in the jail yard, but it didn't keep the punishment from happening. Mrs. Ruskin must have been feeling poorly though—she was increasing and was far along—for her mother took over the chores, including beating the cook.

There was a feeling within him as he watched the incidents of daily brutality that he must have been sent somewhere far from civilization. A land where people spoke a language similar to his, worshipped in churches like his, wore clothes like his, but were some other species, something strange and bizarre and divorced from his reality. It was like reading Polidari's tales of vampires—creatures similar to us but not human at all.

He had to keep his strength up for his rescue, and each day he thought about that event, and the woman who'd take him away from this hell. He wished he were an artist so he could draw Mattie and gaze on her likeness, but that would be dangerous. He was a writer, so instead he engraved her in his memory with words. *Vibrant. Exciting. Fascinating. Heart-stirring.*

The other half of his soul. He loved her, but what could he offer a woman like Mattie? Would a marriage and wedding ring shackle her spirit as much as the iron shackled him?

It was colder now in northern Florida and he shivered on his pallet, his troubled sleep leaving him bleary-eyed when the jailer unlocked his door.

"Time for court, Woodruff."

He gave him the clothes counselor Hamilton brought, and after he dressed, the jailer shackled him, hand and foot, in case he tried to get away. Black clouds and a sharp breeze scudded in from the east as the wagon took him to the courthouse. Oliver barely had time to register his surroundings before he was taken by the arm, hobbling up the steps. Hamilton met him at the door of the courthouse and sharply told the jailer, "Take those shackles off him."

The jailer spat tobacco out the door, then rummaged through his pocket for the key, unfastening the chains. Oliver straightened, feeling he could finally draw a full breath, but he still moved slowly, aching in his joints from his confinement in the chains for so long.

It was chill outside but the courtroom steamed from all the men packed into the small space. There was a great deal of muttering as he entered, his steps slow and measured as he re-accustomed himself to free movement of his limbs.

The jury was seated, witnesses were called, and even before the judge called a recess for luncheon Oliver had no doubt of what the outcome would be. Marshal Torres calmly talked about Oliver's companion, whom he suspected was a notorious slave stealer disguised as a woman. The wanted poster of Mattie was entered into evidence.

Ella's owner testified about her value to him.

"That thief cost me, your honor." Curtis Chase glared at him from the witness stand. "Ella was a skilled cook, and I could've bred her up too. She was worth at least four hundred dollars, maybe more. And the child was worth three hundred! I already had a buyer lined up for her in New Orleans."

Hamilton muttered to Oliver, "He's inflating her value. That's high, even for a mulatto child."

Oliver stared at him.

"Daisy is his *sister*. They have the same father. That's why she's half-white."

Hamilton squirmed uncomfortably in his seat.

"I don't hold with that sort of thing, but it doesn't matter. The child's still his property."

Oliver shook his head in disbelief.

"I want to testify on my own behalf," he told Hamilton during a brief recess so the judge could use the privy.

"Unless you're going to get on that stand, throw yourself on the mercy of the court and beg forgiveness of Florida Territory and all its good citizens, I strongly recommend against that course of action."

"I need to have my say. People need to know—"

"Know what? That you're a thief? That your actions might encourage murder and insurrection? That you're a foreigner come here trying to upend our peculiar institutions? Woodruff, no one will hear you. No newspaper will spread your words. Look at them." He gestured at the courtroom. "The only story coming out of today's events is how justice was done and miscreants punished. Now, keep your head down and your mouth shut, and we'll try to get through this with your skin intact."

Oliver fisted his hands on the table, and stared at his wrists, rubbed raw by the shackles.

"You talk of the right of the property owner, and I talk of the rights of human beings. Someday, Mr. Hamilton, the world will listen, and know."

"It ain't today, Woodruff. Not for you. Now shut up and let me do my job."

It took the jury thirty minutes to find him guilty of the charges of slave stealing. Hamilton muttered he was surprised it took that long. The temperature in the crowded courtroom had risen to fever levels and sweat plastered Judge Prine's scant hair to his forehead as he glared down from the bench.

"You and the other British incendiaries, motivated by fanatic zeal, fomenting insurrection. You enter our land, pretending to be here for legitimate purposes, but all the time you are plotting theft and rebellion, corrupting our slaves and enticing our people to run off. If you had your way, this land of ours would be overrun with your nigger troops from Jamaica. We're not safe in our beds, our womenfolk aren't safe in their homes with you people threatening all we have, our very way of life.

"We don't have your partner or those runaways in custody, but we have you, Mr. Woodruff," he said grimly. "My pap came down from Tennessee with General Jackson to teach you Brits a lesson, but I can see it didn't take. Maybe this one will, and make you think twice about coming here stirring up trouble and stealing our property.

"Your sentence is thirty days in jail and a one hundred fifty dollar fine."

Oliver relaxed. "Not as bad—"

"Quiet, the judge's not done speaking," his attorney said.

"In addition, your hand is to be branded with the letters 'SS' for 'slave stealer.' The sentence is to be carried out immediately, Marshal. I need to move on to the next town."

The judge rose from his bench and exited in a flurry of black robes. There was a cheer from the assembled men in the courtroom, and Oliver stared at Hamilton, who looked down at his papers, a troubled expression on his face.

"That—that can't be right. It's barbaric," he whispered.

Hamilton wouldn't meet his eyes.

"It's allowed. The Criminal Code is specific in the punishments for slave stealing." He cleared his throat. "You got off lightly. You could be fined one thousand dollars and jailed for six months."

"Branding a man—it's been decades since England's done anything so horrific in its courts!"

"Then you should have stayed in England! You heard the judge. You think you can waltz into our land, our homes, and do what you want, destroy our way of life? We won't allow it, Woodruff."

The marshal came over and took him by the arm.

"Let's go. It's best to be done with this. Do you have the money for the fine?"

Oliver's ears were buzzing, and he just stared at him.

Torres sighed.

"Maybe you can write someone to send the money, get you out of jail sooner."

The crowd of onlookers was still crowding the courtroom, some of them gleeful, one or two looking pensive, and Chase was in the front, grinning like a hobgoblin.

"You go back home to England, Woodruff. You tell them we don't hold with you stealing our goods."

Oliver straightened, and looked the slaveowner in the eye, then looked around the courtroom.

"I will tell them. I will tell them of everything that I saw in Florida Territory. Of that you can be certain."

There was some muttering and shuffling of feet, and

Hamilton said, "I'll stay here 'til it's done. I'll send word to your bank, and you can get the money for your fines, but it may take some time. I sent that letter to the British minister in Washington like you asked, but there's been no word back yet."

"Thank you for what you've done for me, Mr. Hamilton. I know it wasn't to your liking, but you tried. I'm ready, Marshal."

Torres took him back to the prisoner's box and was handed a coil of rope by the jailer.

"There's no need to tie me."

Torres shook his head.

"You will be tied, Mr. Woodruff. It's better that way—safer for you and for me."

He lashed Oliver's right hand to the railing in full view of the assembled crowd. Part of his mind still refused to believe this could happen, but part of him was making note of all the details, storing it in his memory. The brazier with its red coals and the handle of the iron sticking out, the rank smell of the crowd, the musty odor of wet wood from where the roof leaked, and the muttered comments of the men. The branding iron had a wooden handle, and Torres grasped it now, pulling it from the fire, the end of it glowing crimson.

He told himself he wouldn't cower, but he was glad to have the railing at his back as he watched the iron draw closer to him.

"It might be easier if you look away."

"I will not, Marshal. Do your duty."

Torres nodded. He placed the iron on the ball of Oliver's hand, searing the meaty flesh below his thumb.

It spatters like salt thrown on the fire, one part of his

mind registered as his skin charred.

Then his world exploded into a white sun radiating outward, near blinding him from the pain as the marshal held the iron to his hand, but he would not faint, he would not cower. He looked into the eyes of Curtis Chase, who watched with great delight as Oliver's flesh was branded for his crimes.

None of them knew that as Oliver struggled to stay conscious, what tore through his mind was disbelief and regret. Not over his alleged misdeeds, or the punishment, but over a greater betrayal.

Mattie St. Armand had not come for him.

CHAPTER 22

"IT'S OVER, GO HOME NOW," Torres told the crowd as he untied Oliver. They weren't happy the entertainment had ended so quickly, but the taverns were doing a brisk business since it was court day and the men thinned out. The jailer returned with his shackles.

"Marshal, is that necessary?" Hamilton said.

Torres looked at Oliver, who cradled his hand against his chest. Sweat streaked down his forehead as he swallowed the bile in this throat, trying not to vomit at the pain and the roast pork smell of his burnt flesh.

"No, I don't believe he needs to be shackled. You might want to stay with your client until he's settled. The doctor's away at St. Augustine, but maybe Mrs. Ruskin will give you some butter to put on the burn."

Hamilton didn't look pleased to be stuck with Oliver for a minute longer and wouldn't meet his eyes, but he gently held his left arm, steadying him as he walked down the courthouse steps past the jeering crowd, helping him into the wagon.

"I'll meet you at the jail."

When they returned Oliver to his cell, Hamilton

asked for salve for the burn, but all he had from Ruskin was a pail of water and some none-too-clean rags.

"If his hand becomes putrid, Marshal Torres isn't going to be happy with you. At least see if there's some lard or a raw potato he can put on it."

The jailer spat out the door.

"The marshal don't pay me, counselor. If you want more, you can see to it your own self."

Oliver sat gingerly on the chair, not willing to look at his damaged hand with them there. Hamilton sighed and put his hat back on.

"You take care of yourself, Woodruff. If I hear anything from the British Legation, I'll contact you immediately."

"Thank you for all you have done for me, Mr. Hamilton," he said hoarsely. He swallowed again, willing himself not to vomit in front of his adversaries.

"I'll come back in thirty days, make sure you get home to England. You don't want to stay around here once your sentence is up."

Oliver didn't reply to that, just nodded, and the door closed behind his attorney and the jailer. Finally, before it was full dark, he dipped the rags in the water and gingerly wrapped them around his hand.

Thirty days. I can survive thirty more days. With or without Mattie St. Armand.

CHAPTER 23

THE ODDS OF OLIVER SURVIVING his jail sentence were looking worse. Within days of the branding his hand scabbed over, but it was inflamed, blistered and swollen with yellow pus and fluid.

He asked the jailer for salve and was ignored, so he used some of his drinking water to make a cold compress to soothe the burn. He could barely stand to touch his right hand and at night he'd jerk awake at the slightest movement jarring the injured limb.

It was hard keeping track of the feverish days, and he idly wondered if his sentence was finally up when he heard raised voices outside his cell door. He blinked against the sudden light pouring in through the unlocked door, then it was blocked by Marshal Torres standing there and staring at him.

"Christ, Ruskin, what have you done to him?"

"I ain't done nothin'. He's just mopey from his punishment."

"Did you have the doc come by to see him?"

"Nobody gave me money for doctoring him."

Torres glared at the jailer, then came over to Oliver, taking his arm in a surprisingly gentle grasp.

"Shit," he said softly, staring at the infected hand,

then straightened up. "Mr. Woodruff, I'm taking you to Fort Marion. We've received a letter from the British Legation asking about you and it would be better if you were housed in the fort. And they have a surgeon," he added, almost as an afterthought. "Can you ride? I can put you on a horse with a lead line."

Oliver stood, black dots blinking before his eyes from fever and exhaustion, but he stayed upright, his hand cradled against his breast.

"I would crawl if that's what it took to get out of this hellhole, Marshal."

"I'm going to round up a couple men to ride with us."

The marshal glared again at Ruskin, who called to his back as he was leaving, "If'n you wanted him at the fort, you shoulda taken him there in the first place. Save me money and aggravation!"

The news he would be leaving jail, even if it was going to the federal fort, brought him hope for the first time in days. He'd stopped looking for Mattie. She wasn't coming for him, but if the British government stepped in and assisted him home, he vowed he would still do all he'd planned, writing of his experiences, letting the world know more of the evils of slavery.

He didn't need her. She was the catalyst getting him to this point, but it wasn't because of her that he'd speak out. He sat again until voices outside brought him out of a feverish doze. He lurched over to his window to peer into the yard. The marshal was there with two men, and Oliver smiled to himself again at what a desperado they must think him, to send him off with an armed escort. At this point he suspected he was weak enough that the jailer's mother-in-law could take him down.

Torres led him from his cell, helping him onto his horse. When Oliver saw the faces of the men the marshal deputized from the streets to ride along, he wondered whether he'd make it to the fort or whether violence on the road would bring an end to his pain.

His mount was a gentle gelding, one of the sturdy, short horses he'd seen the cattle drovers use. It wasn't fancy but it was sure-footed, and that was what he wanted as they followed sandy roads south. The marshal didn't relax his vigilance until they were well out of Fernandina, and the two deputies kept to themselves. Oliver kept his eyes off of them, not wanting to stir up trouble so far from civilization, focused instead on staying in the saddle and not jouncing his wounded hand. The wind picked up, swirling the oak leaves on the road and shivering the branches.

"We're going to push on before—" The sound of two pistols cocking silenced Torres. He put his hand on his gun and turned in the saddle to look at the men he'd deputized.

"You boys don't want to be planning anything stupid now. I'm expected at Fort Marion with my prisoner, and if I'm not there by Friday they're going to wonder why."

One of the men, older and weathered from years in the sun said, "We don't want trouble either, Marshal. We brought some friends along to make sure that doesn't happen."

The sound of hoof beats from the south brought Oliver's head around as a party of masked men came through the trees. They had bandanas pulled up over their lower faces, and their leader raised a hand to stop them.

"Marshal Torres. We've come to take your prisoner

off your hands."

Torres shifted in his saddle, then scratched his chin. "You know I can't let you boys do that, but I'm regretting offering these yahoos a dollar each to work for me."

"Let them take me," Oliver said, watching the armed group. "Don't shoot the marshal. He's an honorable man."

The leader looked him over and seemed to mark each bruise, each shadow, and most of all, the hand bandaged and cradled to his chest.

"No, you don't look like you're going to put up much of a fight, mister. Torres, dismount, easy now, and this won't end with your blood being spilled."

"Don't make me responsible for your death, Marshal. I beg of you. It's better this way. I'll leave knowing you did all you could to protect me."

Torres looked at Oliver, then looked again at the men willing to shoot him to take the Englishman away. He dropped the lead for Oliver's horse and dismounted, but before he could do more, one of the men he'd deputized hit him over the head, knocking him unconscious.

"Take him off the trail, but don't hurt him, and leave his horse."

The leader rode over and pulled down her bandana.

"I promised I'd return for you, Oliver."

CHAPTER 24

MATTIE SEETHED AS THEY RODE to the river and the boat waiting for them. Oliver's condition—his face hollow and wan from confinement and the poor food they allowed him, the pus-stained and filthy wrappings of the hand he cradled to his chest—tempted her to shoot the marshal and any other Florida resident with the bad luck to cross her path.

Nash, who along with Daly had "volunteered" when the marshal was scrounging the streets for deputies, held the lead for Oliver's horse.

"When I saw you and Mr. Nash in town it was the first glimmer of hope I had in weeks," Oliver rasped to Daly.

His words flayed her like a cat-o'-nine-tails. *Useless!* Mattie castigated herself as she rode in silence. She'd once termed him useless, but it was she who could not do what needed to be done, who'd abandoned him when he needed her most.

The rain started as they rode to the river, but she couldn't stop, even though Oliver looked like he'd keel over if the rain came down any harder. Ezekiel Factor met them, taking charge of their horses. They'd never be returned to their owners, and that suited her down to her bones. If she had her way they'd raid and pillage Fernandina like the residents hadn't seen since the days of Luis Aury's pirate republic. If only she'd found a way to take him with her, if only she'd never roped him into this scheme.

Once on the water she pushed the men, blasting them for not rowing harder to get them to the *Prodigal Son*, but they finally came alongside the schooner gleaming in the moonlight.

"Cap'n, we need to rig a chair to get him aboard," Nash said softly to her, and she only nodded.

Oliver watched her, as he'd been watching her since the rescue. She knew him well enough to know that he too was waiting until they had privacy to talk, but she'd dealt with many wounded men over the years, and talk could wait. His survival was foremost in her mind.

"Take him to my cabin," she said once they were aboard, and she went down to the galley.

"How is the boy?" the cook asked.

"He is not a boy! He's a man!" She ran her hand across her face. "My apologies, Mr. Holt. I should not have snapped at you."

"Cap'n, you haven't slept, hardly eaten a thing these past days. I understand." Concern furrowed his already wrinkled brow.

Mattie sighed.

"Now the hard work begins. Boil up that water and make strong tea, as we discussed. I'll need vinegar also."

She returned to her quarters, hesitating outside her door. Then she took a deep breath, wiped her hands on her trousers to dry her sweating palms and entered. Oliver sat on her bed. He looked up at her, his face shadowed in the lamplight.

"No matter what happens, do not cut off my hand."

"Oliver—"

"Promise me! You owe me, after all," he finished harshly.

She closed her eyes for a moment against the pain stabbing her heart, then moved into the room, lighting the lanterns to get the space as bright as possible for the work ahead of her.

"My goal is to keep you alive. When we get to the islands, that's when the real work will begin. If you want to keep your hand, be prepared to suffer."

He watched her darkly, still cradling his hand against his chest.

"I've already suffered. I can put up with more abuse if it allows me to keep my hand."

He might hate her by the time she finished with him. Mistrust her more than he already did. So be it. She couldn't offer him soothing words or false hope. That wasn't what he needed. She could offer him what skill she had, try to make amends for ruining his life.

After a knock on the door, Fong entered with the slipper tub she used at sea. The crewmen filled the tub, glancing at Oliver but not saying anything. They'd all served aboard vessels where a man losing a hand or leg was just another day on the water.

"First, we're getting you out of those clothes. You're likely carrying a boatload of vermin with you."

"I'd rather someone else bathed me."

"I'm not giving you a choice."

She knelt at his feet, breathing shallowly from the rank odor of his unwashed body as she removed his boots, then she stripped his clothes from him, cutting his shirt off with her hunting knife. Even so, he shivered and drew in a sharp breath when his hand was jostled.

There was none of the playfulness of the last time, when he'd undressed her before they set out for their rendezvous in the woods. It seemed like a lifetime ago, almost as if they were two different people. Maybe they had been.

With her assistance he stepped into the tub, his injured hand resting on towels on the chair she placed alongside him. She worked soap into a cloth and bathed him. He leaned back, his eyes closed, and let her serve him, until finally he cracked an eye open and croaked, "At least if I die, I die clean."

She ignored this, silently cutting his hair and beard as close as she could. After drying him off and wrapping him in a blanket, she called in the crewmen who'd been waiting for her. They took the tub and the filthy water out, Fong's usually impassive face carrying a frown as he looked at Oliver, but he left and returned with the supplies from the galley and clean cloths.

"Sit at the table. Are you hungry?"

He shook his head.

"I have no appetite."

"You're fevered. After I see to your injuries, you will try to eat some broth. Nothing heavy yet, but you need to keep your strength up for what lies ahead. Now, place your hand on the table."

He did as directed, and she set some shears and her knife alongside his hand. His glance skittered across the blades.

"Hold extremely still. I can either tie your arm down, or call Fong back in to keep you from moving."

"The marshal insisted on tying me before he branded me," Oliver said, looking deep into her eyes.

"I told him I wouldn't move, but he did not leave me a choice. Do not cut across—" He swallowed. "I want to see it. Every day, I want to be reminded of what happened to me."

Mattie suppressed the shudder running down her spine, holding his gaze with her own.

"I cannot risk your jerking under the knife."

"I will not flinch."

He couldn't promise her that, of course, but she honored his bravery.

"Look away then. It will help me concentrate."

She wiped her knife and the shears with a vinegar-soaked cloth, then put his hand palm up against the table atop a cushion of clean rags. He turned away from her and she snipped at the befouled bandages. The oozing wound made her swallow bile. His hand was hot and puffy with infection, just as she'd feared. She took a deep breath, and her razor-sharp hunting blade flashed out, slicing through the swollen flesh, pus and corruption gushing out in its wake.

He made a guttural sound, and a quick glance from under her lashes showed his face was bleached white as a fishbone as he gripped the chair with his other hand, his knuckles cracking under the strain. But he didn't move, and she worked swiftly, taking fresh vinegar-soaked cloths and using them to press gently around the burn and her cut, pulling out the poison, draining the wound. She followed it with warm compresses soaked in the strong tea.

"The doctoress told me tea helps heal burns, and it can draw out infection as well. I don't want to bandage it yet. Let the compresses work."

He nodded, and they sat in silence. She was afraid, afraid in a way she never had been before. If he started talking, would his words gush out covered in poison, hatred and disdain for her for not being there for him when he needed her most, when she'd given her word?

"Captain—"

"I will give you laudanum. It will help you sleep," she babbled, trying to stop him from saying words she'd never be able to unhear.

"No. Laudanum makes me sick to my stomach. I will manage."

Now she felt worse than ever. She couldn't even offer him relief from his pain.

Useless.

She replaced the compresses with fresh ones, and examined his hand, far less swollen, but still reddened and inflamed. Worst of all, the fingers were curled in and stiff.

"Open your hand. Go slowly."

He gritted his teeth and his fingers twitched, but she stopped him from doing more.

"Stop. You'll tear the skin open."

"It's like a claw," he said in a low voice.

"One step at a time. First we keep you alive, then we deal with…with the rest. Will you eat something?"

"I just want to sleep," he said wearily.

She nodded and helped him into a clean nightshirt, enveloping him in folds of cotton.

"Mr. Turnbull loaned this," she said, rolling up the sleeves. "Given the difference in your sizes, I thought it might not be too uncomfortable."

He looked at her, a tired frown on his face, and she could see he was barely keeping his eyes open. She helped him into her bed, and within minutes he was out, his wounded hand resting atop the covers.

All around her were the sounds of the *Prodigal Son* under sail, the music of her life for so many years. Tonight it brought her no pleasure. A ship at sea depended on the wind and current as much as the skill of its crew, and the sounds only reminded her of her failure to get to this man who depended on her, who had trusted she'd arrive in time to save him.

She grabbed one of the pillows from the bed and settled into a chair alongside him, keeping watch through the night.

Oliver didn't remember the rest of the voyage. The illness brought on by his ordeal in Florida raged through him, almost as if his body had been holding it at bay until he was safe. There were moments of lucidity, or maybe those too were fever dreams. Joe Carpenter holding him down while Mattie cleaned his wound. Someone screaming. There was a night where he opened his eyes, disoriented and scared, thrashing, until he realized he was being held in strong arms and a voice whispered in his ear, "Hush now. Go back to sleep."

He thought broth was dribbled into his mouth, water—he remembered water, clean and cool and tasting of lemons—but even that couldn't put out the fires in his system.

The worst of the fever nightmares involved Turnbull and the captain, Turnbull's rumbling voice telling her the hand needed to come off, and the captain cursing the mate and ordering him from her cabin.

The next time he woke, he was flying, flying away from the ship. Then he realized he was in a sling being lowered into a boat. He shivered as the salt spray soaked his blankets, but he was lucid, for now, and as he was carried onto a wagon ashore he knew they were going to Mattie's home. The sun rose over the pink manor, warming it, making it glow like roses in the dawn.

"You're awake, then? Thought our next task would be to shovel the dirt over you, boyo."

Oliver turned his head slowly on his stiff neck. Daly sat in the wagon with him, grinning, his red hair poking out in spikes from beneath his cap.

"Cap'n said when you woke you'd be parched. Here, sip this. Slowly now, I have no need to see you spew all over my shoes."

It was the lemon water, and he gulped it, and would have taken more if Daly hadn't removed the flask.

"The cap'n rode ahead to the house to make sure all is in readiness for you. Believe me, we had our ears blistered with promises of what would happen to us if we didn't treat you like spun glass."

The wagon was padded with palm fronds covered with a section of canvas, and they rustled beneath him as he shifted. Holt was at the reins, taking his time so as to not jostle the patient.

None of that mattered, because Oliver had confirmed what truly mattered. He still had his hand. Daly pretended he didn't see the moisture leaking from Oliver's eyes and wordlessly passed him a rag clean enough for him to dry his eyes and blow his nose.

"What is that song you Englishmen sing in the Royal Navy?" Daly asked. "The one about oaken heads or somesuch?"

"Do you mean 'Heart of Oak'?"

"Aye, that's the one. That's you, my lad. A heart

as solid as those navy ships. What you did is all the talk on the streets. We know what happened to you in Florida Territory. The islands have been buzzing with it."

They did not know what happened to him. No one knew of the daily brutalities he witnessed, the degradation of people whose owners claimed they were childlike and docile and needed to be kept in bondage for their own good.

They did not know, but they would.

CHAPTER 25

OLIVER BLINKED HIS EYES OPEN, staring at the high ceiling above his head, disoriented as to his surroundings. A child sang about meeting a band of angels. He hoped it wasn't a portent.

"Mister, there's a bird here who thinks he a cat, but if'n you want to see him, you got to wake up."

Oliver cleared a throat dry as parchment.

"Daisy?"

He turned his head carefully, but at least it no longer felt like it was floating off his body. He remembered the fever climbing after he was taken to his room in Mattie's house. There were moments he recalled—opening his eyes to see her in the chair beside him, insisting he drink water. He remembered too the fever breaking, the sweat soaking his nightclothes, and her wiping him down with cool cloths.

That had not been a dream. He was awake now, desperately thirsty.

"Careful, that parrot cat likes to bring mousies and leave'm for you. See, I made you a drawing."

He picked it up with his left hand, which had a tremor to it but was strong enough to hold the piece of paper she passed him. On one side was a list of household supplies in Wellington's neat writing. On the other was a pencil drawing of stick people, and a black blob up in the air. He suspected it was supposed to be the aforementioned parrot cat. In the corner of the drawing was written "Daisy." The *s* was backward and the flower over the *i* resembled an insect track, but she'd written her name.

It was Captain St. Armand who'd said they couldn't help them all, but they could make a difference for some. The proof sat next to him, safe, cleanly dressed, her hair braided and her cheeks plump from good food.

"Mister! Mister! What wrong with you?"

The door flew open and Mattie rushed in, sword in one hand, pistol in the other, her eyes wild as she scanned the room for danger. She only lacked a knife between her teeth to look the complete pirate. Oliver wiped his streaming eyes on the sheet and took a gulping breath. He saw relief flow over her like a cool shower as she said, "Daisy, wait for me outside the door."

"Aye, Cap'n," the little girl said, bare feet pattering across the floor.

Mattie closed the door behind the child, then placed her cutlass and pistol on a table before moving to his side, putting a hand on his forehead. She poured him a cup from the pitcher beside his bed and supported his shoulders while he drank. It was cool and fresh, and so welcome it nearly made him cry again.

"Do you remember anything since you arrived here?"

"Bits and pieces," he croaked. He took another sip, clearing his throat. "I remember you wiping me down when my fever broke. Was that last night?"

"Yes, but you have been here for four days."

"Days? I thought it was yesterday that we arrived. No wonder I'm so parched."

And no wonder she looked worn to a nub if she'd been with him the entire time.

After he drank again she helped him out of bed, but fortunately he did not need her assistance to manage the pot she retrieved from underneath.

He felt more human then, able to focus on her with more attention.

"I want to go home."

"If I put you on a boat now you'd be dead within a fortnight. Sooner, I'm guessing. Sit, I'll send Daisy for breakfast," she said, walking to the door.

"No cabin boy?"

She jerked and looked back over her shoulder at him, and the look on her face was one he'd never seen before. Wary, almost vulnerable. Even in Florida, disguised as a slave girl, he'd never lost sight of her being the captain. She would have had an insulting comeback to his question, a smart answer to put him in his place.

"No, no cabin boy. Wait here."

It was an unnecessary command. He was still limp as a piece of seaweed washed ashore, and he dreaded unwrapping his hand. It throbbed, but not like before. He had to believe just being away from the miasmic despair of the Nassau County Jail sped his recovery. He thought about hobbling over to the window and looking out over the water to reassure himself that he was far from the Florida coastline, but Mattie returned, followed by Joe Carpenter carrying a tray.

"I wanted to see for myself that you was still among the living, Woodruff."

The freeman looked more piratical these days, decked out with a golden medallion at the end of a heavy chain and a wicked-looking knife on his hip. But what was truly different about him was his demeanor. After being surrounded by slaves in the county jail, Oliver saw how freedom affected a man in every way. Joe met his eyes directly without his own glance looking down. He wasn't trying to be self-effacing, to disguise himself so as to not bring attention to his person or his actions.

More than anything else though, it was his air of confidence. On their first meeting Joe had displayed courage and anger, but with wariness, like a creature freed from a trap. Oliver couldn't compare what he'd suffered to what the slaves experienced every day of their lives. His life would never be like theirs. But his experience in Florida had taught him things he'd never thought to learn, sights he could never forget.

If he was going to make a difference, he'd bring those lessons to his writing.

"My coat!" he said to Mattie, struggling to sit up. "I had papers inside my coat!"

"They're safe," she said, as Joe placed the tray down and exited the room. "The coat's a lost cause, but we found the papers and the bits and pieces you had on you."

He worked his way over to the table and just looked at the food. Broth, rich with chicken and vegetables, fresh biscuits so light they nearly floated away, and a small dish of custard with a sugared top. There were orange sections and tea with honey, and he nearly burst into tears again at the sight of it all, so simple, yet so welcome.

But when he reached for the spoon, he stopped, and

stared at the food.

"You have to let me feed you," she said. "It's necessary if you want the food inside you, and not down in your lap."

"I have to become accustomed to using my left hand."

"No. You will allow me to feed you. That's an order." She brought her chair next to him and dished up the soup. "Now, stop glaring at me like a brat and open wide."

He wanted to glare at her, but the food smelled too good, and with her aid he made short work of it. But he hated the helplessness of his situation.

"Time to take another look at your hand."

His muscles tightened at the thought, but he nodded, and she left to fetch her supplies. He tried to move the hand within its bandages but stopped when the pain seared across his palm.

Joe followed in the captain's wake, carrying a can of hot water. It was worse today, because he knew how much it would hurt to have his burn treated, but Oliver gripped the table as Mattie unwrapped the wound.

"Better, but still healing." She delicately poked at the flesh below his thumb and he tried not to whimper when she attempted to straighten his cramped fingers.

"We need to deal with this, but the most important thing is keeping the wound closed."

By the time she finished he was sweating heavily and did not argue her order to return to the bed.

His first visitor was Roscoe. The parrot flew into the room, fortunately without a mouse in tow, and landed on the bed, walking up the covers with a rolling gait reminiscent of Mr. Nash after the grog ration. The parrot peered at Oliver, cocked his head as if trying to place him, then whistled.

"Poor baby! Poor baby!"

"I'm doing better. Don't throw me out with the dead mice yet," he told the bird solemnly.

"Give Roscoe a kiss?"

He scratched the bird on its head and Roscoe purred in satisfaction before walking all over the bed, investigating it carefully. Then he flew behind Oliver's head to perch on the bedrail, muttering to himself as he watched the patient.

Various shipmates wandered in and out when he was awake. Nash was sharing some town gossip when Daly dropped by with a draughts board he plopped down atop the covers.

Once the quartermaster left, Daly leaned forward.

"We're not aboard ship, mate. What d'you say we make this game more interesting?"

"I suspect 'more interesting' is a euphemism for 'let's wager coin on this.'"

"Not sure what 'yoofumissing' means, but aye, the game's more fun when there's more at stake."

Oliver had found his money with the other possessions he'd left behind when he went to Florida. It seemed so long ago.

"I thought the captain was going to send us all to Davy Jones' locker," Daly said.

Oliver raised his head and looked at the Irishman sharply, but he had his eyes glued to the board, his nimble fingers jumping a piece forward and relieving Oliver of another of his men.

"Squalls and headwinds like I've seldom seen this time o' year battered us on the journey to New Providence. I've been on this ship long enough to see

Captain St. Armand laugh during a hurricane that had hardened salts puking their guts up and praying for mercy. I've seen him thumb his nose at not one, but two *Costa Garda* sloops pursuing us. But I have never heard such cursing from the captain as I heard on that voyage. We could see it was eating him alive, the delays in getting back to you."

He shook his head. "But there are some things even bloody Captain St. Armand cannot command. Only a real arsehole of a lubber would hold a grudge over the wind being in the wrong quarter."

He looked at Oliver genially as he collected his winnings.

"I had more sympathy from the parrot," Oliver grumbled.

"He's a birdbrain, matey. You're not, or at least I don't think you are."

CHAPTER 26

"**M**ATTIE! WAKE UP!"

Her eyes burst open and she leaped to her feet, knife in hand, breath heaving in her chest. Oliver lay in bed, pushed up on his good hand. He looked at the chair next to him, the quilt crumpled on the floor.

"You slept here, still."

She nodded. She'd spent every night by his side since Florida.

"Bad dream?"

Mattie sheathed her knife and ran her hands through her hair.

"Once I wandered away from my mother in the market. In the dream I looked around for her, but never found her, no matter how hard I looked."

"But you found her."

"She found me."

Mattie never forgot that day in Marigot. Her *maman* thrashed her for wandering away, then hugged her fiercely like she'd never let her go.

"Nearly dawn," she said, looking at the veranda. In the pre-dawn glow she saw him sit up, wrap his hands around his knees.

"It's early yet. Don't rush off."

"Get dressed," she said, leaving him before her heart overruled her sense.

She spent more time than usual dressing, fretting over her clothing choices like a young maiden. She chose buff moleskin trousers of the newer style, with a vertical flap buttoning in front. As a concession to the climate she left off her coat, dressing in a linen shirt and a pecan-brown waistcoat over it, but the shirt was open at the neck.

Roscoe rode on her shoulder when she returned, and the bird eyed the naked man struggling to get into his trousers.

"Big pike!"

"Thank you for that compliment. Now shoo," Oliver said, waving the bird away.

Roscoe settled himself on the perch Joe had made for him, dangling from the rope and whistling to himself.

"Poor baby, poor baby."

"If that concern is for me, I am doing much better, thank you. Except that I'm holding conversations with a parr—cat, so I may be losing what's left of my mind."

Mattie smiled, then stepped forward. "I'll help you dress—"

"Stop coddling me!" he snapped. "I am not an infant and I can manage for myself!"

Well! He *was* feeling better.

"Have at it." She leaned against the table—taking her knife out and pulling a stone from her pocket—and began honing the edge while she watched him from beneath her lashes.

His mouth was a grim line of determination, and he managed to get into the loose duck trousers the sailors favored, even fastening them with one hand. The shirt was more of a challenge. He pulled it over his head, buttoned it, but the sleeve flapped over his left hand since he could neither roll it up nor fasten it.

He looked at her in exasperation, and she walked over and rolled up his sleeve.

"No, you are far from an infant," she said gently. "And there's nothing wrong with getting an assist until you're healed."

"I'm tired of this, tired of not being able to use my hand, tired of being tired!"

"Hold that thought. The real work begins today."

He held onto the chairback, slipping his feet into the leather sandals he'd purchased in the market weeks back. She didn't have to say anything about him still being weak, it spoke for itself. However, being dressed appeared to help him feel less like an invalid. What he needed most of all was more food and moderate exercise. She sent Daisy, who'd been waiting outside the room for her commands, and the child ran off to get a footman with their breakfast. There were crisp strips of bacon, shirred eggs, slices of guava, and plenty of coffee. Thick slices of toasted bread arrived buttered and spread with marmalade.

They ate in silence until the first edge of hunger was gone and the coffee did its job.

"Thank you," he said.

She looked up from her coffee.

"I didn't make this. Ella did."

"I doubt it was Ella who thought of sending food a man could eat with one hand."

She didn't say anything to this, but poured them each more coffee, then fetched her medical supplies and shooed Roscoe away when he came to investigate.

The bird pronounced her a scrub and flew off in search of Daisy, mice, or both.

Mattie unwrapped the bandages. The hand was clean, the skin pale but pink with health. She took some sweet oil and poured it into her hand, working it well over her fingers and palm, then took his hand in hers and gently massaged more oil into it. She avoided the scar with its letters clearly legible, the thin line of her cut beneath them like an underscore. As she worked she concentrated on massaging his fingers loose from their cramped position, stretching them without stressing the wound.

She worked in silence, the only sounds were his small grunts as nerves and muscles that had been neglected and abused were called upon once again.

"I think"—he gasped—"I think that is all I can handle for now."

"Open and close your fist."

He tried, but he couldn't fully close his hand. Mattie said nothing but reached for a clean cloth, wiping off the excess oil. She fetched a paper and pencil while he sat there, staring down at the brand on his hand.

"Write your name."

When he tried to grasp the pencil, at first it rolled out of his hand. He picked it up again, his brow furrowed as he attempted to position it in his fingers. Finally, he let it fall.

"I cannot."

"You cannot today. You will tomorrow."

"What if I cannot tomorrow?"

She made a rude noise that brought his head up.

"What if Blackbeard decided it wasn't a good day to pillage the Carolinas? What if Henry Morgan thought himself too tired to rob the Spanish? What if

Bartholomew Roberts was a weakling who'd rather die of old age than go down in history as Black Bart, the scourge of the Leeward Islands?"

He looked bemused at her analogies, then with a small smile looked down at his hand.

"With examples like that to live up to, how can I fail?"

"Indeed. Think less like a milksop and more like the pirate I know you could be! Now, pick up the bloody pencil and write something!"

He picked up the pencil with his left hand, positioning it against the crook of his right, where the thumb and fingers met. Sweat popped out on his forehead, but he closed his fingers enough to write shakily on the paper before him.

Mattie couldn't see what he wrote but noted his smile of satisfaction as he folded it and put it in his pocket.

"What did you write?"

"I will show you someday. Maybe. Another piece of paper, please."

He spent an hour practicing loops and swirls and letters, until Mattie told him to stop and stretch.

"You're as pallid as a squid's arse. We're going out."

"*Are* squids' arses pallid?"

"Don't try my patience, Woodruff. Get your hat."

It was a perfect day for strolling on the sand, and she could see the sunshine and fresh air was better than any medicine for Oliver. They talked about inconsequential things—the activities of the sailors, new words Roscoe learned from Daisy…and vice versa…how the child and her aunt were fitting into the household.

"Mrs. Oldman and her daughter moved to Jamaica,

so Ella's our cook now," Mattie said. "She's butting heads with Wellington, which is entertaining to watch."

"They don't get along?"

A smile lifted the corner of her mouth.

"Don't tell anyone, but I suspect those two are scrapping because they're attracted to one another and don't want to admit it. Ella doesn't trust men, not after the way she was used, so if Wellington wants this to advance he'll have to work for it. He does spend part of each day teaching Daisy her letters, and that's winning him some approval, but it will take time."

They did not discuss Oliver's experiences in Florida. Most importantly, they did not talk about themselves. They did not talk about the future. It was too much like a reef. If they didn't navigate with the utmost care, they could be smashed to pieces.

Her heart could be smashed to pieces. She feared it was inevitable, no matter what choices they made. She would put it off as long as she could.

CHAPTER 27

DAISY AND ROSCOE JOINED HIM as Oliver sat at his desk that afternoon. The bird kept trying to take his pencil and eventually was banished to the captain's room. Daisy fetched her own pencil and he worked with her on forming her letters, both of them doing the same exercises.

"Your writing look like mine," she said critically.

"We're both improving with practice, child."

He did not know if the memories would ever fade, but he feared it would be too easy to slip back into a comfortable routine and put off the unpleasantness of documenting his travails in Florida. Now that he was healing, recovering his strength and not in danger of keeling over dead, a new passion burned within his breast to tell his story. The abolition societies sent speakers around Britain, raising funds and raising awareness of the plight of slaves. A writer's efforts could go where a speaker could not, traveling by ship and mail to readers far away. When he'd spouted off platitudes and arguments in Manchester, he'd only been repeating what he'd heard. Now he brought experiences to the argument. No one could tell him it was exaggeration or a lie. He'd seen it, lived it. It was branded in his flesh. That was the most powerful argument there was.

He'd also be naïve if he didn't acknowledge what Mattie pointed out in the tavern weeks back. He was a white man, and a man of status and privilege, allowing him access to society that Mr. Turnbull or Joe Carpenter or Cicero Holt would never have. It allowed him to enter parlors whose doors would be shut to a bastard colored woman dressed in men's attire. Mattie would be viewed as a novelty, but the only way she'd be taken seriously was at knifepoint.

That night he joined Mattie in the dining room. It was just the two of them, with some new faces waiting table.

"Adam moved to the governor's mansion, replacing one of the staff who left for England."

He looked at his food in bemusement.

"Fried chicken?"

"Ella's specialty. I like it because it can be eaten with one's fingers—as far as I'm concerned, it's the only way to eat fried chicken. Just be glad it's Wellington's afternoon off and he's not here to see it. He sticks his nose in the air when we eat 'picnic' food for supper."

The chicken was delicious, and he could manage it with his injured hand. In addition, there were slices of yam and molasses pone, hush puppies, ale to wash it down. Even though the menu had been deliberately chosen to facilitate eating with his fingers, he used his knife and fork, pleased with the returning dexterity.

He was still tired, but it was a good feeling, a feeling that he was tired because he was gathering his strength. After supper she had him practice picking up individual grains of rice from a pile on the table, shifting them to another pile while she quietly sat and read shipping periodicals.

At bedtime Mattie massaged more oil into his hand, as she did each morning, and he went through the stretching exercises she'd shown him.

He pulled back his hand, flexing it, closing it. A breeze ruffled the light draperies at the door leading to the veranda, and he looked out at the starry night before he looked back at Mattie.

"There were days in that cell I would dream of fresh air and seeing the stars, and I'd dream of simple foods, nursery foods like toasted bread and cheese. But most of all, I'd dream of you."

She looked away from him.

"I failed you," she said in a low voice. "I promised I would return to save you. I did not."

It was the truth. He knew he'd been chosen because he was necessary but expendable. And yet, here he sat, fed, clean, healing. Most of all, he was with her. He put his left hand atop hers on the table.

"Look at me."

She brought her gaze down to their joined hands first, then up to his face. She appeared worn down, the air of command she carried about her person tarnished.

"Am I an automaton, incapable of deciding for myself what I want to do with my life? You gave me multiple opportunities to leave, Captain. You cannot take all of this on yourself. As you have pointed out, I am a man, and I am able to choose my destiny, for good or for bad.

"We need to talk, Mattie, talk about us. There are things I did not say in Florida…"

She pokered up, but he would not be deterred. As she rose to leave the table, he grasped her wrist. Even on his best day she would have been able to break his hold, but she didn't resist.

"Talk will not fix anything, Oliver. Talk will not give you back the weeks you languished in that jail. Talk will not repair your hand."

He released her and pushed himself to his feet. In the silence of the night he stroked down her cheek with the knuckles of his right hand, the hand she'd fought to save and heal, and she lowered her eyelashes, covering her expression. She was correct. There were times when words could not be said, when words would not fix what was broken. A kiss though...

He moved closer and she stood still, almost as if she was afraid, afraid to move, afraid of what they might have, afraid of what was lost. But he wouldn't let her run, and to capture her he lowered his head and lightly moved his mouth across hers, relearning the contours of her lips, the soft exhalation of breath as she opened to him. He could think himself a wordsmith, but actions said so much more. He angled his head to deepen the kiss. She was quiescent, not the assertive lover he'd come to cherish, but as he took his time, not hurrying, she softened in his hold, and she crept her arms around his back to hold him closer.

At her small noise he pulled his head back. Tears trickled down her face, leaving tracks that shimmered in the light, and he gently thumbed away the moisture. She looked at him in horror at the weakness she showed.

"Don't worry, my love. I'm here. I'm safe."

She tried to pull out of his embrace, but he wrapped his arm around her and held her to his chest. That brought more tears, but it was soundless crying, and he wondered how often this strong woman had had to cry in silence, unwilling and unable to let her emotions show in front of others. So he let her cry it out because it'd been a long time coming, he knew, and if he could do nothing else for her, he could hold her as she wept, rocking her gently in his arms.

Eventually the well was emptied, and they stood there in silence. She cleared her throat, but her voice was small and clogged when she said, "If this ever leaves the room, I will run you through."

"It is only what I would expect from the fearsome pirate St. Armand."

He knew now they had time ahead of them, time for talking, and for more. But he still had healing ahead of him as well, strength to regain, so when she pulled from his embrace he kissed her on the forehead and let her slip away in the night.

CHAPTER 28

AFTER DAYS OF GOOD FOOD, rest, and exercising his hand, it didn't surprise her when Oliver said during luncheon, "I want to go to town."

"The governor would rather you didn't," she said calmly, buttering her bread. "The Americans are unhappy one of their prisoners disappeared, and since he's an Englishman and a known agitator, they suspect he might be somewhere in the islands."

"I am not afraid of the Americans."

"Believe me, they're far more afraid of us invading Florida than we are afraid of them causing trouble in the islands. However, I want to maintain my good relations with the local authorities, so you'll do as I say and stay here for now."

He set down his fork, looking at the implement he'd used almost unconsciously, a marker that he was mending and his hand was returning to full strength and dexterity.

"If you're finished, we're going for a walk, and then a swim."

She rose and left him there, taking the steps two at a time up to her room. She knew she was avoiding him, avoiding the questions he'd ask her. She grabbed toweling and met him downstairs, heading off toward a secluded cove. The tropical water beckoned, and Mattie turned from taking off her boots to see Oliver, his eyes closed as he lifted his face to the sky.

"I covet the sunshine," he said softly. "We take so much for granted in our lives, don't we?"

He opened his eyes, the blue silvered by the sunlight, the burnished hair gleaming with renewed health, and when he held out his right hand to her, she reached out and took it, turning it over in the light.

The tender skin was pale, and the "SS" brand stood out clearly beneath his thumb, and below it, the thin line of the scar where she'd cut him.

"This will never fade."

"Nor should it," he said. "Over time the remembrance of what I saw might fade, but this will always be there to remind me."

He brought her hand to his lips, kissing it and startling her. He stepped closer, wrapping his arm around her and holding her to him, his hand cradled in hers.

"I haven't been fair to you, Mattie. I've judged you harshly. You don't deserve that."

She closed her eyes and leaned against him in the sunshine. She would always think of him this way, her golden man.

"There are those who'd tell you what I deserve is to swing from the gallows."

"They don't know you. Not like I know you."

He nudged her chin up and she opened her eyes to see him looking at her tenderly. She took her hand, the hand that had doled out pain and misery and bloodshed over the years, and she traced his firm lips, his chin, memorizing the details of his face.

She knew what had to be done, but for now she savored the moment, and the sunshine, and him. When he brought his lips closer, almost questioning after she'd been so diligent about avoiding him, she answered by bringing his head to hers for a kiss.

The warmth from his mouth flowed through her like the tropical sunlight, reaching into the dark corners of her soul, lighting her heart. If she could not give him forever, she could give him these memories.

She lovingly removed his clothing, and he returned the favor, and they silently slipped into the water of the cove to embrace again. No words were spoken as they bobbed in the aquamarine warmth, their bodies slick and slippery as they explored each other. It was as if Oliver was relearning her, what made her gasp and shiver, what touches she craved. She relearned him as well, the hard angles and jutting hip bones, the line of hair shining in the sunlight as it arrowed down to his hips, his shaft rising strong and ready for her touch. He leaned her against a sun-warm rock, waves lapping at her ribs as he bent his head to taste her, suck her.

Her breasts, too often confined and hidden, swelled at his touch, the nipples hardening, welcoming his hands and the sunshine he carried with him. Oliver was all she had ever wanted in a man—strong, handsome, intelligent. He was the man she'd never known she longed for. One who was steady and capable, who put others before himself.

She knew she shouldn't do this, that the best thing to do would be to cut herself off from him, make it easier to let him go—as if that were possible—but she'd been a pirate too long, too used to satisfying her hungers and desires without thought to tomorrow.

Like buried treasure, the memories would be there for her to uncover and savor. She couldn't have him forever, but she too could have these moments.

She maneuvered him against an outcrop of rock where he was mostly out of the water and she ran her hand over his chest with its light scattering of hair, smoothing it over his belly, exploring the delineation of muscle and bone at his hips. His lips were pressed together and sweat gleamed on his neck and forehead, not from illness, but from the tension of her explorations. He didn't say anything, but she knew he wanted her to hurry. She could tell from his body's response, the moisture seeping from the head of his cock. When she put her hand beneath his balls, cradling him, then stroking up to spread the moisture from his body over her hand, he spread his legs wide, his hips rising.

"Please, Captain—"

His mouth looked so pretty when he implored her, and other parts looked pretty as well, so pretty they deserved a kiss. She leaned down and took him in her mouth, and his hips jerked off the rock as he swore, using one of Roscoe's favorite words. She couldn't say anything about his expanded vocabulary because she was busy, and he seemed to be enjoying her ministrations.

Mattie was enjoying herself too. Satisfying bed partners of either sex was a skill she'd honed over the years, but with him it was a new experience. She thought about him when he wasn't in her arms, and when he was in her arms, she thought of nothing but him. With others she'd been desired. With Oliver, she was cherished.

When he pulled her up and nudged her legs apart,

she opened her eyes as he paused at her entrance. He was backlit by the sun, glowing with health and vitality, and she tipped her head back and took him inside her, all of him, savoring their connection.

She'd injured him, yes, but she'd also brought him back, and she could take satisfaction in that. And satisfaction was what she had as he worked her with strong, steady thrusts. All her senses were alive as she cherished the moment, the memories they created— the taste of the salty sweat on his neck, the lap of the warm water, the sounds he made as he pushed her to completion, the slick feel of his hips where she gripped him, and finally, the explosion of color behind her eyelids when she climaxed in his arms.

He followed her a moment later, calling out her name, clutching her curls in his hand and holding her, embracing her. A flock of pigeons disturbed by the humans whirled away. She watched them as he gasped, his lungs working to pump air back into his strong body, a body no longer in need of her healing.

Dear heaven. She clutched him to her. *So this is what heartbreak is. And sacrifice.* Putting the one you cherish before yourself, wasn't that was love was? She'd never thought it would be her lot. She was quick and clever, too clever to fall in love.

But there were some blows even Captain St. Armand wasn't quick and clever enough to dodge.

Everything took on a special glow for Oliver that night. Some of it was the feeling of being himself again, regaining his normal good health. But mostly it was a feeling of rightness as he looked at Mattie across the table. They'd enjoyed a fine supper, laughing and exchanging childhood stories.

"So your childhood wasn't as bleak as I feared?"

She shook her head, her black locks glowing in the candlelight. She'd washed her hair earlier and didn't slather on the pomade she normally used to keep her hair close to her skull, instead lightly working it with her coconut oil. Now the soft curls sprang out from her head, corkscrewing with life and vitality, inviting him to wrap them around his fingers, to hold her still for his kisses, which he'd done during an afternoon of lovemaking back at the house. Her amber skin had glowed against the white linen and she was a goddess, strong and powerful, so he worshipped her, lavishing kisses along her arms, her legs, laving her breasts with his tongue in the manner he knew she loved.

Her words brought him back to the present.

"No. I had good friends. The vicar's daughter and I were childhood chums, playing pirate, of course, and when her family moved away from our village I was devastated."

"What of your parents? You never talk of them, but I've heard tales from the men that you're not the first Captain St. Armand to helm the *Prodigal Son*."

"Once I took command of the vessel it was a convenient name to use. A bit of mystery never hurts when one's establishing a reputation in these waters. I have returned to my family for visits, but I'll always have some sand in my shoes bringing me back here. But tell me more of your youth, Sunshine. You sound like an absolutely beastly brat, especially to your sister. I believe that boy and I would have done well together as playmates."

"No doubt you would have been right there, helping me catch frogs to put in her bed. But I do not want to discuss the past, Mattie. I want to discuss the future. Our future."

Her eyelids fluttered down, veiling her expression as she took a sip of her wine.

"Your future is to return to England, to the life you will make for yourself there. I am not a part of that. I am not the girl you marry. I'm the adventure you had, the wild island girl you'll talk about in your club when you're an old man reminiscing with other old men.

"No, before you tell me I'm wrong, think about this carefully. Think about introducing me to your friends in Manchester. Think about taking me to church. Think about introducing me to your mother, and your sisters, and the men who depend on slave cotton for their mills."

"I told you, it will be different when I return."

"That is why you do not need me dragging you down. You can accomplish so much, Oliver! Napoleon said he feared newspapers more than bayonets. You can make that happen. You can bring the truth of slavery to light and people will listen to you. I belong here, with my ship. Here, where the men of the *Prodigal Son* accept me."

He rose, grasping her arms and pulling her to her feet.

"The men accept you as their legendary Captain St. Armand. Would they accept you as the woman, as Miss St. Armand? Would they accept her command of the ship? They call you 'sir' because it's easier for them but I want all of you, not only the capable captain, but the woman, the one who likes pink flowers and parrots and who smiles at my jokes. I love the woman and I love the captain. I love your softness and I love your strength, Mattie St. Armand, and I want you for always."

He pulled a paper from his pocket.

"This is what I wrote, that day when you made me pick up the pencil and try again. I've kept it with me ever since."

The paper was crumpled and worn, but she unfolded it like it was the finest parchment. Inside was scrawled in a barely legible hand, "My captain."

"Oliver—"

"You know this is the right thing, Mattie. You know we belong together." He got down on one knee, holding her free hand while the other clutched his note. "Will you marry me, Mattie St. Armand, and make me the happiest of men?"

She looked down at the paper, swallowed once or twice, and then brought her gaze to his.

"If you are certain this is what you want, Oliver, let me sleep on it and I will give you my answer in the morning."

He saw something in her eyes then, resolution, determination, and his hopes rose as he smoothly stood. Roscoe flew to his shoulder, a weight he'd become accustomed to, the bird looking down at Mattie from his perch.

"Pretty captain."

"Yes, she is," he said softly. "The prettiest captain afloat."

Hand-in-hand they walked upstairs, and Oliver placed the protesting parrot in his room, closing the door and window to the veranda. In Mattie's chambers he found her looking out at the dark ocean, her arms crossed over her chest, her head bowed. When she turned to him he fancied he saw the gleam of tears in her eyes, but then she blinked and smiled at him, and he forgot everything else. It wasn't the usual sardonic lift of her mouth, but a smile full of tenderness.

He hoped it was a smile full of love, but he could take it one step at a time. One did not rush. He'd learned aboard ship that patience was a sailor's skill, understanding the vagaries of the wind and the sea and waiting until the optimum time to hoist sail or bring the vessel about.

"You appear pensive."

"I am relieved, relieved that you are fully recovered from your wound and you are ready to return home."

"*We* are ready to return home and *we* will tell people the truth," he said, looking down at the brand.

She walked over to him and he smelled the sandalwood scent of her soap, the coconut oil on her hair, fragrances that would forever be Mattie to his senses.

"It is part of who you are now, Oliver."

"So much of what I experienced is part of who I am now. This mark, a parrot who thinks he's a cat. My captain."

She lowered her lashes and took his scarred hand, kissing it softly, then folding his fingers over the kiss. The fingers moved easily now, his writing firm again, thanks to his hard work and her ministrations. They'd done it together, and he wrapped his other arm around her, holding her to him in the night.

Together.

Tonight he wanted to show her, he had to show her, together could be for a lifetime, so he took her to her bed, and tenderly undressed her, laying her back against the cool sheets.

"When I see you like this," he said softly, gazing

down at her, her eyes as deep and dark as the water lapping at the shore, "it makes me want to kiss every inch of you."

"Nothing is stopping you, Sunshine," she said huskily.

He joined her and propped his head on his hand, gazing down at her body. She called him Sunshine, but she was the ocean. Dark and mysterious in the night, warm and embracing in the sunlight, always shifting and changing, holding secrets and danger in her depths.

One could not hold the ocean, or know it in its totality, but he could explore it, and he did, starting at her slender ankles and working his way up her long legs, legs that could wrap around him and hold him within her body. He showed her with his mouth and his hands how much he worshipped her. He took his time, moving from her legs and her strong thighs to her arms, her neck, the sensitive skin below her jaw.

"You have made me a new man, Mattie," he whispered, and she slowly shook her head on the pillow, her tongue darting out to lick her lips.

"You were that man all along. You just needed to find him."

She pulled his head down and her mouth opened beneath his like a flower, filling him with sweet nectar kisses, exploring him at her leisure.

He placed his hand between her legs, felt how ready she was for him, how her desire flowed out of her like the honey of her kisses. He'd told her his hand was returned to full dexterity and now he demonstrated, stroking his fingers inside her, finding the sensitive spot that with the right pressure would make her tighten and gasp and call his name as she climaxed.

"I would have waited for you," she said when she caught her breath.

"Coming first is the captain's prerogative."

She purred with satisfaction at his words as she lay back, relaxed, ready for him again. His balls were so tight he feared they'd explode, but she was worth waiting for, worth all the tension and frustration and anticipation she brought him.

"I love you, Mattie St. Armand," he murmured as he slipped inside her, into her welcoming warmth. Her eyes, black rimmed with blue fire, widened at his words and his joining himself to her. Then she tightened her arms about him and he began moving within her, smoothly at first, reveling in the strength he brought to her, propping his hands alongside her shoulders so he could gaze down at her beauty as he worked himself inside her, the curls sticking to the sweat across her brow, the flush of color through her cheeks and neck. This, this is what coming home was. She was all that was in his heart, and he knew winning her would not be easy, but what prize worth having was?

He knew, even if she did not realize it yet, if she would not say the words back to him, he knew she was not only the right woman for him, he was the right man for her. She did not need a pirate by her side, she needed someone who would balance her, light to her dark, open where she was closed. He knew himself now, better than he ever had, and she would complement him as no other could.

"My captain," he whispered to her again, and her eyes closed as she tightened around him, holding him, embracing him as his own climax built within him, rushing out from his body, pouring all his love into the captor of his heart and of his desire.

CHAPTER 29

M ATTIE REINED IN THE GELDING she'd hired from the livery stable and gazed on the Tudor manor. The dark house was imposing, even when lit only by starlight. She thought of the people living there. Complacent, snug in their beds, no doubt thinking themselves safe from housebreakers in the night.

She tied the horse far enough from the house to not alert anyone, then sneaked around to the back, eyeing the easiest spot for entry. As the wind shivered through the trees, she pulled her coat closer. It had been easy to forget how miserable northern England was but the chill kept her alert, reminding her she needed to grab what she could and be gone before anyone in the house realized they'd had an unexpected visitor.

Tightening her gloves, she climbed an oak next to the upper windows. A large branch jutted out, just the right height for a nimble pirate, well-experienced in climbing the mainmast. The window was unlocked and slid open easily, no telltale squeaks to give her away.

However, she had not counted on the guard dogs.

"Hush. Down, Bijoux! Yes, I love you too. Stop licking me, Bebe."

A mild "koff" alerted her to the presence of another person, and she turned slowly, her arms full of wriggling, squirming, ecstatic, frantic bichons.

"I'm home."

"I can see that, Mathilde," her mama said dryly.

She set down the bouncy white dogs and walked over to embrace the woman who, if she hadn't carried her in her body, was still the one who'd carried her in her heart through the years. Mattie towered over her, and when warm tears pattered the back of the woman's neck she said nothing but hugged her tighter.

"I am so tired, Mama."

"Shhhh…whatever you need to tell me can wait. For now, let me get you settled for the night."

"I was going to take some of my things and leave."

"*That* is not happening. Home is where we take you in no matter what adventures you've had. You will stay here, Mathilde, and we will sort this out, together. You are too old to keep running away," she lovingly scolded.

"Is Papa here?"

"He is in London on business. I expect him back tomorrow."

Mattie sighed and nodded. Her plans to flee, to hide in some port city and lick her wounds until she figured out what to do with herself…they drifted away like the evening mist. For now, she would let her family take care of her, a luxury she'd denied herself for too long. The *Prodigal Son* was safe under Mr. Turnbull's watch, and all her other problems were across the sea.

It did not alarm Oliver to awaken alone in his bed, as he expected to see Mattie at breakfast. But the dining room was empty, a letter propped at his plate. He stared at it, at his name on the front, a chill running down his back. No one was in the room— no footman nearby, no food, no Wellington or Daisy or crew from the ship.

He broke the seal.

Dearest Oliver—

By the time you read this, we will be underway and I will be gone. You are more precious to me than anyone, my Sunshine, and that is why I am leaving you. You will make a good life for yourself. You do not need me weighing you down, holding you back from accomplishing great things.

I couldn't say the words to you before, but I cannot leave without saying them here so you understand: I will love you always and forever, Oliver Augustus Woodruff. You are the finest man I have ever known. Try to think of me fondly in the future, if you think of me at all.

Mattie St. Armand

"You bloody coward!" Oliver snarled to the empty room as he crushed the note in his fist. He stormed off to the kitchen, where he found the staff, silently and apprehensively watching him.

"She told you not to say anything, didn't she?"

Wellington looked at the others, then stepped forward.

"Yes, Mr. Woodruff. The captain gave us strict orders."

Daisy was next to Ella, clutching her aunt's skirts, eyes wide. He remembered the sights the child had witnessed in her short life, the harm an angry white man could inflict. He took a deep breath.

"I do not hold any of you responsible for her actions, Wellington."

"The captain left with Mr. Turnbull in the middle

of the night."

"Of course. This was all planned well in advance."

The butler looked at him with understanding, and sympathy.

"My instructions are to continue to assist you, for as long as you wish to be our guest."

Oliver smiled, but when he saw the child's eyes grow even wider he knew it wasn't a friendly expression.

"I will not be staying any longer than is necessary to secure my passage to England."

He turned on his heel to leave, calling over his shoulder, "I've lost my appetite, Wellington. Have a horse saddled, I'm going into town."

The first stop was the docks to confirm for himself the ship had sailed. He was a fool for not anticipating this. Of course she'd abandoned him. She was a pirate, flying false colors when he told her he loved her, when he asked her to marry him, to make a life together.

When he went to Government House the governor's secretary told him they would do all they could to help him return to England. No doubt they were anxious to have him off their hands and away from Florida and the angry Americans as quickly as possible. A letter of credit at a local banking house allowed him to return to the docks to book passage on the next packet to Liverpool, but it would not sail for three days, the purser of the *Rose of Sharon* told him, maybe longer if the storm brewing kept them in the harbor.

Even the weather conspired against him.

He returned to the house and sat down to luncheon, restored to good health thanks to that lying, deceiving jade he could not live without, and if he was going to catch her he had to keep his strength up. He put his head in his hands, thinking about all he'd have to do in England.

He whipped around in his chair as he heard a familiar voice croon, "Poor baby, poor baby."

"Roscoe?"

The parrot perched on the sideboard, nibbling on a dish of nuts. Wellington entered the room, clearing his throat.

"The captain's instructions were that Roscoe belongs to you now, Mr. Woodruff. You're to take him with you to England."

"I am, am I?"

But when the parrot flew to his arm and nuzzled him, he sighed and scratched the bird where he liked it. Roscoe purred like the cat he thought he was.

"Roscoe loves captain."

"So do I, dammit, though I suspect that makes me a bigger bird brain than you. Too bad you're not a bloodhound instead of a kitty. I could use you to track her scent."

CHAPTER 30

O LIVER TRUDGED UP THE WORN stairs of a Liverpool boarding house smelling of cooked fish and wet woolens, but it was near the docks and relatively clean. He'd become a familiar sight to the sailors and the residents of the city, the parrot perched on his shoulder as he roamed the taverns and shops asking for word of Captain St. Armand.

His hand ached from the damp as he clutched the latest letter from his mother and his uncle ordering him home to Manchester. They couldn't force him and he wasn't returning, not until he knew what happened to Mattie.

So he spent his days buying drinks for sailors and talking with merchants. The bad weather that kept him in port in Nassau meant the *Prodigal Son* set sail from Liverpool before he arrived. Some said it was in Belfast, some said the ship was en route to London, others said Calais, and one salt thought he heard talk of New York.

He unlocked his door and struck a Congreve match, then paused. His first thought was his life had indeed changed if he could now identify the sound of pistol being cocked in the dark.

"Finish lighting the lamp, Mr. Woodruff."

He did as told and turned to the intruder.

"Pretty pirate! Pretty pirate!"

"Silence, you annoying chicken," said the man sitting in the chair next to Oliver's bed, one booted ankle casually propped over his knee, a pistol pointed at Oliver's heart.

"He's not a chicken. He's a cat."

Roscoe flew to his perch, muttering "buggering beets" and turned his back on the humans in the room. The stranger ignored the bird and said, "I have heard you are seeking Captain St. Armand. I am he."

"Bollocks. You are not *my* Captain St. Armand."

The man raised his brows at Oliver's emphatic *my*, but there was no mistaking who he was. The resemblance was startling—blue eyes with deep lines at the corners, sharp cheekbones, hair the color of polished ebony, but his was threaded with silver at the temples.

"I know who you are. You're the bastard who fathered Mattie!"

"I am quite legitimate. It is Mattie who's the bastard."

He raised his pistol when Oliver advanced on him with his fists clenched.

"Do not be foolish, young man. I am holding a loaded pistol. If you have spent any time at all around my daughter, you know better than to attempt anything."

"I don't give a damn for you and your threats! You threw your child out of your home, driving her away and sending her to sea. She may indeed be a bastard and not white enough to be part of your family, but she is a better person than you will ever be!"

"*That* is what she told you? What an interesting version of the truth. Mathilde always did tell a good story. Regardless, she is home now, warmly embraced in the bosom of her family, and she made it clear to me she does not want to be disturbed. You would do well to return to your own family and the running of Moffett Mills. Do not look so surprised. Did you think I would not thoroughly investigate a man whose existence is upsetting my daughter? You should be careful, Woodruff…"

"I know, I know, I could fall down a well, accidentally stab myself in the back, roll off a cliff… I've faced more fearsome pirates than you," he sneered, crossing his arms over his chest.

"You *do* know Marauding Mattie."

"That is why I will not stop until I find her. You tell her. Tell her we have unfinished business."

"You claim we threw out Mathilde because she did not fit in with our family," her father said, not unkindly. "Can you possibly believe she would fit in better with yours?"

"I am so tired of hearing this argument," Oliver walked into the room, ignoring the pistol. He was weary to the bone, weary of fighting for someone who kept pushing him away, but he knew she loved him. She said so, and he had to convince her that they needed each other now, just as they had in Florida.

"Mattie is strong enough to face the future," he said, looking into St. Armand's face, so similar to hers. But his was a lighter shade, faded from years under a less intense sun than what he'd encountered in the Caribbean. Eventually, Oliver's browned skin would fade as well, while Mattie would always carry her island heritage with her.

"Now that she's back in England, and you say welcomed and safe, what will she do with herself? Where will she go?"

"That is not your concern."

"You are wrong. When you love someone, you worry about them, and you do not stop worrying simply because they are far from you. Tell her that. Please."

Mattie's father sat, watching him, and Oliver knew he was evaluating him and his words. The pistol never wavered, but he stood and motioned for Oliver to back away from the door.

"For heaven's sake, I'm not going to attack you!" he snapped, raising his hands in the air to show he was weaponless. St. Armand's eyes were drawn to the letters branded on his hand, but he only said, "I have not lived this long, Mr. Woodruff, by taking these things for granted."

The pirate paused near the door and with his other hand pulled a card out of his pocket.

"You will not find Mattie in Liverpool. Write to her, care of my man of business in London whose address is on this card, and she will receive the letter. Whether or not she responds is up to her."

He put the card on the table and left, closing the door behind him. Roscoe mumbled an obscenity and tucked his head down, settling in for the night on his perch.

Oliver put down his hands and walked over to the battered table where he wrote at night. The white pasteboard shone in the lamplight like a beacon calling him to action. He picked it up, looked at it, then tapped it against the wood. He prided himself on having the right words, knowing what to say, how to communicate clearly. This could be the most important letter he'd ever write, and he had to choose with the utmost care what to say in it.

Finally, he smiled and sat, pulled out a sheet of stationery and dipped his pen. When he was satisfied with the message, he sealed it to send out in the morning's post, then packed his valise to return home.

.

CHAPTER 31

"I DO WISH YOUR PARROT WAS not quite so ill-mannered. Today he said, 'Good morning, dollymops!' to the girls."

"I am afraid I was given custody of the animal too late to have a positive effect on his vocabulary, Mother. For now, I suggest not taking him out in public, or having him about when you host the Ladies' Society for Relief of Orphans. It's probably better that way."

"Those women could use some excitement in their lives, Oliver. A salty parrot may be just what we need."

Henrietta Woodruff watched his hand as he poured himself more tea. When she had first seen the brand she cried, and he assured her it no longer hurt. That was a small lie. Sometimes there a twinge, sometimes an ache when the weather turned, and it was a constant reminder of what he'd gained, and lost, on his voyage to the West Indies.

He was home, but it would never be what it once was for him. A reminder of how he'd changed was calling on the tailor to make new jackets, jackets accommodating his more heavily muscled arms and back, his trimmer waist. His experiences in the islands and in Florida had hardened his body, and hardened his resolve.

The writing was happening, slowly, and for every two steps forward he'd have to take a step back, but he was putting it all down on paper—his experiences, the notes from jail, the comments of Joe Carpenter, Ella, Cicero Holt, and the others. He kept his writing about Captain St. Armand in the masculine to protect Mattie, but also to not distract from what he had to say. Even here at home he put her at risk if he wrote about her slave stealing operation. He would find himself asking, "What would Mattie do?" as he wrote of his adventures, but since that often ended with someone bleeding, he kept her involvement in the story to a minimum.

His mother's usual routine was to have a tray in bed for breakfast, but since Oliver's return she'd sought opportunities to spend time with her only son. She fussed over him, and he let her because he knew it made her happy. His uncle Braswell "harumphed" a great deal, and his sisters cooed over the bird, who adored the attention. Truth be told, it cheered him to know he still had a place here.

"You have told me much about Roscoe and your travels, Oliver, but you have not talked to me about your young lady, not really."

Oliver smiled to himself to hear Captain St. Armand described as a "young lady" but it was a fair question. If he was ever to find and woo Mattie, it couldn't simply be about his wants and desires. He was part of a family, and it appeared she was as well after his meeting with her father. Marriage brought families together and he owed his mother some understanding of the young woman she would be expected to welcome as a daughter.

"Mattie—Mathilde," he corrected, "she is not like any woman you've ever met."

"I gathered that from Roscoe's vocabulary," his mother said dryly as she spread marmalade on her toast. She wore a morning gown of a soft periwinkle blue, her white hair covered by a fine linen cap, the lappets framing a face softened by time, and very dear to him. "Tell me about her. Your Mathilde St. Armand."

"I hope she will someday be mine. She is the bravest and most intelligent woman I know. She's a leader. People trust her and put their lives in her hands. Her crew, the Anti-Slavery Society, the people she rescues, they have good cause to trust her."

"You said she is a colored woman and," his mother's voice lowered, "a bastard." She set her bread down, hesitated, but then looked straight at him. "This is not what I envisioned when I thought of you marrying and bringing a woman into our home. I fear it will be a misalliance you will regret."

"I will have no other. I love you, and I love our family, but she is the woman I love, Mother." He said it firmly, facing the issue head-on.

His mother still looked troubled, but said only, "Are you going to the mill today?"

He set down his fork and looked into her eyes, a softer, grayer version of the eyes he saw in his own mirror each day when he shaved.

"I need to meet with Uncle." He hesitated, then continued. "It will not be an easy meeting."

People who did not know his mother well thought her quiet and biddable. She was quiet, yes, but she had a spine and an inner core of fortitude which had stood her well through her years of widowhood. Now she looked at her son and said, "You are a man grown. You want to do what you think is best, but you also have to weigh the consequences. However, I will support you in whatever decisions you make. I have confidence in you."

"No matter what happens, you and the girls will always be safe and provided for. I've already made provision for that."

"Yes, but we are not the only ones involved, Oliver."

Her words echoed his own thoughts and he rose from the table, his appetite gone. He gathered his coat, hat and gloves. The weather reflected his mood, gloomy and gray, but he always walked to the mill unless the weather was truly horrific. It cleared his head and was valuable thinking time.

He had received no answer to his inquiry except for confirmation from her father's solicitor that the letter was delivered. He'd even traveled to London to see if he could bribe information out of the man, but he was close-mouthed about his client's affairs.

"Good morning, Mr. Woodruff," John Hobbes greeted him as he entered and removed his outer gear. "You received a note today from a gentleman wishing to meet with you at your earliest convenience. He's staying at an inn in town and asked me to give you this."

Oliver looked at the letter in puzzlement, then opened it.

"Huntley? I do not know a Huntley, do I?"

"That would be Lord Huntley, a baron from Lancashire. He's active in shipping and canals, and I understand he's an investor in rail lines as well. Good English family, solid stock."

Oliver raised his brows as he looked at the secretary. Hobbes was a diminutive man, balding and bespectacled, but his mind was like a calculating machine and he forgot nothing. It had been a fortunate day when Oliver hired him.

"Wealthy, is he?"

"Loaded with it."

"Very well, Hobbes, set up a meeting for two this afternoon."

"You are scheduled to meet with your uncle at four," the secretary reminded him.

"I have not forgotten." Oliver sighed. "I will be in my office until then."

As the afternoon shadows lengthened, Oliver looked down at the papers on his desk, wearily rubbing his hand across his eyes. His office was piled with ledgers and correspondence, neatly organized by the admirable Hobbes. It wasn't that Moffett Mills wasn't making a profit, it was, and a tidy one. The issue was how to make that profit without cotton from the United States.

The steady thrum of the looms was the music of his existence, the clatter of the machinery reminding him of all he had, and all he could lose. The sharp scent of the dyes, the taste of dust in the back of his throat from the motes hanging in the light filtered through the skylights, it was who he was. His office looked out over the floor and the machines ruling his life, but machines also giving him the fine food on his table, the fine fabrics on his skin. If he wasn't careful, his incendiary writing would be as much of a danger to these mills as a careless fire.

At least his uncle no longer accused him of harboring Chartist sympathies. He approved of Oliver coming to the mill each day, and to Oliver's surprise, they managed to talk without it ending with raised voices. Indeed, he respected Braswell's business acumen, his strong connections with the local merchants' associations and the Conservatives.

"Good. You don't have the chicken with you."

The other Captain St. Armand, Mattie's father, stood in his office doorway, looking out over the mill floor with interest. He was dressed in the first state of fashion, but with a flair that would make him stand out on the streets of the city. His gray beaver hat, tail coat in wine broadcloth with a high, black velvet collar, and pale gray trousers and boots were all perfectly correct. Then one noticed the black silk neckcloth was held in place with a sizeable sapphire, a matching stone drawing the eye to his earlobe. These clothes could only have come from London's finest tailors, and the trim older man did them justice.

He also carried a cane, which Oliver suspected contained a blade. He did not appear to need it for stability. He paused as he removed his hat, his eyes narrowing at Oliver's waistcoat. The brown satin with gold stripes was one that belonged to *his* Captain St. Armand. If her father demanded it back, he'd have a fight on his hands.

"What are you doing here?"

"According to your Mr. Hobbes, we have an appointment."

"You? You are Huntley?" Oliver said, rising slowly to his feet.

"I am Robert St. Armand Huntley. Mattie never told you, did she?"

"I am beginning to believe there's a great deal Mattie did not tell me, and I'm wondering how much of what she did say was the truth."

Huntley came into the office, closing the door behind him.

"That is an issue you can discuss with her, if she ever responds to your letter."

"She received it then?"

"Indeed she did, and—let me make sure I am quoting her correctly—you are a 'bloody buggering beet who deserves to be keelhauled and marooned on a desert island.' If those aren't the exact words she used, you at least have the gist of it."

Oliver's lips curled up at the corners. His letter would not have received that reaction if she did not care. He wished he could have been there when Mattie read it. On the other hand, if he'd been there, he'd likely be missing his spleen now. He motioned his guest to a seat, and returned to his own chair as Hobbes opened the office door, alarmed as he looked at the visitor.

"I'm sorry, sir. He must have slipped right past me."

"Good to know I still have a skill or two," Huntley murmured.

"Thank you, Hobbes. That will be al— Do I have any rum here?"

Hobbes looked startled, but capable man that he was he said, "Not that I know of, sir, but we do have some whisky from over the border."

"Excellent. Bring the bottle and a pair of glasses, and then I'm not to be disturbed."

"Your uncle—" He stopped when he saw Oliver's expression, and only nodded and said, "Of course, Mr. Woodruff."

Huntley was looking at him with approval, and Oliver didn't know if it was because of the anticipated whisky or the way he'd issued orders. Nor did he care. The *Prodigal Son* may have been the domain of the captains St. Armand, but this was his mill, and he was in command here.

"This appears to be a thriving operation, Woodruff."

"What do you want?"

Huntley's brows rose at the brusque language.

"I am out of patience with members of your family, Lord Huntley. What is the reason for your visit? Is it to assure your daughter that I have a life without her, that I am not wasting away for the love of a pirate?"

The last words came out louder than he intended, for there was a startled "clink" of glassware as a large-eyed Hobbes waited in the doorway, balancing a tray with a bottle and crystal tumblers.

"Just set that down."

"Yes, Mr. Woodruff."

Oliver wondered as he poured whisky for himself and his guest whether gossip would spread back to his uncle, then decided he didn't care. That's what came from consorting with ruffians. He passed a glass to his guest.

"Please don't label my daughter a pirate," Huntley said mildly. "It makes me want to shoot you."

"Of course it does. I would expect nothing less," Oliver said, taking a generous swallow of the whisky.

Huntley adjusted the crease of his trousers and leaned back in the chair, his hands clasped over the top of the cane.

"I have come here today to discuss business with you. Not to talk about Mathilde."

"Business?"

Oliver paused, then set the tumbler aside. As always, it benefitted him to keep a clear head around members of the St. Armand family.

"Yes. The business of cotton. I do not need to tell you that eighty per cent of the cotton coming into Britain is from the United States, and slave-grown."

"Certainly I know that. Look around you." Oliver waved his hand. "This mill runs on American cotton. I cannot afford not to buy it from the brokers in New York."

"There are other sources of cotton. In addition, I would think looms and machines can be retooled and refitted to handle other fabrics."

"Even if I had the money to buy new looms, there's still the issue of costs for the raw goods. Shipping cotton from the east is far costlier than shipping across the Atlantic."

"Quite correct. What you need is an investor. Ideally, what you need is an investor who owns his own ships. I have ships. You have a mill that needs material. I can bring cotton from India and Egypt and eliminate some of the costs of brokers. You would produce a singular fabric, specializing in quality over quantity. You might even refit your mills for other fabrics. The point is, you do not have to abandon your family or your workers for some quixotic quest against slavery. There are other sources of cotton besides the United States."

Oliver was stunned at the proposition and worked hard not to let it show. He wasn't a pirate with years of experience lying to people, and he needed to think about this. It could be the answer he'd sought, but it could be a trap.

"Moffett Mills is owned by my family. We have never taken in outside investors."

"And yet, you want to make changes here you

know your family cannot support, not wholly, and
certainly not economically. With an investor and a
shipping company as part of your expanded operation
you can grow. At this time you're limited, unless you
somehow come into a substantial amount of money.
As much as your mill is currently thriving, I do not
see that happening for you, with or without my
investment."

He looked satisfied and smug, and Oliver wanted
to punch him, but if what he contemplated came to
pass, brawling with Huntley would not be a good
beginning to their relationship, business or otherwise.

"You are avoiding discussing the one thing—
the one person—we both know is at the heart of
this, Huntley. Does it matter to you that Mattie St.
Armand abandoned me in the islands and has nothing
but insults for me now? For if your offer is contingent
on her approval, I cannot discuss it further. I will not
dance to her tune, or yours."

"The offer is from me alone, and it is genuine. No
one will believe a mill can wean itself off American
cotton until someone makes the effort to do so. I
confess, there would be pleasure for me in tweaking
the noses of the mill owners and others who say it
cannot be done. Stirring things up is an enjoyable
pastime. I have a personal stake in this because of my
daughter, but I would not propose this arrangement if
I did not believe it will be profitable."

Huntley rose, and finished his drink, setting the
glass down with a clink.

"If you want her involved, getting Marauding Mattie
aboard this scheme is for you to handle, Woodruff. I
cannot solve all your problems for you."

Oliver rose to his feet.

"Send me your proposal and we will talk. I am contemplating your offer, with or without Mattie's involvement. She has to make up her own mind as to what she wants to do with her life, and it would be a foolish man who thinks he can steer her in a direction she does not wish to go."

Now Huntley looked at him with clear approval and took Oliver's hand in a firm grasp when he offered it for a handshake.

"In that case, I wish you luck in *all* your endeavors, Woodruff. Good day."

The very efficient Hobbes had the door open for the baron as he strode out, and Oliver watched him leave. Even a generation older than them, Huntley drew the eyes of the women on the floor, who nudged each other as he passed by.

"Your uncle?"

Oliver looked at the secretary and said, "Yes, I am ready to meet with him. Sit in on the meeting and take notes, Hobbes. We will have much to discuss."

CHAPTER 32

THE KNIFE HIT THE WOODEN target with a satisfying "thunk," and Mattie picked up the smaller blade. Its lighter weight allowed her to throw with greater accuracy, and this time she hit the drawing of the one-eyed pirate right in the eye-patch.

"Well done. It's reassuring to know that ruffian is no longer a threat to us."

Mattie turned to her stepmother with a grin. "You could take a turn. We could wager on it."

Lydia Huntley shook her head, the ribbons of her Brussels lace cap fluttering in the air of the gallery. She wore a deep blue plaid merino dress, and the spectacles perched on her nose couldn't disguise her keen gaze.

"You were always more skilled than I, Mattie. Come, sit with me."

Mattie rotated her arm, trying to be comfortable in the confining sleeves of her dress. The deep red ponceau wool flattered her coloring, but the current dress designs put a crimp in her range of movement. Nonetheless, she practiced in her women's clothes because when she was home, she dressed for her life as Miss St. Armand. It pleased her stepmama and took the wind out of Caroline's sails when she couldn't make sarcastic comments on her older sister's fashion choices.

A footman entered with a tea tray, setting out fresh scones and currant cakes. Mattie cleaned and put up her weapons as her stepmama prepared a plate for her. They sat in silence, enjoying the moment of quiet, a shared jewel of peace between the two of them. It had taken Mattie shipping off to foreign lands to appreciate how fortunate she was to have people who loved and cared for her. Once upon a time a quiet cup of tea might have had her itching to run off and see what kind of trouble she could raise. Now she treasured the opportunity, especially as her siblings were away from home and it was just the two of them.

When she was a little girl she'd been the focus of her father and stepmama's attention. Then they started having babies of their own. Babies born in wedlock. Infants as white as the lace on their christening gowns.

Mattie adored her sister, and later, her brother, but she knew everything had changed. She saw the fuss the ladies in the village made over the babies, how they were instantly accepted, where the same ladies hadn't all been so welcoming toward the darker, illegitimate child. The love her parents showered on her didn't change, but she had to share it. It wasn't enough to ease the hurt from the rest of the world reminding her she was different from her siblings.

But having her mama to herself now was like those halcyon days when they first came to Huntley from the islands. Caroline was on a shopping expedition with a family friend—a wealthy widow who bred the bichon puppies Mattie'd romped with growing up. The two were no doubt raiding and pillaging

London's finest shops.

Nicholas was with school friends at a house on the Cornish coast, and she wondered if they'd hear he was picked up by excise men for smuggling. Actually, she hoped that might happen. Tall, solid, resembling his Huntley ancestors more than his father, Nicholas was a placid young man most interested in maintaining the estate. He needed some adventure in his life before he settled down to become a country gentleman.

That made her think of another fair-haired Englishman who longed for adventure before he settled down. She frowned at her cup.

"I'm growing old, Mama."

"Aren't we all? The key is to do it with grace, and not become a bore."

"I don't think you need to fret about boredom, especially with Papa around."

"He does enjoy adding excitement to people's lives, even now," she said, delicately sipping from the Wedgewood cup. "Talk to me, daughter. Tell me why you're so set against your young man. It's clear you have strong feelings for him."

Mattie turned the cup in her hands, staring into its shimmering depths as if the tea held the answers. "You can tell, can you?"

"Your language when you received his note was… impressive, even for Marauding Mattie. But I can tell from your demeanor," she added gently. "You smile, but… Well, I can tell."

Mattie's eyes rose, but her mama sat patiently, not judging, but waiting for her to unburden herself.

"You saw the note he sent me. He called me a coward!"

Mama folded her hands in her lap and watched

without speaking.

"You agree with him?"

"I think a better question is… Do you agree with him?"

Mattie pushed back her chair. She couldn't think when she was sitting, and the gallery had been her haven on rainy days, space where she could run back and forth until she exhausted herself, or practice knife throwing until her arm ached. There was something about the repetitive "crack" of a good knife going where it was supposed to go that helped her think and work off some of her anger and frustration. She returned now to the knives, picking up one of her favorites—the dagger her father gave her for her tenth birthday. She kept it here at the house, a reminder of who she was.

Also, it was just good planning to have a knife in the headboard of the bed in case of attack. "One can never have too many weapons at hand" should have been the family motto.

"You know why I left. I was itching in my skin, skin that's the wrong color for the people here. I had to leave, and you can call it running away if you want, but I called it running to something, running to find myself."

She glanced over her shoulder. Mama's face was shadowed.

"We all love you, Mattie. We always did. Your brother and sister missed you when you left."

"I know. But sometimes love isn't enough. It should be, but it isn't. There's a world out there that's hard on people who don't fit in. In the islands, aboard the *Prodigal Son*, I fit in, far more than I could here."

"And now?"

Mattie set down the smaller blade and picked up her Spanish hunting knife. It was almost a short sword and not at all suitable for throwing, but it amused her to try. It was akin to throwing a hatchet. With this beauty the key wasn't accuracy but impact. To her satisfaction it landed in the target, not in the eye-patch, but in a more dramatic area, quivering between the "pirate's" legs with a satisfying "whap!"

"Oh dear. I trust you were not thinking of your young man when you did that. It could definitely put a crimp in your future together."

Mattie snickered, and retrieved the blade.

"Speaking of futures, the morning's post arrived. You are searching for answers. This may help."

Mattie walked back over and took the card from her mother. It was good quality stock, an invitation for Lord and Lady Huntley, and Miss St. Armand.

"A ball?"

"In Manchester, hosted by Mrs. Albert Woodruff, celebrating the homecoming of her son, Oliver Augustus Woodruff. I don't know Mrs. Woodruff. But if I had to hazard a guess, I'd say she wants to show off her son to the community, and to eligible young ladies, because that's how doting mothers think when their boys reach a certain age. So it's clear one person is interested in getting to know you better, Mathilde, and I consider that a positive sign."

"Or her son pressured her into sending me an invitation."

Mama rose and gave Mattie a hug. Even though Mattie now topped her by at least a head, it felt good knowing she had a safe harbor, someone who would hug her at the end of the day and tell her all would be well.

But her mama was also good at speaking truth.

"Was your Oliver correct when he sent you that inflammatory note?"

Mattie cleaned her knife and put it back in its sheath. One of the first lessons she'd learned at her father's knee was how to properly care for the tools of the trade.

"I have stared down the American Revenue Marine and outwitted the *Costa Garda*. I've fought in dockside taverns and I've kept the fearsome reputation of Captain St. Armand alive across the Caribbean. And now I fear to meet one middle-aged lady from Manchester. Before, only my life was at risk, and that was a risk I was willing to take. Too often, for your satisfaction."

"Now your heart is at risk."

"Yes. Not just my heart, but Oliver's. His future with someone like himself would be safe and assured. His future with someone like me?"

Mama patted her on the arm. Not the weapons arm, she'd been a part of the family long enough to know better than that.

"Mattie, it may distress you to hear this, but as an island girl you're simply not that outrageous or extraordinary. Englishmen have married brides from other lands since Roman times. They brought home Indians, Egyptians, Turks, Spanish, Greek ladies... even Americans. Men have a penchant for returning with souvenirs from their travels."

Mattie eyed her sideways.

"Is that supposed to make me feel better? That I've been reduced from captain of my own vessel to the status of a carved coconut? Or a parrot?"

"All I'm saying is, don't exaggerate the consequences.

Of course, you don't have to get married if you do not want to. You also do not have to run away anymore. You're not a little girl who doesn't fit in. You have carved a place for yourself in the world and your father and I are so very proud of you. Never doubt it!"

Mattie swallowed around the lump in her throat. She knew the choices she made sometimes distressed her mama, who'd tried so hard to raise a young lady rather than a pirate. Her praise and her approval meant more than she would ever have expected it to.

"Your life is what you will make it, just as you always have, Mattie. It's up to you, and maybe Mr. Woodruff, to figure out what you'll do with it."

CHAPTER 33

GASLIGHT LIT UP THE NIGHT, making jewels glitter and white linen shine as gentlemen and ladies exited carriages for the ball. The Woodruffs were well off but didn't boast a ballroom for the grand entertainment tonight, so assembly rooms were hired to welcome home their wandering son.

Mattie stood at the entrance, gazing at the colorful crowd and clutching her fan painted with an island scene of palm trees and flamingoes. It was a gift from her stepmama and complemented her new ball gown from the same London modiste her sister favored.

She bemoaned the style hampering her shoulders but was pleased with her dress. The deep rose shade of the silk skirt made her smile, and the paler blush of the bodice—the same shade as the shells scattered on the beach outside her house in New Providence— made her feel like Mathilde again. As she grew into womanhood she'd come to appreciate the pleasure of being that person instead of the pirate St. Armand. Mathilde had no one looking to her for orders, no one looking to her to save them, no nightmares over the ones who could not be saved or the men who died in her service.

She smoothed down her skirts, lingering over the ribbon knots, the open skirt trimmed in more rose velvet and framing an Ottoman satin underskirt the same shade as the top. A froth of ivory lace flowed from the deep bodice. The dress was cut quite low on the shoulders, barely covering the bullet scar on her arm. She'd considered using paint or more lace to hide the ridge of raised flesh below her neck where she hadn't dodged a dagger quickly enough, but decided against it, just as she opted not to hide the scar on her face. Her scars were part of who she was. Oliver and his mother and the good people of Manchester could accept her in all her glory, or not at all.

Long white kid gloves embroidered in yellow and pink roses covered her arms, and jeweled combs pulled her hair forward, parted in the middle, the curls lapping over her ears. Her stepmama's pearls glowed against her skin. While Mattie had her own jewelry, some of it actually purchased rather than "found," it pleased her to accept the loan of the pearls with their sapphire clasp—a gift from her father to the woman he loved.

She scanned the ballroom as her father adjusted one of his wife's hairpins, whispering something in Lady Huntley's ear that brought a wash of pink to the fair cheeks, but then her father looked at her sharply.

"Is something wrong, Mattie?"

"I thought I saw someone I knew."

"A pirate?"

"No…never mind, I'm probably mistaken."

She turned and saw Oliver staring at her from across the room. He was in a line with an older woman, likely his widowed mother, and a thin and grim-looking man she guessed was his uncle.

But it was Oliver who drew her eyes. His golden head glowed in the lamplight, and she was struck by his demeanor. The cabin boy she'd taken from a brothel was gone. In his place was a man, broad-shouldered and elegant in his evening ensemble. His island tan had faded, but his face and form were honed by his experiences.

"Shall we?" her father said.

She took a deep breath, nodded, and the trio traveled across the floor to their hosts, her gaze never leaving Oliver. His mother watched her, looking more intrigued than horrified, a good start to the evening. The widow wore deep lavender, flattering her fair complexion, and her stylish dress befit the owner of a successful mill. Fine pleated muslin in the bodice framed a mourning locket of gold and onyx, and a cap of violet velvet covered her hair, ribbons in the same shade as the dress dangling over her shoulder.

"Mother, Uncle, may I present to you Lord and Lady Huntley, and Miss St. Armand."

"So pleased to meet you, Mrs. Woodruff. I know you're happy to have your son safely home."

"I am indeed, Lady Huntley. Oliver means the world to me."

Papa picked up Mrs. Woodruff's hand to kiss it and a becoming blush added color to her wrinkled cheeks. Mattie nearly rolled her eyes. Her devastatingly handsome papa felt compelled to prove he still had what it took to make ladies young and old sigh, and her stepmama took it in stride.

"You cannot make a peacock into a house sparrow," she'd once remarked to Mattie, to which her father had said, *"Why ever would you want to?"* as he'd admired his reflection in a silver teapot.

"Miss St. Armand. I am so happy to meet you at last. Thank you for assisting Oliver in returning home to us," Mrs. Woodruff told her.

It was said with sincerity and some of the tension left Mattie's stiff shoulders. "I am pleased to meet you as well, Mrs. Woodruff."

The older woman's face crinkled up into a smile as she patted Mattie's hand.

"I look forward to getting to know you better. Will you and your mother call on me tomorrow?"

"It would be our pleasure," her mama answered for both of them.

Then Mattie came to the person she most wanted to see. In a receiving line they could not say, they could not do, what each wanted. To embrace, to kiss, to tell the other how much was lacking in their lives since their absence from one another.

Or, at least, that's what she thought. Oliver greeted her and her family with all due courtesy, and a genuine smile for Lady Huntley.

"I have heard so many wonderful and entertaining tales of you, ma'am. I suspect raising young Mattie was an adventure in itself."

"Indeed it was, Mr. Woodruff. Thank you for assisting Mathilde in returning home."

His head swiveled back to her, eyes narrowed. "We have much to discuss, Miss St. Armand. You will save the supper dance for me."

"Are you giving me orders?"

"Yes."

Her back pokered up. She did not take orders from the cabin boy, but then she looked down at his gloved hand holding hers, and she swallowed the rash words that almost spilled out of her.

"Until then, Mr. Woodruff."

They continued to greet Oliver's family, his uncle Braswell, stiffly correct in greeting the guests, and Oliver's sisters, barely out of the schoolroom, who giggled at meeting Lord Huntley, made a pretty curtsey to Lady Huntley, and thanked Mattie for Roscoe.

"He is so entertaining!"

"He says the most scandalous things!"

"We want to take him with us everywhere!"

"Roscoe believes he is in command and will rule the roost if you let him," Mattie pointed out.

"Perhaps he truly is a cat after all," her father said with a wink at the girls that had them blushing crimson above their maidenly bodices.

As they walked out into the room, both ladies flanked Huntley, a hand on each arm, and he said, "I am the most fortunate of men, escorting the two most beautiful women here."

He was looking at his wife as he said it, and her mama did look wonderful, her bronze and sage Pekin striped silk gown highlighting her auburn hair and eyes the same shade as the king's ransom of emeralds dangling from her neck. For all Mattie knew, they had been a ransom seized by an enterprising pirate.

Her father turned his head and said to her, "You look absolutely charming, my dear. That gown is very becoming to you."

"How am I supposed to throw a dagger with any accuracy when my sleeves restrict my arms and shoulders this way?"

"I cannot imagine why modistes do not take those needs into account when designing this year's fashions. Ideally, you will not have to call on those skills this evening."

She smiled at that because she knew he was carrying a small arsenal on his person, as he did every day. He'd taught her many years ago, *"Blades are cheap, life is dear."*

"Cap'n St. Armand?"

"Yes?" said two voices simultaneously, but as Mattie turned, a wide smile split her face.

"Titus Waters! But what are you doing here?"

A footman stood next to them, balancing a tray of drinks. His dark face gleamed with perspiration and an answering smile for Mattie.

"I work here, in Manchester, Cap'n. The hall employs me and I am the assistant manager," he said with pride. "We're all pressed into service for a large affair like this," he gestured at the full ballroom.

"Titus worked for me in New Providence," she explained to her parents.

"Mr. Wellington and them, they all fine?" Titus said, his speech slipping back into island rhythms.

"Indeed they are, and when I write him I will let him know I saw you."

He returned to his duties and Papa turned to Mama, inviting her out onto the floor to join in the quadrille. Mattie unfurled her fan, her back to the wall as she watched the dancers on the floor. She saw some women eyeing her and whispering behind their own fans, but that was to be expected. The warm greeting she received from Oliver and his family fueled gossip at an affair like this, and tomorrow she would be discussed in detail. However, having Lord and Lady Huntley beside her was as good as an eight-pounder, blowing holes in any speculation that she wasn't the right social class for a Manchester merchant's family.

Oliver was also on the dance floor, partnering first his mother, then his sisters. They were charmingly unaffected girls, lovely in their figured muslin gowns, the fine fabric a product of the family mills. The ladies were of a class and society with the ones he would have partnered as a young man…before he'd fallen in with pirates.

He'd said he wanted her, but now that he was home, in his natural environment, it made no sense. He did not need her, and she certainly did not need him. She could make a life for herself, as her father had offered her management of their shipping business.

"You are the best qualified person to take charge, Mattie. Your brother will be Huntley, and he'll be an excellent steward of the land. He does not love the sea though, not like you do, and he doesn't have your head for business or your experience."

It did not take Mattie long to think about it. She was ready to turn command of the *Prodigal Son* over to Mr. Turnbull, who wanted to stay in the islands.

So she stoutly told herself she did not need Oliver Woodruff in her life. She did not need his soft blue eyes, or his burnished locks, or his lovely hip bones and muscled chest, or his kisses or his…

She did not need his love. He was better off without her, and while she smiled at her parents and exchanged small talk with the lady beside her, inside she was bleeding because she knew she had to cut it off with him. She would let him make the life he needed to here, without her dragging him down. Her past followed her like a shark. Titus was one reminder. There was also the other familiar face she'd seen—it would continue to happen over time, and each person who knew her as Captain St. Armand would be a reminder to Oliver of the sort of woman he'd married.

The ball was in full bloom and Oliver could tell his mother was gratified at the number of people attending and would pronounce the evening a success. There were fellow merchants and mill owners, some of the local gentry, the bishop and his family, a peer or two. They were the new face of England, the lines blurring as men—and women—found sources of wealth and status, not in land passed down, but in commerce, where bold steps and a drive to succeed could take one far.

Nonetheless, knowing Mathilde St. Armand was the product of an old and well-respected barony, even with her color and birth on the wrong side of the blanket, it would help his mother and his family make room for her in their hearts and homes.

"She is not what I expected, Oliver."

His mother looked up at him as he escorted her to the side where her friends waited to share gossip with her.

"Were you expecting someone who'd swing down on a line from the balcony, clutching a dagger in her teeth?"

"Your sisters were rather hopeful, especially after getting to know Roscoe." She sighed and patted his arm. "I can see though that any thoughts I entertained about your harboring a *tendre* for Miss Langley were mistaken."

He considered Miss Annabelle Langley, a charming young lady who could paint fine watercolors but would be absolutely useless in a knife fight. Then he considered how corrupted he'd become by his experiences in the past year, and it made him smile.

"Frankly, I was a tad surprised you invited Mattie and her family tonight."

"Her mother and father are well-respected, and let us be frank—Lord Huntley would bring substantial connections to our lives, connections benefiting you in business. Miss Langley is all that is charming, but it would not be a marriage advancing the family. It would be a comfortable choice, but not the best one."

"That's a rather...mercenary stance, mother."

"Is it? I suppose I'm thinking about what's best for Moffett Mills, not just what's best for us."

Perhaps his dismissing Miss Langley for not being good in a knife fight hadn't been so farfetched. His mother now...

"Then I look forward to your getting to know Miss St. Armand better. I am beginning to suspect you two have more in common than you know."

He passed her off to her cronies with a kiss on the cheek, and went to track down the pirate in question. She was deep in conversation with his sister Augusta, and he feared for what kind of information and advice Gussie might pick up from Mattie.

"They love to be scratched on the head and enjoy nuzzling..."

He hurried closer to where they stood.

"And don't feed him oranges or lemons, even though he will try to snatch them from you. He's fond of apples."

Roscoe, not men. Much safer.

"Does he really believe he's a cat?"

"All I know is we needed a mouser more than we needed a bird aboard ship, so we've never tried to convince him otherwise. Good evening, Mr.

Woodruff."

"May I take Miss St. Armand away?"

"Only if you promise to bring her back, Ollie. I want to get to know her better." Augusta smiled.

"Good," he said with satisfaction, putting Mattie's hand on his arm and walking with her. She smelled of sandalwood and coconut oil and citrus. She smelled like herself, different from all the other women here tonight with their floral scents.

"I suppose you like seeing me this way, in a dress, like other women."

"Are you fishing for a compliment?"

He turned and looked at her. She wore no paint, her rich skin and ripe lips needing no enhancements.

"Yes, you are beautiful in that dress. You are beautiful in breeches. You are even beautiful knocking me down into the sand. You are always beautiful to me."

She smiled. "I doubt you thought me beautiful when you met me in Mrs. Simpson's parlor."

"On the contrary. You were the embodiment of masculine beauty, and that scared me in a different way."

It was a conversation he could never have with another woman, only with this woman, yet another reason he needed her in his life again. They needed to talk and he needed to breach her defenses, but for now it was sufficient to enjoy the moment. There was a beautiful woman on his arm, he was recovered from his experiences in the West Indies, and the musicians were playing the first notes of the next set.

"Dance with me, Miss St. Armand."

"Orders again," she murmured, but she let him escort her onto the dance floor.

It was a waltz, and she realized as he put his hand on her waist and took her gloved hand in his that this might be one of the biggest mistakes of her life. She loved to dance. She especially loved to waltz. It was the closest she could come to the feeling of flying across the waves, the wind carrying her to adventure. But that only happened when she waltzed with a competent partner.

Oliver was more than competent. He was the perfect partner. The perfect partner for her. He wasn't tall, he might be a smidge shorter, even in her dancing slippers. But he was graceful. She'd seen him move, she knew how he could use his body, and this would be one more reminder of what she was pushing away from her life and from her heart.

But oh, she wanted this! To be held in his arms one more time, to look into his eyes capturing the light of the lamps brightening the room. Waltzing in Oliver's arms, she discovered a closeness she'd never experienced before. There was something beyond intimate in moving around a dance floor, looking into each other's eyes, sharing a moment that despite the public setting, despite their being fully clothed, rivaled all the delicious moments they'd shared together up until this point.

Perhaps too it was because it was a public declaration of sorts. One did not waltz with just anyone, at least not in her mind. One waltzed with a man whom you trusted, one you would let take your weapon hand and hold it, constrain it, yet treasure you.

He held her the correct distance as the music swirled about them, as the colors of the ladies' gowns flashed past her vision. She looked into his eyes and saw he wanted this moment, here, with her. She wanted in turn to say to him that she never expected to find this, to find not just passion, but closeness and caring and consideration. Instead, she let her eyes speak for her, content, for once, to let this man lead her where he would take her, just as he'd led her into his heart and soul.

"We need to talk—"

"Not tonight, Oliver. Not now. This is your celebration, your mother's celebration of you. I do not want to spoil that."

His brows rose, and she took a moment to admire his face, to drink him in. He was clean shaven, and he smelled of cedar and himself. She inhaled the masculine scent, the scent of him, to hold in her memory and to treasure. All too soon the dance finished, as waltzes do, and he escorted her back to the side of the room because he'd promised his sister the next dance.

"We will talk," he told her sternly. "This is my mother's night, but you and I have unfinished business, and I will not let that go by."

"Your ordering me around is getting to be a habit, cabin boy."

He stopped walking.

"Not tonight. Tonight I am Oliver, and you are Mathilde. I will say what I must, and you will listen. We will be a man and a woman, not commander and crew, not separated by color or birth or any of those other barriers you throw up between us."

His eyes did not leave hers as he raised her hand for a kiss, then released her.

"Until then, Mattie."

She watched him walk away and unfurled her fan, gently wafting the air in front of her face. It was chill and raining outside, but the room was crammed full of dancers, couples strolling the perimeter, matrons and spinsters exchanging gossip, young men sneaking about for a smoke or a nip of something stronger than the punch. The cold outside reminded her that in the Bahamas right now it was sunny and pleasant.

But it was also lonely. She had the staff at her house, acquaintances in town, but Captain St. Armand did not have friends there, not real friends. Here she was loved, by her family and by Oliver, and his sisters and mother were surprisingly open and friendly toward her. Maybe Oliver was correct and she'd been wrong to think they could not work it—

"Captain? Gentleman asked me to give you a note."

"Thank you, Titus," she said, lifting the paper off the silver salver he held out to her.

She read it, read it again to be certain it wasn't a jest in bad taste, then straightened her back and took a deep breath. Getting through the evening without killing anyone looked like a slim possibility now. Oliver wasn't in sight, which was a good thing, because he did not need to be involved. This was a job for a pirate, not a gentleman.

CHAPTER 34

"I SEE YOU RECEIVED MY NOTE. It was prudent of you to join me here."

Mattie slipped into the room, closing the door behind
her with a soft click. The room was sometimes used
for cards, but now it was largely empty, the darkness
lit only by a low fire. There were two winged chairs
facing the flames, a table for card players, and a larger
table in the shadows near the windows.

"What are you doing at a ball in honor of Oliver
Woodruff?" she said.

Nelson Lowry posed in the center of the room,
looking nauseatingly smug as he eyed her from her
jeweled combs to her slippers, his eyes lingering on
her bodice and the pearls resting there.

"My cousin was invited. She's bosom-bows with
Claire Woodruff and wanted an escort this evening.
Imagine my surprise when I saw a colored woman
dancing with that mill boy. It was easy enough to find
out who you are, Miss—or should I say 'Captain' St.
Armand?" he sneered. "Easy enough too, to expose
you for an unnatural creature, someone who whores
her way around the islands dressed in trousers."

"What is it about stupid men that they always think

a woman acting in a less than conventional fashion is selling her body? No matter." She walked over to the larger table, perching herself on the edge, not an easy maneuver in stays and a ball gown. She swung her foot back and forth as she thought about his threat.

"You will expose me? What will you expose me *as*? Are you assuming the Woodruffs do not know who I am?"

"They may know who your family is, but I saw you, drinking and gaming with low men in that tavern in Nassau. I recognize you now. You were disguised, behaving in an outrageous manner. It was easy to get that colored footman talking about Captain St. Armand in the islands, and how *he* trains blacks for service in English houses, as if we aren't already overrun with enough darkies. And now, here you are, flaunting yourself, dancing with weaklings like Oliver Woodruff. I should tell him, tell everyone, warn them about the disreputable creature in their midst. However, for enough of a consideration, I might change my mind."

She pursed her lips as she thought.

"When you say a *consideration*, I assume you mean financial compensation. I do want to be clear on this. However, as you might imagine, I did not bring a purse of money with me. I did not plan on being blackmailed at a ball."

Lowry looked frustrated now, poor idiot, and ran his hand through his hair. This was clearly not the reaction he anticipated, but he brazened it out.

"You can start by giving me those pearls. We will call it a down payment."

"And if I don't give you these pearls?"

"I will expose you as a deviant—or, better yet, I

will tell Lord Huntley that I will expose his black bastard for what she is. He'll pay well to keep this hushed up."

"*That* is a conversation I would pay to see! But it is immaterial. It's clear you're new at this, so I will explain blackmail and extortion to you... It only works when the person you are blackmailing feels threatened by exposure. I do not find you threatening. I find you annoying."

She gently smiled at him, because he really was an idiot, and soon he'd be a dead idiot. "Let me ask you something, Lowry... How do you intend to back up your threats? Better yet, how do you intend leaving this room alive? Did you bring a knife? Or a gun? Or friends with guns?"

"What?" he said, taken aback. "I don't need a weapon to take on a woman! I certainly don't need a gun!"

"But you see, you do, because while I may not have brought money to this fight, I did bring a gun."

He stared as she reached into her beaded reticule, a birthday gift from her sister, and pulled out a small pistol, a birthday gift from her papa. It held only two shots, but it was sufficient for dispatching vermin.

"You can't shoot me! The noise will bring everyone running!"

She shrugged. "I am certain I can spin a good tale. How about this one? You are despondent because I recognized you as a bumboy who sold his arse to sailors in Nassau. You shot yourself because you couldn't live with the fear of discovery. Better yet, I will tell them the truth—you are a scoundrel who cheats with loaded dice. The shame of discovery tonight caused you to take your own life."

"No one will believe a nigger pirate!" he gasped out.

"Maybe. But you won't be around to see it," she said as she raised the pistol.

"That will not be necessary, Miss St. Armand."

Two men rose from the winged chairs in front of the fire. The speaker was a figure out of a William Blake etching, tall and broad and substantial, a white beard covering his chest. His heavy brows lowered as he looked at Lowry, prepared to rain down fire and brimstone on the worthless sinner standing before him. The man other was Oliver, looking as murderous as she'd ever seen him. It was a good look on him.

"My Lord Bishop!" Lowry squeaked.

"Nelson Lowry," his deep voice rumbled through the room like thunder. "I heard the rumors you were a cheat, but to find you attempting to blackmail this young lady is beyond outrageous."

"She's no lady, sir, she's a pirate!"

"She's my lady," Oliver said, stepping forward, fists clenched. "You didn't check to see if the room was empty, you dunce. Titus thought there was something off about you, and fetched me here before he gave your note to the captain. Since I know you for a lying cheat, I brought a witness. Now you and I will go outside and discuss what happens to swine who insult and threaten my woman."

"Don't risk your hand, Oliver. Just quietly knife him in the guts. You did bring a knife?" she added, just in case.

He flashed her a smile. "Of course. I learned my lessons well. Do not worry about me, I just intend to kick him a few times."

"That's not sporting!" Lowry protested.

"Sporting? You're fortunate I don't knife you simply for annoying my lady. Sporting is letting you live."

"Wait, use these." She rummaged through her reticule and light flashed on the metal as it flew through the air. Oliver caught the brass knuckles neatly, slipping them onto his hand.

"An excellent fit. Thank you, my dear."

"Use the side door, Woodruff," rumbled the bishop.

Oliver grabbed Lowry by the collar, dragging him out of the room. While he attempted to free himself, he was no match for her man, who used a well-placed knee to make the miscreant more tractable. It warmed her heart to see Oliver put his lessons to use that way.

"Are you all right, my dear? Shall I fetch Lady Huntley?" the bishop asked.

Mattie jumped off the desk, taking a deep breath to compose herself and smooth down her skirts. It was probably for the best. While she was prepared to carve out Lowry's liver, it would have been hell getting bloodstains out of the silk.

"No, I am quite well, and involving my parents would make all this unpleasantness too public. That swine's family does not deserve to be dragged into his mess. Thank you for being a witness, though. He should not escape unscathed."

"He won't. You might be surprised by the power a bishop wields in certain circles and at certain clubs. I was pleased at the way young Oliver handled himself there. It's obvious his travels have had a profound effect on him. Incidentally, you look absolutely lovely, my dear. It is a pleasure to see you again."

"It is wonderful to see you also, Bunny."

CHAPTER 35

WHEN OLIVER RETURNED TO THE library the bishop was there, but Mattie was gone.

"She left to find her parents, Oliver. Miss St. Armand is a most interesting young lady."

Oliver paused from sucking on his sore knuckles. He'd passed on using the brass because, despite Mattie's best efforts, it struck him as a bit piratical for his tastes. And there was something deeply satisfying about using his bare hands.

"You approve of her, sir?"

His older cousin, someone Oliver had always considered the stodgiest of individuals (and a little frightening, truth be told), poked at the fire warming the smaller room.

"Miss St. Armand is active in anti-slavery efforts, as is her family. I approve of that. She comes from solid stock, one of the oldest baronies in the north. Lord Huntley has an excellent reputation in business circles as well."

He looked at his cousin with new appreciation. The bishop was fiercely conservative and highly respected, and his approval would go far in helping the rest of Oliver's family, and society, accept Mattie as his wife.

Not that it mattered. The only way he was going to let Mattie go was if she convinced him she did not love him. Everything else was an obstacle to overcome, not an impediment to marriage.

"You understand, sir, my intention is to ask her to be my wife."

"If you marry Miss St. Armand it will not be easy for you, for a variety of reasons. There are many women you could marry who would please your mother and your uncle Braswell."

"She is who I need, sir. I intend to write about my experiences in Florida and the islands and talk about it everywhere. It is time for us to speak up against the evils of slavery, not pretend that our cotton magically appears from across the ocean. Mattie St. Armand would be an asset. Even if that were not the case, she is the woman I love, and I will have no other."

"Best of luck to you then, boy. Winning Marauding Mattie St. Armand is not a task for the faint of heart."

Oliver was startled at the use of Mattie's pirate name, but he had a woman to track down, so he excused himself from his cousin's presence.

But when he returned to the ballroom, she was gone, like Cinderella fleeing before the clock struck her doom.

Mattie shoved the last of her shirts into the valise, the night outside her window reflecting her mood with its chill drizzle dripping from the trees. But it wasn't night any longer, was it? It was an hour or two before dawn, the darkest hour, and she had to make her escape while she could, before she changed her mind and followed her heart and not her head.

A dangerous path, that. She knew what she had to do, the choices she had to make. She'd always known. The brief glimpse of heaven she'd experienced earlier, waltzing in Oliver's arms, laughing, that was eclipsed by what came later.

Her dress and finery were scattered like a silk explosion across her bed, and she was reaching for the last knife to put in her bag when a faint noise outside her hotel room door brought her up short. There it was again. It sounded like—

"Meow."

She eased the door open. Oliver Woodruff leaned against the wall, his knife in his hand, prosaically sharpening a pencil. His weathered seabag was at his feet, and Roscoe perched on his shoulder, his flaming colors a contrast to Oliver's black and white evening clothes.

"Pretty captain! Give Roscoe a kiss?"

Without looking up from his work Oliver said, "Let me in, or there will be a scandal, Miss St. Armand."

"I am not afraid of scandal!"

"I wasn't thinking about you when I said that. Imagine what your parents would say if they found a man pounding on your door at four in the morning."

She grabbed him by the arm and pulled him in as Roscoe flapped and squawked before flying over to the bedpost, where he perched on one leg, scratched himself, and looked around the room.

"Nice bawdy house."

"Quiet, Roscoe. What are you doing here?"

Oliver put up the knife and slipped the pencil into a leather case, which he tucked back into his jacket. "You are a coward, Captain St. Armand."

Her hands closed into fists. "I have fought my way

across the islands, I have outrun the best navies on blue water, I have faced down a ballroom full of girls who would knife me and climb over my cold corpse to make a good marriage. No one calls me a coward, you...you...beet!"

"You heard me. Coward. Pusillanimous. Timid. Craven. Faint-hearted. I'm a writer, remember? I have a sufficient vocabulary that I do not have to denigrate harmless root vegetables to say what I need to say. You are brave when it comes to doing what's comfortable for you, but you are not brave enough to risk all on a different goal, a different life. A life with me."

He straightened his shoulders as if bracing for a blow.

"I understand that I am not the sort of man you are accustomed to. I am not a swashbuckler, or a great swordsman, or a pirate like you. I'm just an ordinary man who owns a mill in Manchester."

She stared at him, then grabbed him by the lapels, pulling him closer.

"Are you insane? You are the bravest man I have ever met. Any idiot can stab with the pointy end of a knife and call himself a pirate. Hell, I do what I do for money! I do it because it's personal! You're greater than that. You put yourself in harm's way for strangers, for people some would name the lowest of the low, little better than animals in the eyes of their owners.

"You see this?" She pointed at the crescent at the corner of her mouth. "It's from drinking too much and getting into a stupid tavern fight. This..." She grabbed his hand and held it to her bosom. "This is a badge of honor! You deserve better. You deserve a true lady, one who will bring you respect. All I can bring you is snickers and whispers behind hands.

"I love you, Oliver, but love is not enough. Not in your world."

She almost turned away so he wouldn't see her tears, but he was right. She was a coward. She'd forgotten that with this man she did not have to hide, she did not have to pretend, she did not have to be strong every single moment for fear he would no longer respect her.

Oliver had seen her at her worst, and yet, here he stood, heart in hand, as if she was worth it. In all her life, that was the one response from a man she never expected, never hoped for. She wanted to be feared, she wanted to be respected, she wanted to be desired and admired. She had all that.

But until a floundering Englishman washed ashore in an island whorehouse, she'd never been treasured.

"Well then. If you insist on running off, I'm ready to ship out. You need a cabin boy, Captain St. Armand, and I am yours to command."

She tried to pull back, but he held tight to her hand, and moved in closer to her. She swallowed around the obstruction in her throat.

"You can't do that. You can't just run away from your responsibilities. You're not that person."

"Neither are you, Mattie. That's my point. I'm not the person you think I am capable of being, not without you at my side, at my back, making all that happen. And you want to be there too, otherwise we'd both be happy being pirates for the rest of our lives, sitting on a beach, swilling rum and counting our booty. But we're better than that. Each of us. And together, we're magnificent."

He turned his wrist, holding her hand in his, and raised it to his mouth, kissing the inside, where the pulse beat fast. Her hand, carrying its own scars and calluses and marks from life, from fighting, from hauling ropes and hoisting sails.

"We were both looking for freedom, Mattie. You ran away to be free of a life where you did not think you fit in. I ran away to the islands to find some freedom before I settled into the role I knew I would have to take on. What we both found were people in need, whose definition of freedom was very different from ours, and much more basic. I will never cease to speak of what happened to me, Mattie and there will be danger involved. I need protection. I need a strong right arm at my side and guarding my back, defending me. I need you."

She put her other hand up, alongside his face, where new grooves fanned out from his eyes and alongside his mouth. Lines that had not been there before he met her, when his life was far simpler, and far safer.

"Oliver, I love you so much. You're the sunshine in my life, but I *am* afraid. Afraid to risk my heart, risk that one day you'll have your fill of people making comments, people calling me names, or...or...you'll think I'll run off to sea and abandon you."

"I do not expect you to settle into being a pattern card of domesticity. I know of your father's offer. He and I discussed it at the ball."

"You two men are planning my life for me now?"

"Neither of us is that foolish. But it's an offer strengthening our partnership, your ships, my mills, the ability to obtain cotton from other sources. I don't claim to have all the answers. I just know together we're better than we are apart. Together we can accomplish more. Together we will each have the other half of our soul. I want that. I want that more than I have ever wanted anything in my life. No matter what happens, no matter what the future holds, I want to face it with you by my side, Captain Mathilde St. Armand."

She looked away from him, overwhelmed by the glow in his eyes, the love there for her, for the scarred and scared woman who'd never felt like she had a true home. She sighed, trying one last time to save him from himself, and from her. "Don't you worry I will take the family silver and run off to sea?"

For answer he pulled her into his arms, and she sighed again and laid her head on his shoulder, because he was there, because she could, and because being in his arms was the safest harbor she'd ever known.

"No. I don't worry about you running off with the family silver. I worry you will take the family silver and run off to sea without me."

He put his hands alongside her face, warm against her skin, but not as warm as the look in his eyes before his lips met hers. He kissed her, breaching her remaining defenses, boarding her heart and breaking the locks on the final chest, the one where she kept all the love secured inside that she'd never been able to share, because she'd never found the right man. Until now.

"I will take you with me if I take the silver," she said huskily when she came up for air.

He showed his approval by kissing her senseless again.

"And if we have children, I have to insist that we take them as well," he added.

"Oh very well, I'll take you, and the children, and

the silver."

Then she kissed him, because two could play this game of "Drive the other person insane with longing even though your parents are sleeping in the next room…"

"And the cat. Roscoe has to come with us as well when you run off with the silver, and me, and the children…"

"Quiet, Sunshine," she said kissing him again.

And whatever the parrot saw, he refused to speak of it forever after, except to occasionally mutter "buggering beets" when his master and mistress were caught kissing, as they so often were.

AUTHOR'S AFTERWORD

T HERE WAS A REVERSE UNDERGROUND rail-road where slaves fled from Florida by boat to the Bahamas and Mexico. Florida Territory was the wild frontier—a land of rough justice complicated by questions of jurisdiction between the U.S. Marshals and the local sheriffs. The marshals had the support of Governor Call, and mostly ran law enforcement, when they got paid.

I have taken liberties with details of the history of Nassau County, Florida, and changed the names of real judges, marshals, attorneys, and sheriffs. However, the scenes in the jail, the conditions there, and the punishments meted out to slaves are taken directly from accounts of the Pensacola jail by abolitionist Jonathan Walker.

What happened to Oliver is based on real events. Captain Walker was convicted of slave stealing for trying to smuggle enslaved people to freedom. His story was well-known to northern school children in the antebellum period through a poem by John Greenleaf Whittier, "The Branded Hand." Walker was the only man ever punished in such a fashion in a U.S. Federal Court, and his hand was photographed for posterity. He went on to be an ardent abolitionist and public speaker, showing his branded hand as a mark of courage and commitment. You can read more about Captain Walker's trial in the State Archives of Florida, and you can read his biography on Wikipedia.

For more on law and order (or lack of same) in early Florida I recommend *"A Rogue's Paradise": Crime and Punishment in Antebellum Florida, 1821-1861* by James M. Denham.

Also, "Daniel Green" is based on a real Anglo-African woman, known to history as "William Brown." Brown was a hero of the Royal Navy. Her sex was discovered when she was injured, but she returned to service in the navy and after the war served on merchant ships.

About The Author

DARLENE MARSHALL WRITES AWARD-WIN-NING HISTORICAL romance, mostly about pirates, privateers, smugglers, and the occasional possum. Her home and the setting for many of her stories is North Florida, a land of rolling hills, sweltering summer days, and insects that take no prisoners. She enjoys living in a place where she can put the top down on the convertible, drive to the beach, drink *mojitos*, and call it "research."

Marshall loves to hear from readers at
www.darlenemarshall.com

You can follow her on
Facebook at
www.facebook.com/DMarshallAuthor

Twitter at
@DarleneMarshall

Instagram at
www.instagram.com/darlenemarshallauthor

If you enjoyed reading about the St. Armand family, the Fletchers, and the fashionable lady who raises bichons, check out Marshall's award-winning novels, available in ebook and print:

THE PIRATE'S SECRET BABY
(*High Seas, #3*)

"Governess wanted: must exhibit patience and fortitude with precocious little girls, puppies, and most importantly, rakishly handsome pirates. Apply Capt. Robert St. Armand, *Prodigal Son…*"

CASTAWAY DREAMS
(*High Seas, #2*)

A dour doctor (after a fashion), a dizzy damsel (more or less), and a darling (and potentially delicious) doggy, castaway on a desert island. One of them may have fleas.

SEA CHANGE
(*High Seas, #1*)

A war is raging on the world's oceans as two enemies fight an attraction neither can deny.